# DOCTOR WHO

## BUNKER SOLDIERS
## MARTIN DAY

Published by BBC Worldwide Ltd,
Woodlands, 80 Wood Lane
London W12 0TT

First published 2001
Copyright © Martin Day 2001
The moral right of the author has been asserted

Original series broadcast on the BBC
Format © BBC 1963
Doctor Who and TARDIS are trademarks of the BBC

ISBN 0 563 53819 8
Imaging by Black Sheep, copyright © BBC 2001

Printed and bound in Great Britain by
Mackays of Chatham
Cover printed by Belmont Press Ltd, Northampton

*Dedicated to Mum and Dad and Nan –
and everyone else who's helped*

# Prologus
# Separatio

Every day he asked the same question, and every day the answer was the same.

'I would like to see my ship, if I may.'

'Very well. I will arrange an escort.'

Sometimes I accompanied him. Sometimes I declined, for I could not bear the anguished look on his face, and I preferred my own company to his tortured introspection. Either way, the same procession of cloaked figures would make their way into the same expansive chamber, where the wind made the torches throw grotesque shadows on to the cold stone walls.

And, in the centre, was the same blue box, the same 'ship', as the Doctor called it. Our escape route, our home – our *TARDIS*.

The last time I saw it, there was a fine patina of dust visible on the glass windows (or, rather, over that part of the exterior that resembled glass – few things about the Doctor's ship are entirely as they appear). It was a stark reminder of the length of our enforced stay, of the impasse engineered by two polite but utterly intractable wills.

The Doctor would stand and stare, a faraway yet precisely focused look in his eyes. Were it not for his white hair, and the cane he occasionally lent on for support, he would perhaps have resembled a serious-minded student in an art gallery or a museum, where one exhibit unexpectedly takes the breath away and demands close attention. The fervour in his gaze was that of a religious missionary in a strange land, staring at the object of his remembered faith.

Seeing the ship brought him some comfort, a pinprick of

light in the darkness, yet its very existence was enough to remind him of what he had lost, what he was separated from.

I came to realise that, to the Doctor, the TARDIS was more than a means of conveyance. How else could I explain the daily ritual, the contradictory look of pleasure and pain that gripped his angular features? Dodo and I, of course, wanted nothing more than to escape from this benighted city, to leave in the TARDIS and return to that which we had left behind. We had, together, hatched numerous plots and plans, ruses and subterfuges. All had failed. 'Never let your enemy realise the true value of that which is important to you,' the Doctor noted, and he was right. Our biggest mistake was in drawing our captors' attention to the craft. Whether or not they believed it really could allow us to escape, they certainly came to realise its vital importance to us. And desperate men are drawn to the hope of others – a hope which the Doctor resolutely failed to elaborate upon. The TARDIS, he said, *must* remain a mystery to them. We would either leave on our terms, or not at all.

The door remained locked, and the Doctor refused to open it. The TARDIS remained where it was, guarded round the clock, and we were refused unhindered access to it.

But still the Doctor persisted with this ritual, this daily drama of the moth, despite all intentions to the contrary, returning to burn itself in the flame.

For a moment, he would close his eyes, and breathe deeply, as if transported to some verdant hillside where the air is fresh and cool. He seemed to draw strength from his proximity to the machine, as if it afforded him access to limitless determination and patience. Occasionally I thought I saw his eyes flutter beneath his eyelids, as if he was dreaming.

And then he would turn sharply on his heels and return to

our quarters, where he would brood and mutter under his breath.

When the Doctor was in that sort of mood it was best to give him a wide berth. After all, what possible words of encouragement could I offer the old man? If he was starting to run out of ideas, of possible resolutions to the dilemma, what hope did I have? The Doctor would clearly have waited until eternity became cold before even thinking about revealing the secrets of the TARDIS, but he was surrounded by people who had more immediate and lethal concerns. For them, time was running out.

Dodo and I would sit in an upper room, overlooking the square at the centre of the city and watch, in the endless twilight, as preparations continued. Always preparations, round the clock, irrespective of weather, personal health, dwindling provisions. The attackers would show no mercy, no compassion: their eventual and crushing assault was reckoned to be as inevitable as the setting of the copper-coloured sun.

A shroud had settled over the city, and it was palpable. You could feel it prickling at the shoulders of the people who passed you by, hear it in frightened murmurs on the street corner and in the abject prayers of the pious.

It was an undertaker's shroud, preserving the dignity of a corpse, for, by all accounts, the city and its inhabitants were already sentenced to death. What lay beyond the hills was, to the people of the city, alien, unfathomable, and utterly unstoppable.

'How much longer?' asked Dodo, as she looked to the forests and hills for the first glimmer of light, the first sound that would herald the arrival of the apocalyptic hordes.

'I have no idea,' I said, trying hard to hide my own fear. 'At least when the attack begins, this awful waiting will be over.'

'If only we could get back to the TARDIS.'

I nodded. I didn't like admitting it, but if someone had given me a free path to the Doctor's craft, I don't think I'd have spared the city and its inhabitants a second glance. My potential cowardice sat heavy in my stomach.

'Oh, Steven, what are we going to do?'

I shrugged my shoulders, and waited for the darkness to envelop us.

# Codex I
# Cecidit de coelo stella magna

*I, Andrey, potter by trade, and man of God only through such mercies as He has chosen to show me, write this account in my own hand, while the memories are still fresh, and my mind still ablaze with images of heaven.*

*I offer this account to my family and to the future, hoping that one day some sense or use might be found in it, and that all will know how the dark angel came to visit our land. I thank the Lord that I have been taught well enough to capture such things in written words – for the mind and memory seek always to embellish, elaborate or alter, as our consciences allow – but I know that I am not sufficiently tutored to explain or understand what has happened this day. I merely commit to this parchment my own impressions of the arrival of the celestial star, and the angel that it contained.*

*I was busy at work, and deep in thought, when I first heard the cries of terror. By the time I had wiped my hands on my apron and come to the door, the entire village was in chaos. Pigs were running free, women were trying to urge their children indoors, and men stood open-mouthed in disbelief.*

*And the smell – the smell that greeted me was strong and primal.*

*The forest was on fire.*

*I stood in the centre of the village, turning to follow the gaze of those around me. High on the rising slope, almost exactly behind my dwelling, a column of fire twisted in the darkening sky. Trees crumbled into the white-hot flames, ash and burning leaves sparking with the flow of the wind.*

*Leading into the great conflagration, and arcing across the sky like a scimitar, was a line of reddened cloud. It looked to me like a leering grin, an expression of satisfaction as the trees succumbed to the fire.*

*'What happened?' I asked the stout herdsman who stood at my shoulder.*

*As he replied, I saw the flames reflected in his awe-struck eyes. 'I was tending my animals... There came a great noise from the skies, like a multitude of birds, or the very breath of God. I looked, and saw a star falling to the earth. When it touched the trees, they began to burn – as you see.'*

*Others nodded their agreement – it was as the herdsman had said.*

*I turned again to watch the conflagration. I remember only too well the last forest fire, and its awful touch as it raged against our village. If the wind turned towards us, and this time did not ease...*

*Petrov the metalworker, an enormous fellow rendered black by the soot of his furnace, clearly had similar thoughts. He threw some dust into the air, and watched its course keenly. 'The wind will keep the flames away from us – for now,' he announced loudly.*

*I was less sure. In my limited experience, once a fire like this starts it takes on a life its own, moving where it wants, devouring what it wants, and only showing mercy when God Himself wishes it so.*

*I looked back at the flames – just as they blinked into darkness.*

*A murmur went around the assembled villagers. What fire was this, that vanished into nothing in a heartbeat?*

*'By the saints...' I approached Petrov. 'Have you ever seen such a thing?'*

The big man shook his head. 'A miracle. It is nothing less.'

I watched Alexander the village elder sink to his knees. 'Thank the Lord.'

I let out a relieved sigh. 'We should pray,' I said.

'No,' said Petrov firmly. 'There will be time for prayer – later. There may be smaller fires burning that we cannot see. We should take what water we can carry, some brushes. Who will join me?'

Most of the villagers held Petrov in such esteem that they would follow his burly frame to the gates of Hell and back. There was an immediate chorus of assent, brave words flowing forth from people who moments before had seemed resigned to the flames.

I was more cautious than the others, though wary of being called a coward. I became aware of people looking towards me, as if daring me to stay.

I too publicly assented to Petrov's plan.

Alexander's wizened face cracked into a smile. 'You are a good man, Petrov. I shall pray for your safe return.'

Within the hour, the group of men was ready. I could have made excuses then. There were reasons enough to stay and, in time, my decision would have been forgotten.

But, more frightened of the word of men than the Word of God, I set out with them.

As I sit here in the darkness, as the shadows deepen and the wind makes the torchlight flicker, I fervently wish that I had not – or that the Lord could wipe these memories from my mind.

There are some things mortal man is not fit to know.

# I

# Tempestas ex oriens

Dmitri paced the room. His anger and resentment ebbed and flowed beneath his air of well-mannered authority.

'Chernigov and Pereislav have already fallen,' he said quietly, stopping for a moment to glance out over the roof-tops. 'What chance have we?'

Although I didn't recognise the names of the cities that Dmitri spoke of, I had little reason to think they were any smaller, or less well prepared, than the sprawling settlement in which we were trapped.

I looked towards the Doctor. His features were impassive and set, as if carved from granite, and his voice carried little more warmth than this cold stone. 'You say that, and yet you govern the mother of Russian cities? You will not inspire your subjects with such defeatism, sir.'

The rebuke in the Doctor's voice only served to agitate Dmitri further. 'My subjects?' His voice was bitter now, and he seemed about to launch into some tirade, some honest expression of the appalling position he found himself in, when he noticed the soldiers positioned about the debating chamber. I could read his face in an instant: it was unwise to talk about such things in front of the common folk. Status, and apparent status, were everything in this society.

Instead, Governor Dmitri lapsed into introspective silence. I glanced at Dodo, sitting opposite me, and smiled, but we both knew that the conversation was not going well. We were at the mercy of the governor but, though unstintingly polite, the Doctor seemed unprepared to meet the man half-way.

I turned my mind back to our arrival the previous day.

Dodo, feeling a little unwell, had said she needed some 'fresh air'. The Doctor, rigorous pragmatist that he is, complained that the TARDIS's air supply was constantly recycled, purified, modified... But, with a twinkle in his eye, he had agreed to Dodo's request. 'It's not the air, my dear,' he said, 'it is the walls which enclose it that become wearisome.'

The TARDIS had come to rest in the corner of a room just as a family were about to have supper.

As unannounced entrances go, it was one of our best.

We emerged to find ourselves almost alone in the room, as all had fled in superstitious terror. All bar one. I later learned that his name was Isaac, and that he was the head of the household. For the moment, though, he stood meekly before us, clearly afraid, but very much intrigued.

Not knowing when or where we had landed, the first thing I observed was the man's clothing. He wore a black fur-trimmed coat over some sort of embroidered tunic. Dark, narrow trousers led down to large boots of leather. Everything about him was understated, though I guessed that his tunic was of high quality for the time. Given this, the yellow patch of fabric on the man's coat drew the eye, a bright badge against a backcloth of cool sobriety.

I sensed that the Doctor was also drawn to this single identifying mark. He glanced swiftly around the room – no doubt taking in the design of the stone walls, the oak table at which the family had been sitting, the food on the table, the candles that provided illumination – and nodded to himself as if precisely confirming our whereabouts in time and space. The TARDIS's instruments were all very well, but the Doctor was a scientist, an inquirer, who would take nothing at face value, and believe nothing until it had been categorically proved.

The Doctor looked back at the man, and smiled. '*Shalom aleichem*,' he said, inclining his head in a mark of respect.

The man was clearly amazed, barely knowing how to respond to this courtesy. Eventually, he fell to his knees, averting his eyes.

The Doctor chuckled. 'Get up, get up,' he said. 'I am a man, such as yourself.'

(I grinned to myself at this. If only it were that simple…)

'Forgive me,' stuttered the man. 'We were saying our prayers before our meal. I have read of the angel of the Lord appearing to Abraham. I merely thought…'

'Of course you did,' said the Doctor lightly. He indicated the TARDIS. 'Our means of travel might be unusual, but I assure you that we mean you no harm.'

Moments later, Isaac introduced himself, then begged us to stay and join in with the family meal. He insisted – it was his obligation to all weary travellers. The moment we gave him our word that we would be delighted to stay, he scurried off to reassure his servants and family. We found ourselves alone for some minutes – clearly convincing his family to return was no easy task.

I remember the Doctor sitting on one of the benches that surrounded the low table and surveying the food with great interest. Wooden bowls were filled with some sort of vegetable and meat broth, whose smell was a good deal more inviting than its appearance. A platter in the centre of the table bore a pair of pigeons, resting on their backs. Their blackened legs jutted from the cooked flesh like trees after a forest fire. At either end of the table were ceramic jugs decorated with exaggerated pictures of birds and animals. I suspected that they might contain ale, but the contents proved to be a rough red wine that smelt of spices and rich, sun-dried earth.

'Observe how the spoons are placed face up,' said the Doctor quietly.

'So?' I queried.

'In this culture, spoons are often placed face down, so that one does not run the risk of seeing the face of the Devil reflected in it.' The Doctor grinned. 'Such superstitions are prevalent. We are lucky to find ourselves not only in the house of a man of some status, but a man of some thought, some openness.'

'I can't see any forks,' said Dodo prosaically.

'Indeed, no,' the Doctor replied with a smile. 'They have yet to be invented.'

'The Middle Ages,' I stated, probably sounding more confident in my summation than I felt.

The Doctor nodded, but said nothing more as the family returned. They stared at us as if we each had three heads and, I am afraid to say, things did not improve as the evening drew on. Isaac himself was a cheerful and engaging host, but the others were largely silent. They chewed slowly, either staring at us or averting their eyes. I really think that we had put them off their food.

I came to learn that Isaac was a trusted adviser to the city's governor; that his wife was called Rebekah, and his son, Nahum; and that we were welcome to stay as his guests for as long as we wished. He clearly took being a host very seriously indeed.

It goes without saying that we planned to take our leave of Isaac after the meal. If Dodo was looking for fresh air, I couldn't imagine she'd find much of that in an era where the streets ran with excrement, and urine was stored to dye clothing. But events transpired against us. It seems that one of Isaac's servants had been so unnerved by our appearance that he had run from the house to the governor's residence.

I shudder to think what story of magically appearing demons he told; whatever his words, action followed swiftly.

Within the hour, Isaac's home was full of soldiers and

12

frightened officials. Nahum and Isaac tried to defend and protect us, but it was clear that the sanctuary and hospitality they had tried to extend to us was a minor concern to them.

We were questioned politely – though I am not sure that didn't have more to do with our supposed magical powers than the fair-mindedness of the city authorities. But at no point could I entirely forget that I was surrounded by battle-hardened young men in armour who carried swords and pole-axes.

The officials wanted to know who we were, where we came from, what our 'allegiance' was, and whether we knew of the great army that was sweeping through the forests and farmland towards the city. I should not have been surprised by their interest in our method of transportation, but I am afraid that I let slip that we had indeed arrived in the 'blue box'. Their eyes lit up immediately.

I shot the Doctor an apologetic look, but he was turned away from me, trying to convince the leader of the military delegation otherwise. However, given that he could offer no alternative explanation for our arrival behind fortified city walls, still less an idea of our geographical journey, it was obvious that his subsequent comments were little more than bluster.

I knew the authorities didn't have an inkling of what the TARDIS was – but it was equally clear that they would prefer to keep hold of it, rather than run the risk of it falling into the hands of their enemies.

We watched as, with some difficulty, the craft was transported to the governor's house. No one could believe how heavy the 'box' was: the Doctor refused to say anything about the TARDIS. He merely muttered under his breath, took a tighter grip on his cane, and glared at me from time to time.

We were invited to stay at the governor's residence, as

honoured guests of Dmitri. In the morning, he would have a proposal to put us. It was clear that the authorities didn't expect their invitation to be turned down.

I slept badly, my head resting uncomfortably on a pillow stuffed with chopped straw.

Soon after we awoke we were indeed summoned into the presence of Governor Dmitri. He politely asked for the Doctor's help; the Doctor refused. And now, some six hours later, the governor was asking again.

'I cannot force you to help us,' Dmitri observed, eyeing the Doctor closely.

'Indeed, sir. And I am grateful that you have not tried.'

'But I can beg.'

'What makes you think that we are in any position to assist you?'

'Your… craft… It appeared in an instant. Whether you are a conjuror or a magician or an angel of the Lord, it matters little. You clearly have powers that our attackers do not.'

'Your attackers are men, just like you.'

'They are devils! They sweep aside entire cities like the straw toys of children. All the knights of Christendom will be powerless to stop them.'

'I have considerations that I cannot even begin to explain to you,' said the Doctor. 'I am sorry, but I cannot help.'

Dmitri walked over to the window, flanked by his advisers – Yevhen, a broad man with reddish hair and soulless eyes to whom I took an instant dislike, and Isaac, who still bore the apologetic look of a man whose generosity has been abused. He avoided eye contact with us as much as possible. Nahum, on the other hand, who was with his father, was completely engrossed in events. I suspected that he was being groomed to follow in Isaac's footsteps.

'Look upon our city,' said Dmitri, casting a slender hand over the vista. 'Look at its people, the children that play in the streets. Do you consign them to death?'

The Doctor stood at Dmitri's side. Suddenly he seemed very alien to me.

Yevhen seemed to indicate that Dmitri should cease this pointless discussion, but the governor was having none of it. He pointed instead to a building dominated by a large white structure surrounded by twelve smaller towers. 'The Cathedral of St Sophia, the very symbol of who we are as people. It will almost certainly be destroyed by the coming horde. Everything you see will be reduced to rubble.' His eyes blazed with indignation.

The Doctor turned away. 'I can do nothing to help you. You can imprison us, you can threaten us with death, if you wish to descend to that level. But I cannot interfere.'

'Interfere.' I turned that word over in my mind all day. Such a mild-sounding collection of letters, yet from the Doctor's lips it was like a death warrant.

I later found the Doctor sitting in the small garden at the back of the governor's house. Two soldiers were watching over him, though they seemed more concerned with the serving girls who were picking herbs than with the possible escape of their charge.

I sat next to the Doctor on a stone bench, but I didn't know what to say. Instead, for a moment, I listened to the clatter of carts in the street outside, to the bawdy chuckles of the guards. Somewhere nearby a baby was crying. Everyday sounds, but each one was a torture to me.

'My boy, you seem troubled,' observed the Doctor.

'Can you blame me?' I asked.

The Doctor sighed. 'No.'

'I don't understand,' I said. 'How can you consign these

people to their fate?'

The Doctor looked around before replying. 'Fate? What do you know of the fate of these people?'

'Not much. Only what I've heard –'

'We are in a city soon to be under siege,' interrupted the Doctor brusquely. 'A terrifying – you could almost say "alien" – army is sweeping across the landscape towards us. A storm from the east. The army is decimating towns and cities and subjugating everyone and everything in its path. The invaders are known for their astute tactics and advanced weaponry. I'm afraid that they are absolutely unstoppable.'

'But that's no reason not to try.'

'You're forgetting. This is no warped version of the history of your planet, this *is* history. Here and now, we are living in a snapshot of the past. But we have no right to meddle, to interfere, to even think about changing the slightest element. All this, all that will happen tomorrow and next week, next month… It has already happened, it has already been written.' The Doctor tried to sound reasonable, like a teacher explaining to a difficult student that two plus two does indeed equal four, but I saw through this in an instant.

'Yes, but –'

'As you know,' interrupted the Doctor, 'we are in Kiev, in the year 1240. The Mongol army, led by Batu on behalf of Ogedei Khan, will soon attack. If you've read your history books, you will know what will happen next: in time, the Mongols will attack Hungary and Poland. It is the largest invasion Europe has ever seen.'

'But these people will die.'

The Doctor sighed again. 'From the perspective of history, you could say they are already dead.'

'We must do something.'

'We must do absolutely nothing!' The Doctor was almost

angry now – as if stung by the fact that I dared to question him.

He paused, watching a sparrow descend into an ornamental tree. It flitted in the branches, seeming to stare at the servants bent over their rows of herbs, and then landed at the Doctor's feet. It pecked at the dust looking for morsels.

The Doctor looked up. 'Would you save this creature?' he whispered, mesmerised. 'Would you save it from a fox or a cat? And, even if you did, could you save it for ever? Hmm? Like it or not, one day soon, this creature will become ill, and will die.'

'But we're talking about people – not animals!!' The bird flew into the air with a flash of chestnut-brown wing, surprised by the anger in my voice. 'People who, for all I know, will die in agony if we don't help them!'

'People die in agony all the time. Do we have the right to decide who shall live, and who shall be saved?' the Doctor queried. He pushed the tip of his cane through the dust at his feet, watching the marks it left behind. 'I once believed that history is carved in stone… resolute, unchangeable. But it seems that our friend the Monk disagrees with us. Perhaps you *can* change the past. But the ripples, the connections… We owe it to the future to leave things well alone.'

'But surely to save lives –'

'You save the life of a child here, and when you return to the future everything will be changed, and changed utterly. Hitler did not lose the Second World War, an atomic war has consumed most of Asia…' The Doctor paused. 'My boy, it is so complicated – even I can't meddle with the patterns of history. Time is no respecter of good intentions!'

I nodded, remembering our earlier argument after our escape from Paris. But the debate had never really ended, and I didn't want the Doctor to think that the passing of time meant I now agreed with him.

'But perhaps something positive will happen,' I said,

desperate to hear something constructive from the old man. 'Perhaps there is someone here who will discover antibiotics or whose descendants will find a cure for cancer.'

'Believe me, my boy', said the Doctor with a resigned weariness in his voice, 'such changes are rarely for the better. And I am afraid to say that human history is full of such massacres – but no one has the authority to prevent them.'

I got to my feet, indignant. 'I can't believe you're taking such a casual attitude to the slaughter of innocent people.'

'A glimpse of what the TARDIS can do will only fuel their hunger. They will want a piece of it, or of the technology that produced it. They will want to use that technology for their own ends – but they do not have the maturity to use it wisely.'

'Then there's nothing left to say? No way of repelling the attackers?'

The Doctor shook his head as he got slowly to his feet. 'No. In any case, even if you could interfere, would you? From your perspective, Steven, let alone mine, this is a petty local squabble. That's all.'

I held the Doctor's gaze, but he turned away.

'It sounds harsh, I know. But the history of Earth is too important to be tampered with. Our only concern is to get back to the TARDIS.'

'And how long is that going to take?'

The Doctor sighed. 'It may take some time…'

# II
# Labyrinthus

Many weeks had passed since their arrival in Kiev, and yet Dodo still had questions for the Doctor.

'This Genghis Khan bloke,' she was saying. 'He was the first leader of the Mongols, right?'

The Doctor looked up from the illuminated manuscripts he was studying. 'And there I was thinking you paid no attention at school!'

Dodo was evasive. 'I think I saw something on the telly once.'

The Doctor smiled. 'Before Genghis became Great Khan, he was known as Temuchin. He was probably born in 1167…'

'Seventy-odd years ago,' interrupted Dodo.

'… to an insignificant clan on the steppes of Mongolia,' continued the Doctor with barely a pause. 'It was an area rife with tribal herdsmen, made parochial by its geography. Genghis united the clans under one leader, and sent hordes of soldiers out on a grand mission of conquest.'

'He's dead, though, isn't he?'

'Genghis?' queried the Doctor. 'Yes, he died a decade or more ago. Please try to keep up!' he admonished gently.

'So who's the boss now?'

'Ogedei Khan.'

'And he's the one who's invading?'

'No, no,' said the Doctor. 'Ogedei is, if memory serves, residing in the Mongolian capital, Qaraqorum. This campaign is commanded by Batu Khan, Genghis's grandson, along with Batu's cousin, Mongke. Mongke will become Great Khan in…' He muttered to himself, wracking his mind for the date. '1250, 1251, something like that.'

'I'm confused.'

The Doctor seemed not to hear. 'And Mongke will be followed by the greatest khan of all, Khubilai. You're familiar with Coleridge?'

'Unless he's Chelsea's new centre-half, no, I'm not.'

'Pity,' said the Doctor. 'And the name Marco Polo means nothing to you?'

Dodo shook her head, and the Doctor sighed deeply. 'One day I shall have to tell you of the fun and games we had with Polo and Khubilai! Oh yes, a most tricky encounter!'

He rose to his feet, patrolling the great library of Kiev like a teacher.

'In Khubilai's time, of course, the empire is composed of four khanates. It stretches from beyond Kiev, across Russia, down to Baghdad, and then right the way across Asia to China. A vast empire! Yes, an extraordinary achievement!'

He looked round as the soldier who had been watching over them left the room, to be replaced by another.

'But I have said quite enough,' he said in a quiet voice. 'This is all in the future. A little knowledge is a dangerous thing, isn't that right, my dear?'

'If you say so,' said Dodo. 'But I still don't understand why they're so frightened of these Mongols.'

'Oh, my child,' said the Doctor sadly, 'I pray you never have to find out for yourself.' He paused, thinking, then led Dodo to the window. 'Come… come. Look down, and tell me what you see.'

The governor's residence was an imposing building of dark stone, punctured with windows and topped with towers and unadorned battlements. It sat on Starokievska Hill, surrounded by the palaces of Kiev's princes, and afforded a fine view of the city's commercial district and, beyond that, the great cathedral. The library was high up in one of the towers, a series of interconnected and vast circular rooms built one on top of the other.

From the window Dodo saw people moving through the shadows cast by the great building. Some herded animals to market, others encouraged reticent oxen to pull carts of grain. On a street corner a ragged man was trying to sell something, though he ran when a group of soldiers marched smartly down the street, scattering fowl and children before them like dust.

'I see… I see everyday things.'

'Yes, my dear, that's right.' The Doctor's bony finger traced the roof-tops, the chimneys that poured smoke into the grey autumnal skies. 'Over four hundred churches, nine or ten markets, probably some sixty thousand inhabitants…'

'How does that compare to London?' Dodo wanted to know.

'No more than twenty-five thousand people live there, I should think,' said the Doctor. 'Kiev is a fine city, a noble and dominant place.'

He turned to the book shelves, searching for something. He found a great Bible, thicker than an arm, and heaved it from the shelf and on to the desk.

'Let me see, let me see,' he muttered to himself, flicking quickly through the thick parchment pages. Dodo noticed that their margins were filled with illustrations and cryptic comments in Latin; the capital letter at the start of each chapter was enormous and ornate, filled with scarlet and gold, swirling shapes and precisely knotted geometric patterns.

At last the Doctor found what he was looking for. It was an enormous illustration towards the end of the book, and depicted a wounded lamb on a throne, with twelve leaders below and, in a great procession, myriad men and women bowing low. 'Here is the world as these people see it,' said the Doctor. 'It begins with the men and women of what we would term the Middle East and Europe, and extends to the far reaches of the known world. So we see Hebrews, Arabs, Armenians, Byzantines, Romans, Scythians…' He traced a finger along the procession, and Dodo noticed with a start that the people had started to alternate with beasts and monsters. She saw great giants with single eyes in their foreheads; slender girlish figures with extra fingers; men covered from head to foot with hair; grotesques who moved on one single leg, and others with faces in their stomachs. The further along the line her eyes moved, the more bizarre the creatures became, gradually losing their humanity to a dizzying array of seemingly random animal parts.

'Fauns, centaurs, naiads and dryads, monsters of all kinds,' said the Doctor. 'These people are frightened of the unknown, and who can blame them? And the Mongols are a great storm rising from lands they do not comprehend.'

'You mean there's been no contact with Asia?'

'Not quite, my child, not quite,' said the Doctor. 'The Romans returned from their eastern expeditions with silk, though they imagined it was combed from the leaves of particular plants. Alexander marched into India, and described a land of peculiar men and monsters. As you see…' The Doctor indicated the great procession again. 'Merchants persist in telling these tales to this day. They speak of cynocephali, or dog-headed men, and antipodes, who are people whose feet face backwards. Of course, if you follow their footsteps, you will never find them!' He chuckled, then pointed to one of the figures with a single leg. 'Monopodes – well, the name says it all! Griffins, unicorns, vampires, satyrs, Amazons… The list is endless.'

The Doctor closed the book suddenly and, with Dodo's help, returned it to the shelf. 'The Mongols are absolutely unstoppable,' he announced firmly. 'It is little wonder that contemporary accounts talk of flesh-eating beasts and a coming Armageddon. Their fear only makes the Mongols yet more powerful.'

He laid a gentle hand on Dodo's shoulder, and looked at her sadly. 'There are many beasts and monsters in the universe, it is true,' he said. 'But the worst of them is man. No more, no less.'


Adviser Yevhen found the bishop kneeling before the great golden altar, head bowed. The meeting had been arranged the previous night, and Yevhen was not surprised to find the man in prayer. Bishop Vasil was not one to spurn an opportunity to appear pious.

Swallowing his irritation, Yevhen waited patiently for the bishop to rise to his feet. Vasil was not a tall man, but he had an aura about him, a certain haughty bearing that made the most of his wiry frame. A wrinkled face seemed to merge into the dark folded robes that bunched about his head and shoulders and which resembled a dark halo, the inverse of the many bright icons that littered the cathedral. Only his full grey beard brought any colour to the man's features – and that was the colour of decay, of old things stiff with dust.

Vasil straightened slowly. Yevhen genuflected, brushing his lips against the gilt ring that adorned the bishop's right hand. 'God bless you, my child,' said Vasil, his voice cracking like torn parchment. He angled his head to regard the empty pews that stretched towards the door. Yevhen had long suspected that the reason Vasil chose the cathedral for important meetings was because no one would dare to spy within the very house of God.

When Vasil was sure they were alone he lowered himself on to one of the pews, and motioned for Yevhen to sit at his side. 'You wished to speak with me?'

'Thank you, my lord.' Yevhen's voice rang out loudly, for he had nothing to hide.'I am interested to hear if any progress has been made.'

'Progress?' Vasil feigned deliberate confusion, averting his eyes from Yevhen's implacable stare.

'In the response of the Church to this threat. You indicated when last we spoke that a certain... resolution was being sought.'

Vasil nodded. 'Matters are indeed moving forward.'

'But you have no conclusion for me?'

'The governor and his advisers will be the first to know, Yevhen. You must understand that the Church is being pressed on both sides. You are familiar with Prester John?'

Yevhen nodded. John was a legendary Christian ruler from the east, the descendant, perhaps, of the Magi who had visited Christ, who had wanted greater ties with Europe. In actual fact, no one was now sure he had even existed.

'The Church still believes that salvation, not apocalypse, may yet come from the east.'

Yevhen was incredulous. 'But... After the destruction the Tartars have caused... How can you think that?'

'Are they not people, who need to come to Christ?' asked the bishop.

'They are monsters!'

'Augustine said that monsters are part of God's plan. I grant you it takes time to establish their role in things, but...'

'Time is what we do not have in Kiev,' snapped Yevhen.

'Kiev is but one of our concerns.'

Yevhen couldn't help but snort bitterly. 'That's what Prince Michael said, when he fled from the wrath of the Tartars like a frightened animal!'

Bishop Vasil turned sharply towards the younger man. 'Our civil leaders are appointed by God. We must not question their actions – only pray for them, and support them. The fall of Chernigov and Pereislav in such quick succession means that difficult decisions have to be made.'

'Decisions that can be made far better in Hungary.'

'Each of us has to decide how best to deal with the coming storm.'

Yevhen nodded. 'Yes. Yes, that is what I mean. I cannot wait for ever. I have my own… ideas.'

'You have a great concern for the city, and that is as it should be,' stated Vasil lightly. 'But the Church cannot be rushed.'

Yevhen nodded. 'Then I have your support?'

'If you have the support of your conscience before God, you do not need mine,' said Vasil, with something approaching a smile. 'In any event, I do not know the precise nature of your plans.'

'And you are happy that you do not,' said Yevhen, with a hint of scorn in his voice.

'Perhaps.' Vasil's face remained locked in his oily smile. 'While you are here, perhaps you could tell me about the travellers – the old man, the man who shares your name, the girl. I am not allowed to see them, so you must be my ears and eyes.'

Yevhen nodded. 'Of course.'

'They have been here some little while. Are they still resolute?'

'The old man is. He refuses all overtures to open the box – even when he and his companions are offered their freedom.'

'You think this box important?'

'I know only that the old man believes it so. For all his age, he is clearly their leader. The others look to him for guidance in all matters.'

'And the others… this "Steven", this girl. Are they equally strong-minded?'

'No, my lord. It is clear that they wish to leave – at almost any cost.'

The bishop nodded. 'We may be able to use this to our advantage.'

'Indeed.'

'What think you of these travellers? From where do they hail?'

'They themselves do not say, but they are clearly unused to our customs, our way of life. I have heard from the governor's servants that they grumble at their sumptuous imprisonment. Clearly they are used to the very finest of dwellings.'

'Poverty has its uses,' said Vasil. 'It reminds us all of our station.'

Yevhen glanced at the gold-encrusted altar, but said nothing.

'These heathen travellers', continued Vasil, 'seem to have put their trust in the trappings of ephemeral wealth.'

'Some of the soldiers say they came from the very heavens,' suggested Yevhen lightly.

'Do they seem like angels to you, adviser?' queried Vasil, with a hint of rebuke in his voice.

'They seem good and honest,' admitted Yevhen. 'Beyond that, I cannot say.'

Vasil grinned, and got to his feet. 'That is right, adviser Yevhen. You leave thoughts of good and evil to the Church. Your concern is the governance of this city.'

The meeting was clearly at an end, but it had proved less satisfying than Yevhen had hoped. 'And the Tartars?' he called after the retreating figure of the bishop.

The word brought Vasil up short. He turned to look back at Yevhen. 'It is dark,' he commented cryptically. 'You must do what you have to do.'

Taras was waiting for Yevhen outside the cathedral. It was

raining now, which did little to improve the adviser's mood.

'What did he say?' asked Taras.

Yevhen motioned for Taras to follow him into the shadows of the nearby houses, and out of the rain. 'He is a weak fool!' exclaimed Yevhen. 'He tries to manipulate me, yet does not wish to hear my plans.'

'I said it was pointless to turn to the leaders of the Church in times of trouble,' muttered Taras.

'Indeed you did, my friend, and I should have listened.' Yehven watched as two men trudged through the rain under rough woollen capes, and waited for them to pass. 'I had hoped that the prince might be able to exert political pressure... to call for help from neighbouring cities and lands. But what fine neighbours they proved to be!' He snorted. 'The Lord was right when he said, by way of parable, that those who should give you help very rarely do.'

'And now the Church seems just as powerless,' observed Taras.

'They mouth words of support, but provide not a single man to help with our defences.'

'Did you tell the bishop of the legend?'

'He already knows these things. If he wished us to call upon the dark angel of God, he would have done so by now.'

'Bishop Vasil does not strike me as a man who puts much faith in legends.'

'Perhaps so. Any plans he has for our salvation involve this world, not the next.'

'Then we do nothing?'

Yevhen shook his head vehemently. 'No. We have come this far, we should finish what we have begun. Even the bishop said as much.'

'You have his approval?' queried Taras.

'I have no need of his approval.' Yevhen produced a bunch

of rusted, ancient keys from the pouch at his belt. 'I am an adviser to the governor of Kiev, de facto ruler of this city. I can do as I wish.'

'Then we will proceed?'

Yevhen nodded. 'I shall meet you here, with any men you can muster, at midnight.'

Taras grinned, encouraged at last. 'May God protect our endeavours!'

Yevhen said nothing, but watched him as he disappeared into the shadows.

Taras and the others were talking loudly when Yevhen returned later that night.

'I have heard', said one man, flapping his arms excitedly, 'that the horses of these devils snort fire from their nostrils, and that each hoof as it hits the earth thunders like a winter storm!'

'And the Tartars call up such curses', added another, 'that fire falls from the sky like rain.'

Taras nodded sagely. 'I have family in one of the fallen cities,' he said. 'I know in my heart that they were wiped out in an instant.'

'Quiet!' hissed Yevhen. 'You rabble! You want the city guard alerted to our presence?'

He strode towards the knot of men, imperious in his bright robes. They instantly fell into a hush, bowing their heads.

Yevhen looked down at them scornfully – a pitiful bunch, dressed in rags. Was this the best Taras could do? He turned to Taras, who seemed to anticipate his question.

'These are all the men I can trust,' Taras said.

Yevhen shook his head sadly. 'What of Vladimir, of the Rope-Makers' Guild? Alexander? Your cousin, even?'

'All were wary of desecrating the house of God.'

'Desecrating?' hissed Yevhen, loud enough for the others to hear. 'We are not desecrating. We are releasing the angel of the Lord!'

'But the others... They are superstitious.'

'If the people of Kiev were *more* superstitious', spat Yevhen, 'then perhaps God himself would liberate us from the devils on horseback. As it is, we must pray – and be prepared to play our part.'

In silence he led the group to the side of the great cathedral. There was a small door there, facing a stunted row of artisans' dwellings, long since closed. Not a candle burnt in the surrounding buildings, or in the cathedral itself.

'Here, hold that lantern steady,' barked Yevhen as he sorted through the iron keys. He finally found one that fitted and unlocked, then pushed open, the door of blackened oak.

Followed by the men, he stepped down into a small room of yellowish stone. It had once been some sort of vestry, but had long since fallen into disuse. Torchlight revealed one or two simple wooden stools, and a broken storage box containing only a few scraps of clothing.

Despite the room's appearance, and the rat droppings that littered the floor, the men knew they were on holy ground. If they had immediately become quiet when Yevhen appeared, they were now as hushed as the grave.

Taras closed the door behind them, cutting out the scant light of the moon. The only illumination came from torches and lanterns, showing suddenly fearful faces made waxy by the sulphurous glow.

Yevhen pushed open an inner door and led the men into the cathedral corridors. He had obtained a faded map of the building some months ago, from a stonemason who claimed that one of his ancestors had worked on the original cathedral. The plans were, he said, priceless, a family heirloom, though a few tankards of ale soon brought their value down to a more reasonable level.

Yevhen peered at the map. Three main areas, representing the triune nature of the Godhead, were further subdivided into twelve sections, which stood for the apostles of Christ. The entire edifice – its golden towers, its weighty arches, its geometrically precise aisles – rested upon deep foundations riddled with catacombs and tunnels. And one of the tombs was rumoured to contain the very angel of God.

Yevhen led the men through the corridors to another dark door, this one even smaller than the others and surrounded by enormous stone columns that stretched up into the shadows like angular trees. The door had two locks, one old, one recent, but Yevhen had the correct keys for both.

He pushed the groaning door open, releasing the musty air and damp chill of the catacombs. A tight staircase twisted down into nothingness.

Steeling himself, Yevhen bent through the doorway, holding his lamp low to illuminate the unscuffed steps. And began to descend.

He placed his feet carefully on one block after another, grateful for the limited light. As he concentrated on each step, it was as if he was descending in a vertical shaft. Had he been able to see better, he might have realised that the darkness was not the darkness of stone, but the darkness of empty space – and that one stumble could see him pitching downwards into infinity.

Yevhen forced his fears to one side, thinking only of the complex patterns of tunnels and vaults that awaited him and his followers. He permitted himself a deep breath of satisfaction when he finally reached the bottom of the steps. He turned to see a procession of lights descending, like slowly spinning motes above a fire.

He could smell the rats down here, and thought he could hear the scrabble of claws even over the mutterings of the descending men. The walls, cold with decades of neglect, were marbled with filigree lines of fungus. The floor was damp underfoot.

When the men had finished their descent Yevhen again set off without a word. A selfish thought occurred to him – perhaps they should stay here, with provisions, and wait for the Tartar hordes to sweep over them. But then he remembered his daughter, and the countless other sons and daughters who would die if left unprotected, and thought only of the angel of God, and the protection it offered.

He peered at the map again. It showed a number of unmarked tombs, but one in particular caught Yevhen's eye. It was a smallish room surrounded by seven larger enclosed vaults like protective animals. And immediately above it, in the main cathedral building, was the largest altar, the heart of the church.

Surely this would be the one – the legendary protector of Kiev resting at the very centre of the city.

It appeared suddenly in the darkness as the thick stone ribs of the roof descended to form the ceiling of a small tomb. It was square, and seemingly just tall enough to allow one or two people to stand comfortably. Its outer walls carried only the simplest of patterned adornment.

Yevhen nodded, speaking at last. 'Yes, this is it.'

'How can you be sure?' queried Taras.

Yevhen did not answer, for he did not know. Instead, he moved to the door of the tomb, which was held shut by one of the smallest, most delicate locks he had ever seen. He could find no key to fit it.

He turned to Taras. 'Break it down.'

The shock on Taras's face was clear, even in the gloom. 'I cannot do that!'

'You will break open the door,' snapped Yevhen. 'It is only a small lock. It can be replaced once we have been saved from our enemies.'

Taras did not argue further, though his body language spoke of a man whose boyish excitement had turned swiftly to fear. He put his shoulder against the door and, as Yevhen had indicated, the lock snapped almost instantly. Taras pulled at the brass handle, tugging the door open.

The air within was freed with an audible sigh, and Yevhen could feel some of the men behind him take a nervous step back. He began to wonder if it had been right to bring along so many others – perhaps he and Taras could have achieved their objective, and with less fuss, on their own. And, in any case, what opposition was he expecting? He was an adviser to the governor, after all.

He turned to Taras. 'Follow me. The rest of you may stay here.'

Yevhen and Taras ducked through the doorway, then straightened to hold their lamps high above their heads. It was a plain stone room, lacking any hint of finery. And if it had been cold in the catacombs, in here it was colder still. It was as if the entire structure had been carved from ice. Their breath spiralled upwards like plumes of smoke from a fire.

Worse still, a chill of apprehension began to grip Yevhen. For in the centre of the room lay a rounded silver casket.

The more Yevhen looked at it, the more the casket seemed to glow, as if it was greedily sucking on the first light it had been exposed to for decades. But perhaps it was his eyes growing accustomed to darkness, or a trick of the flickering torchlight.

Taras's earlier apprehension had vanished, and was replaced now by an excitement laced with awe. 'You are right!' he exclaimed in a cracked whisper. He stepped forward eagerly, running his hands along the surface of the casket.

Yevhen was about to warn Taras to be cautious, but again he reminded himself – what have we to fear? Are we not upright men, striving to liberate an angel of God?

On closer inspection, the casket seemed less like a man-made structure of metal and more like something that had grown naturally. A flattened dragon's egg, perhaps, or the shell of some great sea-monster.

Yevhen tentatively extended his hands, brushing his fingertips over the surface of the casket. To his surprise, and despite the temperature of the tomb, it was warm to touch.

Taras squatted and ran a probing finger along its outer edge, tracing a fine line. 'There is a joint here. Presumably a concealed hinge.' He drew a sharp knife from his belt, and attempted to force it into the slender gap.

It would not fit.

'We need more than brute force,' said Yevhen, his attention drawn to a series of nodules and depressions along the top of the casket. One pattern, at the centre, reminded him of a hand, though there were only three slender marks for the 'fingers'. He put his own hand in the depression, but nothing happened.

Taras stood up, boiling over with schoolboy excitement. 'Let me.' He ran his hands over the complex pattern of marks and ridges, randomly prodding and tugging. Yevhen noticed increased movement in the nodules; whereas at first they seemed as solid as granite, now they began to give a little, the depressions occasionally blinking with pinpoints of light.

'You see?' said Taras. 'It is a machine of some sort – and it recognises an engineer's touch!'

Yevhen was sure Taras's fumblings at the controls were random guesswork, rather than the studied experimentation of a scientist, but he said nothing. It mattered not if they were being blessed by God, or simply lucky. *Something* was happening.

There was a final pulse of light that made the entire casket burn briefly like a fire, and a clicking noise that they felt rather than heard.

Taras stood back, and Yevhen found himself gripping the hilt of his knife tightly.

The entire top half of the casket began to hinge smoothly upwards. Within, Yevhen could only see darkness, the inky darkness of a night sky with no stars.

Taras was saying something – babbling prayers or simply babbling, Yevhen could not tell which. Yevhen concentrated instead on the motion of the 'lid', which at last came to rest when it was vertical.

There was a sigh as the awesome machinery became silent. Yevhen could feel his heart pumping; could hear the pounding of blood in his ears. His mouth was dry, his mind reeling.

Something moved within the casket.

Yevhen felt movement at his side. He half-turned, to see Taras falling to his knees in superstitious awe.

'Get up, man!' hissed Yevhen. 'We do not know for sure –'

Something came at Taras in a rush of light and shadow. Yevhen caught only glimpses of slender limbs, a sinewy back – and a soulless face angled at Taras's head.

Taras's screams were brutally cut short. His lantern tumbled away, flickered for a moment, and was then swallowed by the darkness.

Yevhen, frozen for a moment, saw the creature turn. He glimpsed a purplish, rounded mouth like that of a leech, and specks of blood over heavily lidded eyes.

With a whip-crack of legs, the creature hurled itself towards him.

# III
# In truitina mentis dubia fluctuant contraria

Dodo was just finishing lacing up the front of her dress. I couldn't help but notice that each tug on the leather strip was more harsh than the last.

'There are servants who will help you get dressed,' I observed.

Dodo snorted in response, but said nothing.

'And perhaps you should consider covering your hair. You don't want to attract too much attention.'

'Steven,' said Dodo with feigned patience. 'We might be here for ever. Perhaps I should think about attracting a husband!'

She was obviously in one of her moods, but I didn't blame her for a moment. There's a world of a difference between examining another culture and actually living it. For both of us, the novelty had long since worn off.

For my part, I didn't like the food, my clothes made me itch constantly, and I shared my bed with numerous fleas and ticks. However, the Doctor was adamant. We were not going to return to the TARDIS for food or clothing, and therefore we had to make the best of it.

Dodo didn't see it that way. 'I can't stand these shoes,' she commented, sitting on a bench to do up the buckles. 'The soles are so thin. I may as well walk around barefoot!'

'There are plenty in the streets who do.'

Dodo paused. We'd had this argument before, and it normally progressed along similar lines. 'Yes, I know I should be grateful!' she continued, indicating her room with its bed covered with thick woollen blankets, its hanging tapestries, its exquisitely carved tables and stools. 'I know this is luxury as far as most people are concerned.'

'And something worse than poverty awaits them.'

Dodo nodded. 'I know, I spoke to the Doctor yesterday. I just wish there was something we could do!' She glanced away. 'I reckon it would be better if we poisoned the lot of them. At least it would save them from the Mongols!'

I put my arm around her shoulders. 'I know. That's why we must help in whatever way we can.'

'Even if the Doctor doesn't approve?'

I walked over to the window and pulled back the shutters.

The governor's staterooms had panes of glass, allowing him to look out over the city and its people. In Dodo's chamber, as in mine, the window was covered with a wooden lattice filled with thin strips of polished horn. The horn felt like plastic, and let in an incredible amount of light, but was not as transparent as glass. Buildings became dark shapes, and the movement of people in the streets was simply a kaleidoscope of blurred colours.

'It looks fine today,' I said, avoiding Dodo's question. 'A good day for drying grain.'

Dodo nodded. She was helping to oversee the storage of food in preparation for a long siege; by all accounts, she was proving to be an excellent manager and co-ordinator, though the men were still not disposed to take orders from a woman, still less one who hoisted her dress above her knees whenever the sun came out.

There was a polite tap at the door.

'Yeah?' answered Dodo gruffly.

It was Lesia, daughter of Yevhen. She had struck an up an almost immediate friendship with Dodo – I think because each recognised something of her own character in the other – and I was glad that they spent a great deal of time together. For Dodo, this was the one bright spark in the whole awful situation.

'Good-day, Steven, Dodo,' Lesia said, the formality of her

words blunted by her generous smile. I'd noticed, too, how she was at great pains to pronounce my name differently from her father's (many were not so careful). I got the impression that she and her father did not always see eye to eye, and that the pronunciation of my name was, therefore, a very necessary distinction.

'Hiya,' said Dodo. 'You ready?'

Lesia nodded and they trouped off, arm in arm, giggling like children – followed closely by the guards who had been stationed outside Dodo's room.

I lingered a while, sitting on the bed. As ever, I ran through my options. Frankly, they were limited, verging on the nonexistent. We couldn't escape; the Doctor refused to back down; and somewhere, distant but drawing close, the Mongol hordes were moving implacably towards us.

We had tried losing our guards, but they weren't stupid enough to fall for any of our ruses. I'd been taught a harsh lesson in patronising 'primitive' people. In any event, the walls and gates of the city were patrolled by soldiers at all times. A mouse could hardly escape Kiev without alerting them.

We had tried appealing to the governor, but he was resolute and, in any case, we didn't want to abuse his generosity. Better this life than an awful languishing in some benighted prison cell – or torture.

I'd even considered cracking the old boy over the head and making off with the TARDIS key – but the point was, only the Doctor could operate the thing. I'm not even sure it would let us in without him.

The only hope I could give myself was that perhaps, just perhaps, the history books were wrong, and the Mongols spared the populace of Kiev – or that we were in control not only of our own destinies, but those of the thousands of innocents around us.

The alternative was too awful to contemplate.

I arrived at the Church of the Virgin some time later. It was a smaller and less grand building than the central Cathedral of St Sophia, resembling a squat castle more than a place of worship.

For this very reason, it had been chosen as the last refuge of the people of Kiev and, day and night, groups of men worked to fortify and strengthen it still further.

Around the base of the church teams of masons worked on huge stone blocks, cutting them to shape with chisels and much cursing. These were then lifted up to their final positions on hoists that were moved by men walking inside, and straining against, enormous wooden wheels. Workers on precarious-looking scaffolding shifted the blocks on to temporary frames of oak.

It was a surprisingly sophisticated operation and, from a distance, it was as if termites were building some great stone edifice. But conditions were poor, and accidents were frequent. I had seen one man slip on wooden scaffolding made wet by a sudden storm, and tumble down to his death. I rushed over to him, but it was too late. I averted my eyes from his face, which had shattered against the unforgiving ground.

The body had been carried away with a stoic lack of fuss.

I tried to clear my mind of these awful memories, hoping that this day would be a safe one, a day of progress.

I asked for Taras, a builder of some repute who was overseeing many aspects of the fortification. It was clear no one had seen him all morning. I was instead directed towards an ever-growing pile of rubble. Lacking the skill to carve the blocks, and the agility to be of much use high up on the scaffolding, I was to sort through the debris for anything that could be reused.

The mound was comprised equally of stone from the original building that had been found wanting, and the 'off cuts' of the contemporary masons. I wasn't quite sure what I was searching for but worked as diligently as I could, piling bits of stone and rock that seemed particularly substantial into an enormous leather bag.

I had been engrossed in my work for some time when I heard shuffled footfalls behind me.

'You don't have to do this, you know,' said the Doctor. 'What are you hoping to achieve?'

'I want to help,' I said. 'I can't just sit around and do nothing.'

'Of course, of course,' nodded the Doctor. 'But how best to help these people, hmm? That is the question!'

'You're not about to change your mind?' I asked, hoping against hope that he would reply in the affirmative.

The Doctor shook his head slowly. 'The governor and I are matched in our obstinacy.' He paused, seating himself with some difficulty on a large block. 'I have great respect for the man, you know,' he said more quietly as he watched work continuing on the walls of the church. 'And for these people. Dmitri feels trapped by the situation he finds himself in. It's no wonder his noble fair-mindedness is tempered with such stubbornness.'

'But you're still not prepared to help?'

The Doctor paused, clasping his hands together in front of his face. His ring flashed in the cloud-filtered sunlight. 'I feel... I feel that something else is happening here, in this city. There is a deeper unease. Desperate men are being driven to desperate measures. Perhaps it involves the TARDIS. Perhaps it involves something far worse than the coming Mongol attack.'

'What could be worse than that?' I queried.

'What indeed?' The Doctor shook his head, as if to clear it of these thoughts, his white hair flowing about his shoulders. 'Do you know anything of the history of this city?' He stared at the church overhead with a steely fascination.

'You know I don't,' I said. I wondered if the irritation I felt was audible in my voice. I wasn't in the mood for a history lesson: if he had nothing more useful to say, then he might as well leave me to my work.

The Doctor continued, regardless of my annoyance. 'Vladimir the Great is venerated as a saint by the Orthodox Church,' he said, in a voice rich with sarcasm. 'He is seen as the ruler who brought a form of decency to a land riddled with pagan practices and belief. And yet records show that his "conversion", and the forced conversion of his people, was for entirely political ends, cementing an alliance with Constantinople. According to legend…' The Doctor paused as a couple of workmen passed, wary perhaps of their reaction to his tale. 'According to legend, Vladimir considered Judaism first – but then he decided he was too fond of pork. He settled on Islam, but discovered that they forbade alcohol, which he was rather partial to.' The Doctor chuckled wickedly. 'He finally settled on Christianity.'

'You don't have much time for religion, do you Doctor?'

'I have no time for hypocrisy,' said the Doctor coldly. 'Sometimes you have to turn the world upside down for it to make sense. And sometimes the least popular course of action is the right one.'

I didn't quite know what to say. It was as if the Doctor was trying to justify his obstinacy to me – to say that moral right was on his side, no matter how petty or difficult it might seem. But I'd heard it all before.

I looked more closely at his angular features. His eyes, as ever, were alive with possibilities, with ideas, with nuances of much that I could not begin to read. But, as he watched the men toiling on the church walls, I did wonder whether he was having second thoughts, despite what he had said.

I decided to change the subject. 'Dodo went off with Yevhen's daughter again this morning.'

The Doctor nodded. 'They have a great deal in common.'

'And Yevhen?'

I must admit, I couldn't bear the thought of Dodo being on the receiving end of either his tongue or his temper.

'If Dodo were a young man, I would fear for her safety,' said the Doctor, with a sly smile. 'But, as it is… Yevhen has a number of other problems to consider.' He got to his feet, leaning on his cane for support. 'The midday sun does not appeal to me. I should be getting back to the governor's residence.'

I nodded, and watched him stride off. I saw, with interest, that the guard who had been watching him from a discreet distance now walked some way behind him. Perhaps they were beginning to trust us. Perhaps they were beginning to believe that even if we escaped from the attentions of the watching soldiers we had nowhere to run to – nowhere, that is, but the TARDIS.

I got to my feet, and looked around with interest. I'd become very used to the idea of one or more guards following me everywhere, but now I came to think of it, I couldn't remember when I'd last seen my own escort.

As far as I could make out, I was alone.

Ridiculous plans for escape ran through my mind. I barely considered each one, for I knew well enough that unless I could find my way past the soldiers assigned to guard the Doctor's ship I might as well stay where I was. And, without the key, without the Doctor…

I was amazed how quickly I had started to forget about the TARDIS, its white walls and clinical beds, its incredible control room stuffed with antique furniture. Sometimes it seemed more alien to me than this world I now lived in – for all Dodo's complaints, sometimes I felt it suited me. It was a simple life, with simple rules and customs, and a clear sense of priority – even more so, perhaps, given the coming attack. People were more important than things, time more important than business, and everything that could not be entirely understood or explained was to be respected.

Compared to the life I had once had – of training, of striving, of never standing still – it had some advantages.

It was for all these reasons, and more, that I felt unable to do anything with even this whisper of liberty, of possible escape.

I sighed, and returned to work.

It was about ten minutes later that I found the body.

# IV
# Eripe me de inimicus meis

*Downloading test signals...*
*Complete.*
*Downloading heuristic diagnostics...*
*Complete.*
*Downloading shared archive 76-FG-92-SD...*
*Complete.*
*Run archive 76-FG-92-SD...*

*Initial summary:*
*Intelligence suggests that target BDR-997-XRF meets all requirements for complete infiltration and subversion of the northern bunker. However, this target is well guarded, and rarely leaves the dome. Other potential targets have been isolated and subjected to rigorous probability analysis, but none can present a satisfactory index of mission success. BDR-997-XRF is confirmed as primary target.*

*Intelligence further suggests that foodstuff staff may present the best hope for ingress into the northern dome (see supplemental material). A range of initial subjects have been suggested, dependent upon situation at arrival.*

The soldier looks around in curfew darkness, keenly observing the landscape of buildings and factories. For once, it is quiet, with only a skeleton staff working through the night. Most of the impure have been sent home, to conserve energy in readiness for the counteroffensive.

An inspection craft droning overhead causes the soldier to instinctively seek refuge in the shadows. It accesses its intelligence and topographical information, skewing the old maps to match the ever-expanding city. Nearby there is a worker who might prove... useful.

A few streets away, a patrol vehicle moves through the litter and the silence, barely disturbing either. The soldier pauses just long enough to confirm its position, and then heads for the edge of the living area. In stark defiance of wartime regulations, an inert-gas light blinks on and off outside a shop closed for business, but the light barely pools on to the street, still less pollutes the air over the city.

The soldier approaches the door, one of countless dormitory entrances in this place. But it is the right one – chances of success will be optimised if this person is subverted.

The first and only problem is encountered when the door-breaking device refuses to come up with the correct access code. The soldier finds a window that hints at curtained light beyond, and taps at it.

There's a voice from within, expressing irritation and surprise. The soldier accesses an official phraseology, dredged from an organic databank, and stands, wondering how best to deal with the coming confrontation.

The door opens a crack. The soldier is not recognised, but is deferred to. Although the words do not flow comfortably, his appearance speaks of authority and power.

The door opens still further. Biocomputers assess the situation, pause for a moment, then order a strike.

An arm snakes into the residence, snapping a neck and pushing the body to the floor.

A weak link has been found and exposed.

The soldier steps over the corpse into the residential unit, and presses the control to close the door.

*Result of action:*

*GHR-678-AAD (provisional assignment) has been attacked and compromised. Mission success index: 52.7%.*

By the time Isaac arrived in the debating room, Yevhen was already there. He sat, hunched, at the table. Parchment maps of the city, and the countryside around Kiev, were laid out before him. He stared at them, unblinking – as if all the metaphysical and alchemical secrets of the world were contained within the ink and information beneath his fingertips.

Isaac sat down facing Yevhen, saying nothing. He had long since accepted that there would never be any semblance of courtesy or comradeship between the two of them.

At length, Yevhen looked up from the maps. He had the drained expression of one who has not slept, or whose sleep had been haunted by nightmares. 'The governor?' he asked, his clipped tones sounding even more brutal than usual.

'I am sure he will be with us soon,' Isaac said. He leant forward a little to better examine the source of Yevhen's unwavering interest, and was surprised to see that the map was not of the Church of the Virgin, as he had expected, but of the cathedral.

Yevhen noticed Isaac's attention, and quickly shifted another map on top of the one he was studying. It showed the rivers, mountains and forests of Russia. From a point just south of the great wall of the Ural mountains, a line of black snaked across the landscape – the path of the Mongol hordes. The line crossed the River Volga at the city of Bulgar, proceeded west towards Riazan and Kolumna, north to Kostroma and Torzhok, and then, mercifully, moved south past Moscow – mercifully, for each city touched by the black line had been obliterated. It was as if a great creature was walking though the land, and wherever its feet touched there was nothing but death, destruction and the smoke of vain prayers.

The line arced westwards again, and passed through Chernigov and Pereislav. Kiev was next, less than a hundred miles away.

Isaac stared at the awesome path carved by the Mongols through Europe. The principalities of Russia had already fallen, and beyond Kiev lay only the quaking states of Poland, Bohemia, Austria and Hungary. At no point had the progress of the horsemen been even halted; at no battle or capitulation had any knowledge been gained that might assist in future struggles against the horde. The situation was worse than hopeless, though Isaac knew it would be unwise to articulate such a conclusion.

'How goes work on the church?' he asked. Even Yevhen's gruff words were better than the awful silence.

'It goes well enough.' Yevhen did not even look up.

'And the Tartars? Where is their army located?'

Yevhen grunted. 'I have had no word from our scouts in recent days. But I believe the horsemen still to be heading towards the city. Doubtless they have permitted one to two souls from their previous conquests to live, in order to advise, to guide.' Yevhen pushed the map of the land away, turning now to a hasty plan schematic of the city walls. He glanced up, his eyes dark with venom. 'Perhaps they will let you live, Jew, if you have something to offer.'

'All that I have, I offer to the prince and his governor,' said Isaac, well used to Yevhen's harsh slights. 'The storage of food continues apace, and will complement the valiant work of your men in making Kiev safe.' Isaac smiled, trying to be as genuine as possible. Men facing death together should at least recognise their common foe, and each other's attempts to save themselves.

'You believe we will be safe from these devils?'

Isaac nodded. 'Of course.'

'Good. I too believe our salvation is at hand.' Yehven paused. 'Your son will not be joining us today?'

'Nahum has other matters to attend to.'

Yevhen snorted, as if to imply that any matters requiring the attention of young men were surely matters of sin best left unspecified.

He was about to speak again when a mass of bodies clattered into the room, the door slamming against the wall. Both advisers looked up, and saw not Governor Dmitri, but the traveller Steven, forcefully held by three soldiers.

'Get your hands off me!' he shouted, struggling against the iron grip of the guards. One raised a mail-encrusted hand to bring it down against Steven's face.

'What is the meaning of this?' exclaimed Isaac. 'This is the residence of the governor, not a tavern for brawling!'

The guard lowered his fist, and behind him Steven and the others fell silent. 'My lords,' said the soldier, bowing with some difficulty. 'This man is a murderer. The governor will wish to sentence him.'

'Will I?' came a powerful voice to the rear of the group. The knot of guards parted to allow Dmitri to stride into the room. Isaac and Yevhen immediately got to their feet, bowing their heads in respect.

Dmitri was a powerful man, whose athletic form complemented the grim authority of his office, but in situations such as this he seemed even more imposing. Isaac had more reason than most to have seen the governor's humour and warmth when the circumstances so demanded – but he also remembered that Dmitri had never ceased to rigorously pursue what he felt was right, even if that brought him into conflict with Prince Michael. On more than one occasion, he had faced being stripped of office for seeming impertinence, only for the prince to eventually concede that Dmitri had been right all along.

The governor smiled at the courtesy shown by his advisers, then turned imperiously to the soldier who had spoken. 'I do not appreciate my dwelling being treated in this way. Nor do I relish being told what to do!'

The man bowed even lower this time, the others following suit. He mumbled an apology but it was drowned out as Dmitri seated himself at the head of the table, his chair scraping across the flagstones.

The governor indicated that his advisers should be seated. 'Your name?' he queried of the lead soldier.

'Mykola, my lord,' said the man.

'An honest and decent man,' added Yevhen. 'A captain of the guard.'

'Bring the traveller here,' said Dmitri. 'And tell me what happened.'

Mykola stepped forward, his hand on Steven's arm. 'Taras the builder has been murdered. This man killed him.'

'Rubbish!' said Steven, indignant. 'I found the body under the rubble I was working through. He'd been dead for quite some time.'

'How do you know when he died?' queried the governor.

'There are signs.'

'Signs?'

'Muscle rigidity, internal organ distension, blood loss if there is a wound.'

Isaac turned slightly to locate the source of this latest comment – it was the Doctor, striding calmly into the room.

'With your permission, sir,' the Doctor continued, 'I would like to examine the body of this poor fellow. We may swiftly be able to clear up this unfortunate business.'

'How can we believe what you tell us?' growled Yevhen. 'You will defend your friend, contrive some excuse to make his "innocence" clear!'

Dmitri raised a hand to forestall any invective that might follow. 'We shall make our own judgement on this matter, but we will allow the Doctor to speak. However, first we must establish what happened.' He turned to Steven and his voice became lower, more friendly. 'Steven. Where did you find the body?'

'As I said, right at the bottom of a pile of stones I was asked to sort through. I pulled him out, but he'd been dead for a while. In fact, it wouldn't surprise me if I've been framed.'

'Framed?'

The Doctor smiled. 'My friend merely feels that the body had been left there, and he had been sent to work on that rubble, with the sole purpose of incriminating him. The murderer hopes to remain undetected while Steven is accused of the crime.'

'There is some foul play at work here,' agreed Yevhen.

The Doctor nodded. 'Unless this fellow died of natural causes, and somehow contrived to cover himself in a pile of stone rubble –'

'And surely we have the culprit in front of us!' Yevhen continued.

'Oh, do stop talking nonsense,' snapped the Doctor. 'You have no proof that things are not as Steven said – that he found the body, and was moments later discovered by one of the soldiers.' He turned to Mykola. 'Did you come across Steven and the body?'

The man nodded.

'Tell us exactly what you saw.'

'I saw Steven crouched over the body of Taras. He had a great rock in his hand. There was blood on the face of the dead man.'

'Of course there was a rock in my hand!' exclaimed Steven. 'I was still pulling the body free.'

'And we must ask ourselves what motive Steven would have for murdering the builder,' said Isaac, his voice of calm authority cutting through the tense atmosphere.

'I have heard it said', Mykola interjected nervously, 'that Steven and Taras often argued.'

'What? I hardly knew him! We'd never argued about anything.' Isaac could see that Steven was becoming a little frenzied now, irritated and perhaps frightened by the statements being made against him.

The Doctor fixed Mykola with his steely gaze. 'Could you produce a witness to testify to the arguments?'

The soldier shook his head, staring at the floor. 'I have only heard it said.' He spoke as if he was reciting someone else's words.

The Doctor looked at Dmitri. 'I ask you therefore to ignore this hearsay and content yourself with the evidence.'

Yevhen turned to the governor. 'Surely we cannot trust the word of this traveller over the word of one of our citizens?'

Dmitri glanced between the soldier and Steven; one refused to meet his gaze, the other stared back with a level gaze, defiant. He turned to Yevhen and Isaac. 'What say my advisers on the matter?'

'The man is clearly guilty!' exclaimed Yevhen. 'We owe no obligation to these travellers who refuse to help us!'

'And yet they volunteer to help with the fortification of the church, with the storing of food,' said Isaac.

Yevhen glared at him. 'We would all do well to remember our circumstances,' he whispered menacingly, as if for Isaac's benefit alone. 'Is it not possible that these travellers are Tartar spies, intent only on learning of our fortifications, our plans?'

'You have said that about us since we first arrived,' said the Doctor. 'I can assure you, we are not spies, nor are we friends... or enemies... of the Mongols.'

Isaac turned his head away from Yevhen. 'In any event, we all know that there are rumours of a Tartar within our city. We should perhaps look elsewhere for their agents.'

The governor addressed Yevhen. 'What do you think we should do?' he asked.

'Execute the murderer,' said Yevhen bluntly.

Dmitri looked at Isaac. The old man was well aware that Yevhen's unblinking gaze had turned in his direction, dark with menace. 'It is your decision, Governor,' he said at length.

Yevhen grinned.

'... but I am mindful of the Doctor's arguments,' Isaac concluded.

Unable to contain himself Yevhen banged the table with his fist, leaping to his feet. 'This Jew offered hospitality to these travellers! He may even be working with them, and the Tartars, to save his own skin!'

'Sit down, adviser Yevhen!' boomed Dmitri. 'This unseemly outburst does you little credit.'

Yevhen looked about the debating chamber, clearly realising he had gone too far. He sat down, his irritation and anger still blazing behind his eyes. 'I am sorry, Governor,' he said through gritted teeth.

Dmitri paused, considering what he had heard. 'It would seem that we do have a murderer in the city. We must not be distracted from our primary task, but if this matter does involve the Tartars it will be well worth our investigation. We shall go with the Doctor to inspect the body.'

'But, my lord...' hissed Yevhen.

Dmitri glanced in his direction. 'Until we are satisfied that Steven is an innocent man, however, he shall be kept in prison.' He turned to Steven. 'If you are innocent, then I am sorry to have to do this.' His voice hardened. 'But if I consider you guilty, then I will execute you, and your friends, publicly, within the hour.'

Lesia looked anxiously up and down the crowded market-place. A subdued feeling of excitement reminded her that there was one face she wanted to observe amongst the sea of people going about their work – so beautiful a face, so noble and handsome! The worried knot in her stomach reminded her that there were many folk she would rather avoid.

Lesia had come to welcome Dodo's presence: in terms of outlook and character they had much in common, and each therefore looked to the other for support and encouragement. When Dodo was busy with her own business, however, and Lesia found herself on her own, she had instead to dig deep to find her own reserves of fortitude and confidence. Until the death of her mother, Lesia had never even imagined that such reserves existed.

She watched as a leatherworker made delicate repairs to a pair of old shoes. Behind him were suspended a host of leather tankards and bottles; wooden pattens, which were worn over shoes when the ground was muddy, rested on a bench to one side, along with rolls of cattle hide and pieces of goatskin. The skins had been dyed – red, yellow, green – and formed a bright point of colour against the drab browns of the stall, like an alpine flower furiously growing on a bare mountainside.

The skins symbolised, she supposed, the hope that burned in the midst of despair. She remembered that certain city officials had questioned the validity of continuing to hold the markets while the Tartars carved their way through the countryside towards Kiev, but the feeling was that the people needed something to cling to, a reminder of their lives before the threat from the east. As long as the markets bustled there seemed to be every chance that life would continue as always, and that perhaps even the Mongols would pass by and leave the people of the city to their business.

'Does my lady require new pattens, new shoes?' asked the leatherworker, looking up from his work.

Lesia shook her head. 'What I have will last.'

He returned to his sewing, disappointed.

'If my lady would only be mine,' came a whisper at her ear, 'I would buy her the finest shoes, the softest stockings, that money could buy.'

She turned to embrace Nahum. 'Why would you do that,' she queried with a smile, 'when your interest would only be to remove them?'

Nahum's face reddened, but he held her gaze as if drinking from her beauty. 'You suspect me of the basest of motives,' he said.

'But am I wrong?'

Nahum shook his head. 'Good lady, do not force me to answer!'

Lesia kissed him lightly on the lips. 'I know your every action is rooted in love,' she said. 'I consider that noble, not base.'

The body had been pulled away from the pile of stones and covered in a makeshift shroud. Isaac watched as the Doctor tugged back the cloth and set to work.

'A shame,' the Doctor muttered as he stared at the man's mutilated face and neck.

'Any death is a pity,' agreed Isaac. He squatted at the Doctor's side, watching attentively.

'I meant that the body had been moved – though you are right, of course,' said the Doctor. 'But it means it will be more difficult to prove Steven's innocence.' He looked over his shoulder to Dmitri, Yevhen and the small group of soldiers who were keeping a discreet distance.

'The men would have wanted to move the body away from the church itself,' said Isaac.

'Ironic for a building surrounded by, perhaps even built on, corpses,' noted the Doctor.

'And for a religion that tells of a dead man returning to life.'

The Doctor glanced at Isaac. 'I am surprised you show such an interest in a dead body. Doesn't your Law warn of –'

'I believe in a god of the living and the dead,' interrupted Isaac. 'Few around here seem to. You were lucky the governor allowed you to examine the body. I am sure Taras's family will not approve.'

'I am sorry this man has died,' said the Doctor, 'but that does not alter my obligation to the truth.'

Isaac nodded.

'Look here.' The Doctor indicated the man's forehead, brown with dried blood. 'This clearly indicates that death took place quite some time ago. It also masks the fact that the attack was centred around the neck and throat.' He pulled at the man's jerkin. 'And look at these.'

Isaac bent forward. 'They look almost like… needle points.' There were three or four puncture marks on the man's neck, and another just in front of his ear. Isaac sighed. 'When the people get to hear of this –'

'Then perhaps they should not,' said Dmitri, who had suddenly appeared behind them. He bent over a little to see the body. 'Better that they continue to think about the enemy without than any demons within.'

'It is clear Steven is innocent,' said the Doctor. 'I'd say this poor fellow was killed as long as a day ago. None of the wounds are consistent with a human attack, even if the murderer was using a large stone or some such. The bone has not been fractured anywhere. Instead, these puncture marks seem to be the cause of death. The tearing around the throat might have become infected, but would not have killed the man so swiftly. It is a peripheral injury.'

'So who killed Taras?' asked Isaac.

'As I said, nothing human,' said the Doctor, pressing his fingers carefully against one of the pinholes in the man's neck. He took a tiny twin-pronged metal object from his pocket, and slowly worked at the wound. 'Unless you are in the habit of killing people with hypodermic needles...' He withdrew a small white sliver from the man's neck, and held it up triumphantly. 'Made of...' He stared more closely, his brow furrowed. 'Bone?'

'You are saying that Taras was killed by an animal?'

'If you use "animal" to encompass everything that is not human... then, yes, an animal is what we should be concentrating on. Not Steven.'

The Doctor got to his feet.

'In any event, look at the man's body – it is covered in dust and dirt from the stones where Steven was working. If the soldier is trying to imply that Steven and this man had an argument, which was resolved by Steven clubbing him with a rock...' The Doctor shook his head. 'No, that's simply not what happened.'

'We should double the city guard,' said Dmitri. 'If a beast is trapped within the city walls, then it must be stopped.'

'That may help,' said the Doctor distantly.

'Do you know what manner of creature attacks in this way?' asked Isaac cautiously.

The Doctor shook his head.

'What is happening to our city?' asked Dmitri. 'What does this attack mean?'

The Doctor began to walk away. 'It means that things are more complicated than I thought,' he said quietly.

* * *

Nahum sat at the table and extended his fingers towards Lesia. She gripped his hands, and smiled. 'I have longed to see you again,' she said.

'And I you.'

Lesia couldn't help but laugh. 'But why an alehouse?'

Nahum looked around him. 'A place of ill repute,' he said, grinning broadly. 'Your father is unlikely to come here!'

'My father,' whispered Lesia, as if the very thought made her flesh crawl.

'How is he towards you?'

Lesia sighed. 'He is polite enough, unless he has drink inside him. Then he sees me as no less evil than the Devil's horsemen who come towards us!'

'Your mother's death changed him.'

Lesia nodded. 'It changed me, but for the better I trust.'

'I know only that you are the most perfect creature I have ever seen. Your eyes are doves, your lips are like a thread of scarlet.'

'Poetry? For me?'

'It is a quotation.'

'I thought the words might not be yours.'

'They are no less true. Hush, there is more. "You have ravished my heart, my sister, my love; you have ravished my heart with but one glance of your eyes! How sweet is your love, my sister, my love; your love is more fine than wine, more fragrant than any spice."'

'The Old Testament?'

'The wisdom books,' agreed Nahum with a smile. 'My father's own translation –'

He stopped, wondering if anyone was listening, but no one was even looking in their direction. And if they were, what would they have seen? Two young lovers, staring wildly into each other's eyes, murmuring the words of gallant love that convention dictated – lovers so lost in each other that every touch was electric.

The Doctor and the others returned to the debating chamber and Steven was brought in from the cells. Dmitri stood at the head of the table waiting for everyone to acknowledge him in silence, then sat down.

He turned to the group of soldiers stationed at the door with Mykola at their head. 'The body may be released to the family for Christian burial,' he said simply. 'Inform them that the poor fellow was killed, and that we have his murderer.'

The Doctor jumped to his feet. 'But you can't still believe that Steven did it!'

Dmitri forestalled his arguments with a gracious wave of his hand. 'I do not wish the people of Kiev to even begin to imagine that there is some other force at work within the city walls. It will do them well to imagine that the matter is in hand, and does not involve animals... Or worse.'

He turned to Steven who stood stoically, surrounded by armour-clad soldiers.

'I am sorry, Steven, but I must ask that you remain in prison. I have wider concerns to consider.'

'But you cannot make Steven a scapegoat!' exclaimed the Doctor, indignant.

Yevhen grinned triumphantly, but said nothing.

Dmitri ignored the Doctor's interjection, his focus remaining on Steven. 'The Doctor's arguments are convincing, but it is also difficult for me to conclude with absolute certainty that you are innocent. The manner of your transport, the machinery you speak of... how am I to know that you do not have access to creatures or witchcraft beyond the normal wit of man?'

'You're making a grave mistake,' said Steven. 'Somebody clearly wants me out of the way.'

'Why?'

Steven was frustrated. 'I don't know,' he admitted. 'But surely it's no coincidence that I found the body.'

'And there is something far more dangerous than Steven at liberty within your city,' added the Doctor. He paused, choosing his words carefully. 'A creature from a faraway land.'

Dmitri nodded. 'There may indeed be truth in what you say. I cannot afford to believe you are in error. I shall be ordering a doubling of the city guard. If there is some animal loose within the city it will be found and destroyed. In addition, my advisers and their families will remain within this building. I do not know when I may need their expertise and, in addition, I wish to keep them safe.'

'But, my lord,' said Yevhen, 'I will be needed to oversee the fortification, and –'

'You will delegate,' interrupted Dmitri. 'You and your family, and Isaac and his, will remain here at all times. These are uncertain days. I will need to rely on you yet more as the Tartars approach.'

He turned to the Doctor. 'I have also instructed that you and your woman will remain here at all times. Steven will be quite safe in the prison.'

The Doctor shook his head. 'I'm sorry. I can't agree to that.'

Dmitri smiled. 'You have no choice.'

'Then I have an alternative proposal to put to you,' said the Doctor. 'I am still not prepared to allow you access to my ship. However, I am now persuaded that something needs to be done about the coming threat of the Mongols.'

Steven looked up sharply.

'Therefore, I wish to travel to the Mongol army and plead for the lives of the people of Kiev.'

Dmitri got to his feet, and walked towards the window. He brought his hands together in front of his face. 'I would rather have you here, old man,' he said.

Steven turned to the Doctor. 'You can't go! You'll be killed!'

Dmitri looked back at the Doctor. 'The Tartars have been known to torture and execute emissaries and diplomats.'

'It is a risk I must take,' said the Doctor calmly.

'Very well,' said Dmitri with a curt nod of his head. 'You are not, after all, a citizen of Kiev. I cannot... should not... order you to stay.' He paused, running a finger along the window frame. 'I shall arrange for an escort, and official papers. You may go at sunrise.'

'Thank you, Governor,' said the Doctor.

Dmitri sighed. 'And may God bring you greater success than those that have gone before you have enjoyed.'


'So we're to be cooped up in here like animals!' exploded Dodo. 'Oh, that's just fantastic!' she added with caustic bitterness.

Lesia couldn't help but smile at her friend's reaction to the news of their enforced curfew. She paused in her sewing. 'We will be well treated,' she said.

'I'm sick of being well treated!' Dodo slumped petulantly on to the bed, pulling decorated pins from her hair. 'I just want to go home.'

Lesia returned to her embroidery, wondering if she should say something, or if silence was the most appropriate response. 'Home *is* important,' she said in a quiet voice a few moments later. 'But I have come to realise that the life you lead, the security you feel – it comes from within, from your spirit. It is not about comfort, or walls, or food and clothing and physical safety.' She glanced up to see that Dodo now had her head in her hands.

'I know,' said Dodo. This time her words were almost whispered, and Lesia had to strain her ears to hear them. 'But I'm so scared...'

'Scared?'

'Scared I'll die here, along with you.' Dodo raised her head, and Lesia could see the tears that were welling at the edges of her eyes. 'And being forced to stay here… makes it feel even more of a prison.'

She rolled on to her back, staring at the ceiling.

'I want a proper bath, I want a toilet that flushes, I want food that doesn't taste of smoke and salt… But even if we were to go – I'd always think that I'd left you behind. Abandoned you all.'

'It is not wrong to want to feel safe,' observed Lesia. 'But fear has been walking at our side for some months now. I am used to it – it has almost become a companion.' She paused, her brow furrowed in concentration. 'Your tales led me to believe you were used to danger!'

'I'm not used to waiting around for it,' said Dodo.

'Then perhaps you would like to come with me later, to pray,' said Lesia. 'There is a chapel where we will not be disturbed.'

Dodo glared at the thick wooden door and the soldiers who doubtless stood the other side. 'And I'm sick of them following us around,' she said.

'Please try to look on our enforced stay in a more positive light,' said Lesia. She put her needlework down, grinning broadly – and was pleased to see a hint of a smile crossing Dodo's features. 'This is a well-guarded building, so we might be allowed a little more freedom… and a little more privacy.'

Dodo sat up, looking closely at her friend. 'What are you planning?'

Lesia felt herself flushing a little. 'There is someone I wish to meet,' she said, avoiding Dodo's gaze. 'Being here may help with our… assignations.'

'You never told me you had a boyfriend!'

'I am in love with a young man, if that is what you mean. But it is best that his name is not common knowledge.' She glanced up at Dodo, not used to the blunt way in which her companion expressed herself. 'You will not tell?'

'Of course not! Who is he?'

Lesia moistened a cloth in a small pitcher of water that stood on a bench by her bed and gently patted it over her face. 'His name is Nahum.'

'Nahum? Unusual name.' Dodo paused in thought. 'Isn't that Isaac's son?' she asked in surprise.

Lesia nodded. 'Our fathers quarrel. You can understand why our relationship must be kept secret for fear of wagging tongues.'

'Of course,' smiled Dodo. 'It all makes sense now. I noticed you staring at him the other day. I thought he had his flies undone or something.'

'Flies?'

Before Dodo could speak there was a tap at the door.

'Who's there?' called Lesia.

'It's the Doctor,' came a muffled voice in reply. 'Sorry to trouble you, my dear, but I would like a word with Dodo, if I may.'

Dodo pulled the door open. 'You didn't have anything to do with us being stuck here, did you, Doctor?'

'Gracious, no,' said the Doctor. He nodded politely in Lesia's direction before returning his gaze to Dodo. 'The governor is clearly concerned for our safety, and that of his advisers. My dear, he really does have the best interests of all his people at heart.'

'Where's Steven?'

'Safe, but in prison. You hadn't heard?'

'I'd heard rumours. I didn't think they were true! What are we going to do to get him out?'

'Nothing,' replied the Doctor. 'As I say, he's safe enough, and –'

'But we've got to do something!' interrupted Dodo.

The Doctor chuckled. 'Oh, my child, you and Steven are so alike – you cannot stand being idle!' He turned towards Lesia, drawing her into the conversation. 'I've tried telling her that some things are beyond even me, and that worrying about them will achieve nothing, but will she listen?'

'We have similar conversations, sir,' observed Lesia.

'Yes, young lady, I'm sure you do.' The Doctor's voice dropped to a precise whisper. 'Now, listen to me, both of you. I have asked for leave to travel to the Mongol army, and plead for Kiev. Now, while I'm gone –'

'But you'll be killed!'

'Oh, really, my dear, this is becoming most tiresome! Yes, Steven said the same thing, but I am confident I shall return in one piece. Now, while I'm gone, the important thing is to be alert to all that happens around you. Staying here, in the governor's residence, is really very advantageous. It is the hub of all that happens in Kiev.' He paused, his voice becoming grave. 'Something awful has been released.' He sighed. 'Desperate men will always make desperate choices... but if only they realised the true consequences of their actions!'

'We'll be careful,' said Dodo. 'But I still don't understand. Why are you going to the Mongols?'

The Doctor paced the room. 'I've told you what might happen if the people of Kiev, still less the rulers of the Mongol Empire, were to gain access to the secrets of the TARDIS. Now I have come to believe that there is something in Kiev that speaks of another world, another time. I cannot let the Mongols have that. Even a hint of its technology might prove devastating!'

He paused, mopping his brow as if in anticipation of the rigorous journey that awaited him.

'I must convince the Mongols not to attack Kiev, or at the

very least to pass swiftly through it.' He turned to Lesia. 'Of course, I hope to plead for the safety of all the citizens. Please be assured, my dear, that my reluctance to allow access to my ship does not mean I am unconcerned by your fate.'

Lesia nodded demurely, but said nothing.

'I will be leaving shortly,' said the Doctor. 'But I will return as swiftly as I can.'

Lesia watched as her friend gave the old man an impromptu hug. Dodo was a slim thing, with little strength, but beneath her embrace the Doctor seemed liable to bend or snap. Lesia could scarcely believe that the fate of their city rested on his ancient shoulders.

Bishop Vasil strode into the vestibule beyond the main entrance of the governor's residence. He looked less than happy at having to leave the cathedral, a fish plucked from water and left floundering on the ground.

Yevhen watched as he reached for a hollowed-out horn that he carried beneath his robes, and drew from it a medicinal preparation. The bishop dabbed the greenish embrocation on to his tongue with a look of unfettered disgust.

'Are you well, my lord?' asked Yevhen.

'I have head pains and a feeling of dizziness,' explained Vasil. He indicated the sheep's horn of medicine. 'It is derived from a wort of some kind. I have found that, on occasion, it works when prayer does not.'

Yevhen drew him to one side, away from the prying ears of the soldiers close to the door. 'I am sorry I had to ask to see you here,' he whispered.

Vasil looked around him with distaste. 'I had heard that the governor wished to limit the movements of his advisers,' he said. A particular shame for you, being trapped in so gloomy a place.'

'It leaves me isolated from the preparations. The governor clearly expects me to do nothing but talk!'

'Whereas you are a man of action,' noted the bishop. His eyes were full of sly innuendo. 'There is doubtless much you would wish to do... or perhaps have already done...'

Yevhen caught the implication of his words. 'That may be so,' he said defensively. He paused, wondering how best to draw the information he wanted from Vasil. 'You know, of course, that the young male traveller is in prison?'

Vasil nodded. 'Yes. Poor Taras.' The bishop chuckled. 'Rumour has it that he was killed within the confines of the cathedral.'

'Nonsense, of course,' said Yevhen.

'Of course,' said Vasil. 'He was found by the Church of the Virgin, was he not? It is no small distance from the cathedral catacombs to the church.'

'The catacombs?'

Vasil smiled. 'The dead man was a friend of yours, no?'

'I have known him for some years,' said Yevhen. 'I wonder...' he added cautiously. 'I wonder what will happen to the murderer while he is in prison...'

Vasil straightened, as if signifying that he had said quite enough and that even Yevhen's allusions were becoming too blunt. 'Some things are known to God alone,' he said, and turned smartly for the door.

As darkness fell, the house descended from hysterical sobbing to near silence. Elisabet listened intently as the boys struggled to find peace underneath heavy blankets; only the dogs that curled at their feet seemed immune to the stresses the family had experienced that day.

It had struck Elisabet as peculiar that Taras had not returned the previous night, but it was not without precedent. In happier times – times before the devilish Tartars swept into

Europe – Taras had had a reputation as something of a wastrel, frequenting taverns and places of ill repute until well into the morning. Sometimes, when he finally returned, having spent money they did not have on the ale she could still smell on his breath, they would argue, in harsh, clipped whispers for fear of waking the children. He would always win her round, blaming Yevhen for his late return and talking animatedly of some scheme, some plan, that would make things better for them.

How she wished he was here with her now. She would rather argue with him for all eternity than spend the last few months of her life as a widow.

Word had arrived just before midday that her husband had been found, and that he was dead. Elisabet had been working, as usual, in the governor's kitchens. She had assumed that Taras had been drunk and had ended up sleeping in a gutter or perhaps in the bed of the one of the whores who frequented the east side of the city. In a moment, as the soldier stammered out the awful truth, her world, and all its preconceived notions of future happiness, had come crashing around her.

She could not remember much from the hours that followed, bar that she would never have believed her capacity for tears. Each time she thought she was in control of her melancholy, she would glance at her dumbfounded children and the crushing sadness would descend again.

As she put the boys to bed, she had been telling herself over and over again that, if she truly believed in the Christ, she would one day be reunited with Taras in a far, far better place – a place not under threat from the horsemen of the very Devil himself! She wondered if the grief she felt would be as nothing to the coming destruction which, quite possibly, no one would survive.

Her thoughts were interrupted by the sound of the night watchmen in the street. She walked over to the window and closed the wooden shutters.

Elisabet stepped carefully through the darkness. There was little point in further delaying the inevitable battle with sleep. She settled on to a mattress.

Almost immediately, a dreaming haze of thoughts and memories enveloped her. She imagined Taras's death, killed by one of the travellers, and then at the hands of some great beast; she remembered the soldier's grim news, told again and again like a grotesque liturgy. She watched herself falling in love, tumbling in the hills around Kiev before the sun was blotted out by the dust of the Tartar's hooves. For a moment, she and Taras were standing in the cathedral, exchanging vows, on a day when God Himself seemed to smile. A flash of imagined, remembered pain brought her to the agony of childbirth, when she wished for death as a kind of release from the torture, the torture of the Fall. Then a noise – an insistent sound, like a drum.

She was in bed again, in that dazed world between wakefulness and sleep. Through the clutter of images and fantasies she heard another muffled thump from the direction of the door.

Her nervous ears were suddenly alert to the myriad sounds underneath the silence of the dark. Perhaps it was nothing – a hound, perhaps, or a thief momentarily pressing himself into the shadows to avoid the night-watch patrols.

Then it came again – this time a much more deliberate tap on the door.

'Who's there?' she called. 'We are all in bed.'

The noise continued, soft taps, lengthy thuds, as if someone outside were trying to communicate with her.

For the first time, a chill slid down Elisabet's spine. She

cautiously approached the door, still not sure whether or not she was dreaming.

'Who is it?'

No reply.

She pulled back one of the shutters, but the fenestral lattice of wood and tallow-soaked linen that it covered showed nothing of the street.

Elisabet gathered her careering thoughts, and pulled open the door.

She was ready to scream, to alert the guards and the watchmen, but even she was not prepared for what she saw.

It was Taras, a kind of lopsided grin on his face, his hands loosely held upwards as if in supplication.

Elisabet gripped the frame of the doorway as her legs weakened and threatened to give way. 'But... but you are dead,' she heard herself stammer.

Taras moved his head slowly, as if trying to pinpoint the source of the words. Still he did not speak. Instead, he opened his arms to embrace her.

Elisabet collapsed into them, the only solid, dependable things in a world gone mad. 'I knew you were not dead,' she found herself repeating over and over again. 'I knew we would always be together!'

Taras's smile became stronger. How beautiful his lips looked, glistening in the moonlight. How mysterious his eyes.

Elisabet raised her head for a kiss.

As her husband brought his head downwards, his mouth was full of needles.

# V
# Confutatis meledictis, flammis acribus addictis

The sleeping arrangements in the prison must have been bad, for they made me think longingly of my rough bed in the governor's home.

I have never had as many nightmares and dreams as I had that first night within the damp, grey walls of the prison. Behind my closed eyes I saw, over and over again, my own execution, played out in various and increasingly grisly forms. On occasions I swear I could smell the fatty stench of flesh burning on a pyre. Worse still, every time my slumbering body moved I would graze a knee or an elbow on the harsh stone floor, and momentarily find myself awake, in darkness and terrified. I had but a thin mattress stuffed with straw for comfort – and, by all accounts, I was lucky to have that.

I awoke to the clatter of bowls being dropped in front of me. They contained pottage of some sort. I had little interest in food, but I had no idea when my next meal might come so I set at one of the bowls with gusto. There was a little water, too, in a tankard of stiff leather.

The other bowl belonged to my fellow prisoner, who had been resolutely asleep since my arrival. I did check on him at one point, fearful that he might be dead, but could just detect the flow of air from his lips.

I suppose it was the sound of my eating that finally roused him.

'What?' he exclaimed, sitting up swiftly. 'Who is there?'

'A fellow prisoner,' I said bitterly. 'You've been asleep for *hours*.'

'Sleep is my one remaining privilege,' said the man. 'Forgive me if I exercise that privilege as often as I can.'

He was a small fellow, little more than protruding bones in a sack of wrinkled skin topped by a mop of white hair and eyes that blinked like a mole's. It was difficult to guess exactly how old he was but, in a society where life expectancy is about thirty years, this man was positively ancient.

'I am Olexander,' said the man by way of introduction. 'Former official to the court of Prince Michael.'

'I'm Steven Taylor,' I said.

'A tailor, eh? My clothes are in need of your skills.'

'No, I'm not…' My words trailed away. It didn't really seem to matter what the old man thought I was. 'How did you end up in here?' I asked.

'It is a long story,' he replied. He came over and sat at my side, and began to pick at his bowl of food.

'I've got plenty of time,' I said.

'To whom is your allegiance?' queried the man, clearly worried that I might have been sent to spy on him.

'I am a traveller,' I said. 'I've been imprisoned on a charge of murder, but I'm completely innocent. Circumstantial evidence has been twisted against me.'

'Who is to blame?'

I paused – this questioning could cut both ways. I had no idea of Olexander's 'allegiance', as he put it. Perhaps he was a plant, placed in my cell to spy on *me*, thus incriminating me further.

I looked closely at his face, at the creased lines of decades and the honest interest of his eyes, and decided that this man was barely capable of wilful duplicity. I trusted him in an instant.

'I think adviser Yevhen may have had a hand in it.'

Clearly I had said the right thing. Olexander's eyes gleamed like polished buttons. 'Yevhen! Is that traitorous dog still up to his old tricks?'

'It would seem that way.'

'Then clearly we have more in common than our current location, Steven,' said the man with a smile. He ran his fingers round the edge of his bowl, and sucked on them greedily. 'My mouth is well accustomed to the food here,' he said, by way of explanation. 'Yours will be so, in time.'

I'd long since had my fill, and pushed my half-empty bowl away. 'I'm not planning on staying here that long.'

'That is what I first said.' Olexander sighed sadly. 'Over a year ago, I think.'

'A year!' I couldn't bear the thought of even another night in the cell.

'I imagine the Tartars will attack long before the next year is spent,' he continued, though his tone of voice implied that death at the hands of the Mongols was preferable to continued imprisonment. I wondered if, in time, I too would share that feeling of desperation.

Olexander turned to me, his small eyes still burning with energy – and, I had to concede, perhaps also with madness or senility.

'What do you know of the coming Tartar hordes?' he asked.

'I'll tell you whatever you want', I said, 'if you tell me how you ended up here.'

'Of course,' smiled the man. 'Do they not say that the enemy of my enemy is my friend?' He paused, gathering his thoughts. 'I was not always as you see me now,' he said. 'I was once a man of status, of knowledge – a trusted adviser, no less! My particular interest has always been the study of languages and religious history. Before I came to Kiev I was a monk in the Church of God.'

'Why did you leave?'

'The Church? It is an imperfect body at best. It is full of fallen men and women, you know!'

He smiled, and I saw a faraway look in his eyes. I sensed that the memories he recalled didn't simply help him tell his tale, but also offered an escape from his current situation.

'I came to the conclusion that although it is easier to be holy in a place where you are shut off from the world, this does not make it a *right* way to seek after holiness. Well, for others, it might,' he conceded, with a rhetorical flap of a bony hand. 'But I wanted something else, something more. Far better to light a candle than to curse the darkness, no?'

He paused, muttering to himself, then exclaimed, 'Thankfully, I had learnt many skills over the years… if only you could see the manuscripts I illuminated!'

He held up his fingers for me to see. They looked normal to my eyes, but I said nothing.

'You can see the gold on my hands from the hours I spent in the scriptorium,' he said.

I nodded. 'All this knowledge would have come in useful in Kiev.'

'It did – but it also led to my imprisonment. Adviser Yevhen had obtained a manuscript of some sort. Now, his family are a rustic bunch, and Yevhen is the first to achieve any prominence. Even so, he could not make head or tail of the text, so he came to me for a translation. Although it was in some obscure rural dialect I could tell immediately that this was no mere note of family history. Yevhen claimed that the document revealed many great secrets, specifically the tale of Kiev's heavenly guardian which had been brought to the city long ago while the cathedral was being built. He was not wrong.'

'What did the manuscript say?'

'Taken at face value, it seemed to confirm many of the details of Yevhen's claim. That an angel had fallen from heaven after some sort of battle against the Evil One; that this celestial creature was contained within a coffin or a casket, but that, though it seemed dead, it was in fact only sleeping. It was waiting for a time of tribulation, at which point it would wake and come to the defence of the people of Kiev.'

'The people who found this "angel"... How did they know all this?'

Olexander paused, trying to remember. 'The manuscript was not specific, though there was a suggestion that the angel had somehow spoken directly to the men who found its casket.' He paused, glancing around him as if to confirm that we were quite alone. 'The manuscript claims to have been written soon after the coffin's arrival. However, I suppose it may have been based on little more than the fanciful stories of Yevhen's forefathers, given permanence by the scribe to whom the task was entrusted.'

'And where is the casket now?'

'The terminology was vague,' said Olexander. 'The vocabulary, the syntax, deliberately obscure. But I believe that it referred to a series of tunnels and chambers set deep in the very foundations of the cathedral.'

'Do these tunnels exist?'

'Some believe them to, though I have only seen them mentioned in the manuscript.'

'They could provide some refuge from the coming attack for the people of Kiev,' I suggested.

Olexander smiled. 'I said as much, but Yevhen was dismissive. He may be right. Yes, a few hundred people, possibly more, could lock themselves away in the catacombs with whatever provisions they could muster. But what then? The food runs out, and they die. Or they emerge from the tunnels – and find the Tartars patiently waiting for them.'

I nodded, taking all this in, though I could not see how either the tunnels or the casket could have much to do with

Yevhen's plans now. Or, indeed, Olexander's imprisonment. I said as much.

'Ah, I was coming to that,' Olexander said. 'Yevhen became obsessed with this angel. It was, he concluded, the only hope for Kiev, the only way we could avoid death at the hands of the Tartars. When I questioned the wisdom of trusting in so ancient a document, he told the ecclesiastical authorities I was a dangerous heretic working on translating the Holy Gospels into base Russian.'

'Were you?'

'No, the idea does not interest me in the slightest,' said Olexander. 'I am quite content with the Latin, the Greek. But my skill with languages, and my background within the cloisters, worked against me. Yevhen had no evidence against me, but there was little I could do to dispute the charges. Bishop Vasil sent entreaties to the prince, requesting my immediate imprisonment on charges of heresy.'

'You were imprisoned by a bishop?'

Olexander paused. 'I believe, in this world, it is important to distinguish between the true and holy Church of Christ, and the fallen and failing human authorities placed before us. It does me little credit to say this, but I am not sure that Vasil is on the side of the true Church.'

'Vasil and Yevhen seem to have a lot in common.'

Olexander nodded. 'And the one was often seen working for the other, though I would not like to guess which partner is the dominant one, and which the subordinate.' He turned to look at me closely, the troubled look in his now tired, milky eyes sending a shiver down my spine. 'If you have been imprisoned here on false charges I am sure it has something to do with one or both of those men, and that the intention is to divert attention elsewhere. While people mull over your guilt or innocence, one can only imagine the plans that Vasil and Yevhen will be hatching together. And the plans of these men are rarely for good.'

As the day passed us by – Olexander said he had become an expert at telling the time merely by establishing the position of the sun as seen through the cell's single window – we spoke further about what little we both knew of the situation in Kiev, and of the coming Mongol army. I was amazed by the breadth and depth of Olexander's knowledge, which didn't seem unduly stemmed by his incarceration. The old man replied that I would be surprised how much gossip one could hear even within a prison, but I had seen little evidence of this so far. This benighted, dark place barely seemed like the hub of Kiev, still less a place of fine conversation and fruitful innuendo.

I told Olexander of the intention to fortify the Church of the Virgin, and the plans that were being made to store food in case of a prolonged siege. As he spoke of other battles he had heard of or seen, I reflected that warfare in this era was often a drawn-out and methodical process. With only the most primitive forms of transportation available, the movement of armies was painfully slow. When they finally met, even a small skirmish could last for weeks and months rather than hours and days. I even got the impression that a kind of unspoken truce was often called at nightfall, or at the approach of winter, though Olexander was quick to remind me that the battles themselves were bloody affairs, an anarchy of indistinguishable foot soldiers hacking away at any movement in a desperate attempt to stay alive. There were, I reflected, no laws here concerning the treatment of prisoners, no arms conventions or pacts on the size of armies or the weapons they used.

In any case, the Mongols were reputed to take little notice of whatever 'rules' might exist. They were interested in nothing beyond their own honourable code, and their total success on the field of battle. Rarely were their sieges prolonged – they were too well equipped, too clever, to be drawn into any extended, resource-sapping campaign. And the reports from the principalities they had conquered underlined the terrible efficiency of their advance thus far.

Later we lapsed into silence, seeming already to have exhausted each other's interest in conversation. There was much more he could have asked me, I suppose, about my home, and the life I had left behind, but Olexander was very precise in what he wanted to learn. He sat in a corner for some time, mulling over what I had said about Yevhen, whispering darkly.

A little later, we both looked up as we heard keys rattling in the lock. The door swung open to reveal a figure dressed in chain mail. I thought at first it was one of the guards with another gruesome meal for us to work our way through, though I could not understand why he remained in the doorway for so long. It was only when he removed his helmet of dull metal that I realised it was Mykola, the soldier who had incriminated me in the presence of the governor.

'What do you want?' I asked. To be honest, I expected him to act as a villain, come to explain his tortuous plan to me from the far end of a sharpened blade. Instead, and despite his grinning visage, I got the impression that he was a simple pawn in a wider scheme. Mykola was, like all good foot soldiers, following orders – and I wasn't entirely sure that he understood their complexity.

As if a certain protocol had to be maintained Mykola unsheathed his sword, which he wafted in my general direction. 'Tell me why we cannot open the doors on your blue box,' he said, completely ignoring Olexander who, I noticed out of the corner of my eye, was now cowering by his makeshift bed.

'I take it you've tried?' I asked. I thought of Dmitri's plan to guard the TARDIS, which was intended not only to preclude our access to it, but also to limit the unwelcome attention of his own people. 'Did you bribe the guards?'

Mykola shook his head against the distractions I was placing in his way. 'It does not matter how we gained access... Tell me how to open the box.'

'Why?' I queried. 'It's just a box. It's full of clothing, one or two bottles of fine wine, nothing more.'

'It is said that it is a means of transportation,' Mykola stated.

'Who told you that?' I asked with a grin. 'That's ridiculous! I mean, where are the wheels?'

'Wheels?' Doubt flooded Mykola's features, furrowing his brow.

'How else could a chest of that size be expected to move around? Think about it.' I took a step towards the man, trying to defuse the situation.

Mykola immediately raised his sword, angling the blade in my direction. (I didn't like the look of the weapon at all. It was not a thing of subtlety, a polished scimitar or beautiful Samurai sword, the triumph of its maker's art. It was a rough-hewn thing, almost too heavy to hold, lacking any semblance of a sharpened tip; in grace and form, it was a match for only a butcher's cleaver. And, whatever the stains along the blade implied, they were enough to make me avert my eyes and look at its owner.)

'I could kill you here,' said the soldier simply. 'I would say you were trying to escape. Away from the governor's residence no one would be on hand to disprove my story.' He flicked a glance in the direction of Olexander, who seemed to be studying the fine detail of the blocks that formed the ceiling over our heads.

'That's why you wanted me away from there,' I said. 'Down here I imagine you can get away with murder.'

'I do not want to kill you,' said Mykola.

'Who are you working for?' I asked, despite the sword that hovered close to my face. 'Adviser Yevhen?'

The soldier refused to be distracted. 'I have been sent to find a key. We have noticed some sort of lock on the side of the box. You must carry a key.'

'I don't have one,' I said. 'If I did, don't you think I might have used it by now?'

Mykola conceded a little ground, stepping backwards, though his words remained bitter with assumed bravado. 'I can kill you and search your clothing if you wish. Or you can give me the key.'

I took another step, forcing him back again. 'Don't you get it? The Doctor's the only one who can open the box. Even if I had a key, and I gave it to you, you'd not be able to open the TARDIS, let alone do anything constructive with it.' I risked another half-step, and Mykola moved back again. 'I suppose you could ask my friend Dodo whether she has a key,' I suggested lightly. 'She's right behind you.'

Mykola began to turn as Dodo brought a huge earthenware water jug down on his head. He grunted once, then slid to the floor with all the grace of a tranquillised bull.

I jumped over his body to embrace Dodo. 'Well done,' I exclaimed. 'Perfect timing!'

Dodo grinned, indicating Lesia who stood at her side. 'We thought we'd come along and see if you needed a hand.'

I grinned. 'I don't think I could have survived another hour.'

'You would have found a way,' observed Olexander from the far end of the cell. 'I did.'

I introduced Olexander to Dodo, but the old man seemed more interested in Lesia.

'Is that you, Lesia? My, how you have grown! And in just a year, as well.'

Lesia curtsied demurely. 'You have been away from us for more than a year,' she said.

'Really?' This revelation seemed to upset the old man, as if another certainty he had relied on had been shown to be false. 'It is so difficult to mark the passing of the days, months and seasons. And yet I remember coming here as clear as this morning's sunrise.' Something like tears prickled at the corners of his rheumy eyes.

I turned to Dodo, impatient to find how she came to be here. 'How did you get away from the governor's residence?' I asked.

Dodo couldn't help but laugh. 'Lesia knows the building like the back of her hand – she used to play in it as a child. It's riddled with tunnels and little passages that don't really go anywhere. She told me about a sort of chute that leads from one of the main corridors into the servant's quarters. From there, it was easy to get out through the tradesmen's entrance.'

'But how did you evade the guards?'

Dodo looked puzzled. 'There was a young guard assigned to us. I happened to mention to him that, where we come from, women's skirts are a little shorter.' She paused. 'Well, quite a bit shorter.'

'I was intrigued,' said Lesia. 'I felt it only appropriate to illustrate!'

Dodo continued. 'While the guard was looking at Lesia, I smacked him over the head with some crockery.'

I glanced at the comatose soldier at our feet. He grunted, rocking his head from side to side.

'I should set up as a neurosurgeon,' I joked. 'With you

around, I could make a fortune.' I led the others towards the door. 'We ought to be going. How many guards are out there?'

'None,' replied Lesia. 'They seem to have been sent away.'

I nodded. 'Allowing our friend here to get all heavy without interruption.'

As I headed for the door Olexander exclaimed 'Where are you going?'

'Anywhere but here,' I replied. 'Come on.'

'But I can't come with you!' said the old man, genuine anguish creeping into his voice. 'Unless my reputation is restored, I cannot leave this place. Without my good name, I am as nothing in the city of Kiev.'

Lesia turned to him. 'But you must come. I have missed you greatly. You cannot rot away in here!' Her affection for Olexander was clear. Given the strength of her reaction, I came to wonder if she had been told he was dead rather than imprisoned.

'I must submit myself to the authorities,' said Olexander. 'But you go, Steven. Clear your name from without while I work from within to clear mine.'

'Are you absolutely sure you won't come with us?' I asked, glancing at the unconscious form of Mykola. The soldier was stirring again.

'You go,' said Olexander firmly. 'I have welcomed your presence, however brief. I sense that things are moving, in the city and beyond – events we may or may not be able to control. We all have our roles to play, our fates to uncover.'

He embraced Lesia warmly and then shooed us away. As we ran through the deserted corridors, I couldn't help but wonder how the soldier would react when he came to and found one prisoner escaped, and another sitting at his feet and looking calmly back at him with those old but wise eyes.

* * *

Even though the other soldiers had been sent away, I was surprised that we didn't encounter a soul as we made our way to the gated entrance to the prison. I suspected that, perhaps, with human resources very much at a premium, all the other prisoners were sent to work on the fortifications during the day. Olexander was too old to participate – and whoever had arranged for Mykola to ask about the keys to the TARDIS clearly had other plans for me.

'We must get back to the residence of the governor,' said Lesia. 'Even if the guard we tricked is embarrassed into silence, my father will notice that I am gone.'

'I'm sorry to have to say this,' I said, as we sought sanctuary in the deep shadows of the city's walls. 'But I think you should keep an eye on your father. Something is going on here, and Yevhen is at the root of it.'

Lesia nodded curtly without a word.

'Leave it to us,' said Dodo.

'Thank you for rescuing me,' I said.

'Try not to get in trouble,' warned Dodo. 'We don't want to have to do it again!'

'Where will you go?' Lesia asked.

I smiled. 'There's a certain bishop I want to keep an eye on.'

# VI
# Rosa rubicundior, lilio candidor, omnibus formosior, semper in te glorior

Night had fallen. The Doctor and a group of soldiers assembled in the shadows of the great gates of Kiev. The men whispered nervously in the light of enormous guttering torches as they sought to reassure the horses; only the Doctor, his long white hair flowing in the bitter breeze, seemed impatient to be off.

Massed footfalls alerted the Doctor to the arrival of Dmitri and his retinue of guards.

'I have grave news,' announced the governor, drawing the Doctor to one side.

The Doctor arched his eyebrows. 'Really?'

'Your friend has escaped from prison.'

The Doctor's face fell. 'I am sorry,' he said. 'Steven is clearly frightened. I implore you not to take that as a sign of guilt.'

Dmitri lowered his voice. 'His flight raises all manner of suspicions in my mind,' he said. 'I am told that when the escape was finally noted the building was almost completely deserted. The soldiers say they were sent away by Mykola, who himself was discovered, unconscious, in the cell. He told some story of the black arts, which I do not countenance. Suspicion points instead to treachery, possibly to Yevhen, and perhaps even to an attempt on the life of your friend.'

'Perhaps Steven is safer now than within the walls of your prison,' noted the Doctor.

Dmitri nodded. 'Indeed. I shall not hunt for him – my soldiers are, in any case, required elsewhere. But I have ordered that

Mykola lead your expedition to the Tartars. He will join us soon.'

'Do you think that sensible?'

Dmitri extended an arm towards the Doctor, perhaps the closest he had yet come to a sign of affection for the traveller. 'You are wise enough to watch for Mykola's trickery. Pray that I am wise enough to do the same with Yevhen.'

The Doctor nodded. 'I understand.'

'I am hopeful of your success with the Tartars,' said Dmitri, more loudly and for the benefit of the soldiers.

'It will be a challenge,' said the Doctor. 'I must first of all win their trust, their respect.'

'You already have mine,' said Dmitri.

The Doctor looked around. 'Though I am impatient to get started, I wonder why we must leave when it is dark. Surely we would make better progress by day?'

'We have no idea how far advanced the Tartar scouts are. Better that you leave now.'

'And get as far as we can before we are spotted?' The Doctor paused. 'Yes, yes… I suppose that makes sense.'

Dmitri turned as Mykola approached. The soldier had swapped his chain mail for a lighter and partial armour of leather. The Doctor noted, with interest, the cut that still bled just above his ear – however Steven had escaped, Mykola would be mindful of what had happened for some time to come.

'The good wishes of our city go with you, Mykola,' said Dmitri.

The soldier seemed less than enamoured by the prospect of the expedition, though he managed a curt nod of respect.

With a last glance at the Doctor, Dmitri strode back towards his home.

Mykola began giving orders to the men, preparing them for

the ordeal that lay before them. The Doctor patted the graceful neck of his mount, a chestnut-brown stallion, and watched the soldier closely. He sensed a crushed resignation about him. Whatever Mykola's role in the arrest of Steven, and whatever had happened since, it seemed unlikely that it had been entirely of his own doing.

Mykola turned to the Doctor.

'I am concerned that the expedition will be arduous. You are old and slow, and many dangers lurk in the forests.'

The Doctor was indignant. 'Old? My boy, you don't know the meaning of the word! In any case, I am quite capable of looking after myself. How do you think I have lived for so long, hmm?' The Doctor made a show of leading his horse towards the city gates. 'Shall we proceed?'

Dodo and Lesia returned to the governor's residence to find Yevhen waiting for them. He was pacing his daughter's room, arms behind his back, boiling with anger. It was like being caught creeping home after a late party, but when Dodo saw the flames that flickered behind Yevhen's eyes, and remembered their situation, her stomach began to churn with fear.

Yevhen fixed his eyes on Lesia. 'Daughter,' he said. 'Thank you for joining us once more.'

'Father, I only wanted to take in the twilight air. I meant –'

'You meant me to look a fool!' interrupted Yevhen. 'The governor has ordered that all of us stay here, where we are safe. I do not like this decision of his, but I am a man of authority, and I live under authority. I respect that decision. And yet I find that you do not!'

'We didn't do anything,' offered Dodo. 'But this place is so claustrophobic! We're sick of having soldiers trailing round after us all the time.'

'They are to keep you safe!' exploded Yevhen. 'Do you have any idea of the dangers we all face?'

'Yes, I do', said Dodo forcefully, 'and it's terrible. But allowing your daughter a little freedom isn't going to hurt anyone.'

'Silence!' bellowed Yevhen, raising a hand as if to strike Dodo. 'I have heard of the "freedom" you espouse – a debauched freedom where womenfolk do and dress as they please.'

'What's so wrong with that?'

'You forget that women are under God's curse. All know that man is nobler than woman, and of greater virtue.' Yevhen stared at Lesia, grinding his teeth in fury. 'Better to have a single good son than a hundred sluts as daughters!'

At this, Lesia collapsed on to her bed in tears. Yevhen went over to her, his face red.

'Do not think I am deaf to the rumours that you've been spreading your legs for some boy!'

'It is not true,' said Lesia limply. 'Father... don't say anything else. You have been drinking.'

'If I ever find out who he is I will tear him to pieces with my bare hands!'

'Oi!' said Dodo, tapping Yevhen on the shoulder to get his attention. 'Cut it out!'

Yevhen swung around wildly, arms flailing. 'Don't touch me, you little whore!'

'Don't you dare call me that!' shouted Dodo, with equal passion.

A silent moment passed as Dodo held Yevhen's gaze, her fists balled as if preparing for a fight.

Yevhen glanced away.

'Now, I didn't really pay much attention to scripture classes in school,' said Dodo in a quieter voice, staring levelly back at Yevhen. 'But I do remember that after all the animals were made, this God bloke you claim to believe in created men, and then he created women. So, if there's a pinnacle of creation, it ain't you lot!'

Yevhen recoiled as if physically struck. 'How dare you!'

Dodo sensed she was in the ascendancy. 'Now get out, and leave your daughter alone, or I will scream so loudly, and tell such stories, that even that bishop of yours will have to act.'

Yevhen glanced back at his daughter, then turned on the spot and marched towards the door without another word.

As the door slammed shut, Lesia began to cry again.

The Doctor's party made swift progress along the plains, the well-bred horses keeping to a dignified half-gallop. Wherever possible the group sought partial sanctuary at the edges of the woods that pockmarked the terrain. Under the great branches of the ancient conifers it was blacker than midnight ink, though the lanterns and torches danced like fireflies in the bitter autumn air. But none of the men grumbled, for they hoped the trees offered some respite from watching, devilish eyes. It was only when there was no cover at all, and they were forced to proceed through the exposed grasslands, that a true sense of awful expectation gripped them.

The Doctor, his body aching with every movement of the horse beneath him, had long since lost track of time. He concentrated instead on the simple practicalities of remaining as comfortable as possible in the unyielding saddle, his ears and eyes alert to the slightest hint of the Mongols. All the while his mind roamed freely elsewhere, turning over fragments, attempting to make a pattern from the puzzle pieces.

The discovery of Taras's corpse had unsettled him even more than he had let on. He was worried for his friends and for the people of Kiev, as the one action of the creature responsible for the builder's death had been to kill rather than strive for communication. Worse still, such a being would not have turned up out of the blue, but must have come in some sort of craft. Even one salvaged weapon, one jury-rigged bomb, could change the course of human history.

The Mongols had already carved out an enormous empire, built in no small part on the expertise and invention of the lands and races they had conquered. The Chin dynasty had provided them with gunpowder, the most advanced weapon the Earth had yet seen, and the Mongol hordes had proved more than adept at finding new ways to exploit the resource. If they were to find themselves in the position to exploit a truly advanced technology, the consequences would be unthinkable.

His thoughts were interrupted by Mykola's order to slow the pace a little. Some of the horses were tiring, and the young captain had every reason to believe the Mongol army was still a distance away.

The Doctor turned to him. 'I imagine you're glad to leave the governor in such safe hands.'

'What do you mean?'

'His advisers, Isaac and... What is the other fellow's name?'

'Yevhen.'

'Yevhen. Yes, that's right. That's right. Do you know him?'

Mykola shook his head, plainly irritated by the Doctor's whispered conversation.

'Well, he seems perfectly capable. If I have a concern, however, it is that Yevhen is quite prepared to do things his way. Bend the rules, the law, if necessary.'

'I know nothing of the work of the advisers.' Mykola paused. 'I do what I am asked.'

'As indeed we all must,' said the Doctor with a smile, furiously trying to build a bridge of understanding with the man. 'Yes, yes. But if different people ask us different things...'

'Then we must decide which voice to listen to.'

'But that can be difficult...'

Mykola shook his head. 'I listen to God, God's people on Earth, the authorities He has placed here... Only then do I listen to the voices of men.'

'But what if the authorities are mistaken, hmm?' The Doctor paused. 'An adviser like Yevhen is no less likely to make an error of judgement than anyone else. These are difficult times. We all might be called upon to perform actions we would rather not perform.'

'Perhaps.' Mykola edged his horse away from the Doctor's. 'But then our consciences must remain strong and hearty. As is mine.' He paused. 'You are asking who told me to lie about Steven, no?'

'Well, I...' mumbled the Doctor.

'I cannot tell you, but rest assured, it was not adviser Yevhen.'

Whatever the Doctor was about to say next was lost to the cloudless sky as a great cry went up over the plains. Man and horse became tense; the Doctor felt his blood run cold.

There was a blissful moment of silence, then the wolves began howling again.

There was a muffled thump at the front door of the governor's residence. The guards, roused from their slumber, looked round in surprise, then guffawed loudly at their ridiculous reaction. Should the Mongols attack, it would doubtless not be prefaced with so polite a sound.

There was another sound, this time a much more precise tap.

One of the soldiers pulled open the wooden door. A dark, cloaked figure stood framed against the pitch-black of the street beyond.

'Who is there?' called one of the soldiers, hefting a cumbersome pole-axe in both hands.

The figure stepped forward, and pulled back its cloak.

'It is Taras's widow,' whispered an old soldier to a less knowledgeable companion. He stepped forward, half-bowing in respect. 'We have heard of the death of your husband,' he said. 'It is a terrible tragedy.'

The woman nodded mutely, her eyes darting from side to side as she took in the chamber, its racks of weapons, its rough mats for sleeping, the small pot of food that bubbled over a dying flame.

'You should go home, Elisabet,' the man continued. 'The kitchen will survive without you... especially when it is so late.'

'There is much to prepare,' said the woman, her voice made husky by grief.

'I am sure. But you need to rest, to grieve.'

The woman turned to the old soldier, touched him lightly on the shoulder, on his cheek. 'You will let me in?'

'Of course, of course,' said the man, blushing furiously. 'Let her through, boys.'

The woman pulled the cloak back over her head, and disappeared into the corridor of shadow beyond.

Immediately the younger guards began to laugh. 'I have heard it said that a widow's bed is warmer than a whore's,' sniggered one.

'Quiet!' snapped the older man. 'We should offer to light the way for her – the corridors are dark.'

But the woman was nowhere to be seen.


'We will make camp,' announced Mykola as the exhausted party found sanctuary once more on the edge of a wood of black-green trees. 'We will be safe here.'

'Are you sure?' queried the Doctor. 'The wolves…'

'The wolves will not attack unless we are sick and they are hungry,' said Mykola. 'The horses, and an hourly watch, will be enough to alert us.'

One of the soldiers helped the Doctor down from his horse. He was, truth be told, more than grateful to be out of the saddle, although he was not sure how well he would sleep in these circumstances.

He watched as the men arranged the animals in a defensive circle, with the supplies and bedding in the centre. Torches were swiftly extinguished; little more was said as the men laid down to sleep.

'I shall take the first hour,' said Mykola.

The Doctor examined his expression closely, striving to read signs of duplicity in his eyes. But the man quickly looked away.

The Doctor tried to put aside his worried thoughts but, as the silence of the plains enveloped them, he could not help but watch Mykola through half-shut eyes.

Isaac looked up suddenly as the door creaked open.

'Father, you should be more discreet.'

Isaac let out a sigh of relief. 'And you should knock before you enter.'

Nahum closed the door behind him, and approached his father. The old man's desk was covered with papers, parchments and leather-bound volumes; his fingers were black with ink. Isaac put down his stripped goose-quill.

'But the authorities could discover your work,' continued Nahum.

'Damn the authorities!' exclaimed Isaac with unusual vehemence. 'They should have better things to consider.'

'Of course,' said Nahum, seating himself on a bench to face his father. 'But if Yevhen already knows…'

'Knows, and delights in reminding me of his knowledge at every turn, as if I am some farm animal that can be led out to pasture only when needed.'

'Do you think he will ever go to the Church authorities?'

Isaac snorted. 'Remember poor Olexander? It is not beyond the man.' He dabbed a cloth at his fingers. 'I do not accept their Church, their beliefs... there are times I am not even sure I accept my own!'

'Which only makes you more vulnerable.'

Isaac looked sadly down at his work. 'It is a shame. If you could only see the majesty of the original words, the text... the beauty of language as it springs from the page as if alive.'

Nahum smiled. 'I must admit, I have had use for some words from the Song of Solomon this very day.'

'Why should the people not have these holy words in their own tongue? "Your breasts are like two fawns, twins of a gazelle that graze amongst the lilies. Until the day breathes and the shadows flee, I shall go to the mountain of myrrh and the hill of frankincense." Who could possibly take offence at such words?'

'There are many,' said Nahum with a smile.

'And there are many sons who would not favour their fathers making such "bawdy" talk!'

'Perhaps. How is mother?'

'She is sound asleep in our chamber.' Isaac paused, his eyes twinkling. 'You are deliberately changing the subject!'

'Forgive me, father.' Nahum bowed his head in mock humility.

'I can forgive you almost anything, my boy. How could any father not say the same?' Isaac grinned at his son. 'I know you are only protecting the identity of your beloved.'

'No, father, I –'

'Very noble, my son, but I will not take offence. You should know that. No matter what her beliefs, no matter what her class…' His words trailed away as his brow furrowed. 'Indeed, an honest serving girl might be preferable to anyone who comes from a family of puffed-up importance and self-justification.'

'Those are the people you now work with,' observed Nahum.

'But I cannot bring myself to think of them more highly.' Isaac got to his feet, stretching his weary limbs. 'It is late. I shall return to my room.'

Nahum stood and glanced back at the table. 'You should clear these away. We are not at home now, father.'

Isaac nodded. 'You are right. The risks are greater while we reside here.'

'That is my concern, father.'

'Your concern is appreciated, but I think you worry too much.' The old man reached up to run his gnarled fingers through his son's hair. 'And I could also ask why *you* are up at so dark an hour!'

'Young men's business,' answered Nahum evasively.

'Young men's business!' exclaimed Isaac. 'I hope with all my heart that this girl is worth your obvious affection for her.' He began to sort through his papers and books before stowing them away. 'And that both our secrets remain hidden.'

The Doctor woke with the sensation that he was being watched. He was not aware of having fallen asleep, and yet clearly he had, and now something had roused him.

He partly opened his eyes, staring through his lashes into the darkness of the hastily created camp. It was warmer than before, with a grey blanket of cloud filling as much of the sky as he could see. But he could make out less than nothing beneath the slate-coloured heavens, merely darker shadows within shadows. Some might be distant hills, some the angles of shoulders and faces in sleep. He could not tell.

He risked opening his eyes completely and turned his head slowly in the direction of Mykola. The young captain had handed over to another soldier, the Doctor remembered dimly. The cloud frayed and allowed some moonlight to fall; the Doctor could see for the first time that Mykola's dark form was turned away from him, and motionless but for the rhythm of his breathing.

The moonlight faded again, leaving the Doctor in darkness and wondering what had disturbed him.

Something made him turn his head in the opposite direction where a number of horses were resting, the air rich with the aroma from their earlier exertions.

He could dimly perceive the dark bulk of the animals. Most rested on the ground, but one stood nervously. Some distance away, visible between the slender silhouettes of its legs, were twin points of light. They were soon joined by another pair, and then another; binary stars ascending and descending and growing bigger all the time.

The wolves were coming closer.

Nahum tried again to make himself comfortable, but he knew that every twist and turn roused his mind and deepened his irritation. He collapsed back on to his pillow, letting out an exhausted sigh, and pondered the source of his irritation.

He and Lesia were living in the same house – but it was almost impossible to contrive an opportunity to see her in private. Yevhen watched her like a hawk – a fascinating image, Nahum decided. He could well imagine Yevhen's teeth descending into bare flesh with all the savagery of a hunting bird attacking a day-old chick on a trainer's glove. Isaac was playing a dangerous game, and Yevhen was an unpredictable foe; and, if that was not enough, the Tartar hordes were coming towards all of them through the shadows and the darkness.

All these concerns, and more, were melding together in Nahum's mind, a bitter core of poison and resentment. They twisted into dreams, and were just calling him to sleep, when he heard the softest hint of movement beyond his door.

He pricked his ears, but heard nothing more. Doubtless it was only a soldier, coming off duty to be replaced by another.

Nahum rolled over to face the door, and was about to close his eyes again when he saw the looped iron door-handle twist.

He stared at the door, unblinking. His forehead was slick with cold sweat; he kept telling himself that he was imagining things and that, if he concentrated with enough conviction, he would be quite safe.

But no. As his fearful eyes widened still further, he saw the twisted handle start to rotate.

Almost unconsciously, Nahum pushed himself into the corner of his bed, wordless prayers on his lips. His terror went deeper than he could articulate, but he knew one thing: something terrible was coming for him.

The door began to creak open, showing at first only the darkness of the corridor beyond. In time, it was fully open.

Behind it stood *something*.

It was tall, and human-sized, and in a dark cape. Pale eyes glinted in what little light there was.

The figure stepped into the room.

# VII
# Mortus in anima

I long ago came to the conclusion that my night vision isn't the best in the world – a particular shame in the darkened city where, lacking even a torch or a candle, I stumbled from wall to wall like a blindfolded drunk.

I was mindful of the increased frequency of the civil night-watch patrols, and the additional groups of soldiers who roamed the streets, but at least it meant that Kiev was swathed in dark silence. As a whole, the population unquestioningly obeyed the curfew, so there was little chance of me running into someone who might alert the authorities. (For all our attempts to blend into this culture, there was a certain alien distinctiveness about us that we could not shake off.)

I headed towards the cathedral – the one structure in Kiev that was big enough to break the grey sky with its own turreted darkness. I was, of course, hoping to find a way to observe Bishop Vasil, whom Olexander felt was not to be trusted. But the old man's mention of the catacombs under the cathedral had intrigued me: I had no idea how to gain access to them, but, if I could, there was surely no more secure place in the whole city. I would be safe from the authorities for as long as I needed to be – or until my food ran out, whichever happened first.

My only concern was the casket Olexander had described, and the fallen angel supposedly contained within it. My travels with the Doctor had pretty much cemented my own mistrust of superstition: everything I had encountered had some sort of rational explanation, even if I didn't understand it. But a rational creature is as likely to kill you as an irrational one – maybe even more so, in my experience.

As I approached the cathedral I realised it was going to be difficult to observe and follow the archbishop. I didn't know the layout of the building, I had no means of contacting the others with my discoveries – and I didn't even know what Vasil looked like. By all accounts he liked to keep a low profile, and I had certainly never met the man. Even so, looking for him seemed a more profitable course of action than searching for the catacombs. In a building the size of the cathedral, stuffed full of rooms and corridors, frescos and tapestries, their entrance could be almost anywhere.

I sighed as I approached the cathedral, wondering for a moment if I should seek out Dodo, or even, heaven forbid, the governor. My anxious thoughts were interrupted by a small knot of men who seemed to appear from nowhere at the side of the great building. Their clothing was dark and they carried only one torch between them, so at first all I saw was a clutch of tiny bobbing heads, moving as one, some distance from me.

I looked more closely, and realised they were arranged almost as a defensive circle around a central figure. They were intent, it seemed, on keeping someone well away from even the most accidental or fleeting of glances. Thus, the single torch and the complete silence in which they moved.

I tried to make my way carefully towards them, but they were already marching away from me. I did, however, catch a glimpse of the central figure, who was covered from head to foot in a dark brown cloak with something like tassels at its base.

I was either going to have to jog after them to make up ground, or let them go. Although intrigued by the stranger in their midst, I settled on the latter. I told myself to concentrate on the task at hand, whatever the diversions placed in my way.

I was about to make my way towards the main doors of the cathedral when two men in dark ecclesiastical robes peeled away from the departing group and began walking in my direction.

I dropped back into the shadows, straining to hear their voices. Though their hands were clenched behind their backs in what appeared to be modest piety, their words, when I could hear them, implied something much less holy. Between the euphemisms, I detected only a dark, festering evil.

'Adviser Yevhen?'

'What of him?' What appeared to be the senior figure paused for a moment, as if checking that he and his companion were not observed. 'He has had his turn to save the people of Kiev. He seems only to have brought more destruction to us.'

'But you allowed him to proceed?'

'I decided I could not stand in his way. His failure underlines the importance of our own… negotiations.' I saw the man turn his head in the direction of the mysterious figure and the men who were escorting him.

'How do the negotiations go?' queried his companion.

'They go well, but slow. We struggle to find common ground in language, still yet of faith and philosophy.'

'But the Tartars' – my ears pricked up at the abrupt use of the word – 'will help us with the southern problem?'

'I believe they will. And the Church of God, united by this threat, will amply reward any who help us.'

'Even these devils that sweep across Russia?'

'We are all tools of the Lord.' With that, the senior figure turned away. 'I have much to attend to.'

They disappeared inside the cathedral, and I wondered if, unwittingly, I had just had my first encounter with Bishop Vasil.

There were smaller doors, to the side of the great arched entrance, and I decided I would try these. They were, of course, open – it wouldn't even occur to the people of Kiev to think of making off with one of the icons, or stealing and melting down the great golden candle-holders or incense-burners.

I stepped quickly inside, and found myself in an enormous cold space where every footstep rang out like gunfire. At first, only my nose gave me any information at all – the musty, sweet smell of ancient incense. Then my eyes grew more accustomed to the mother-of-pearl light that was admitted by the coloured windows and punctuated by one or two lit candles that trailed a path to the great altar. I followed nervously in the footsteps of the faithful, all too aware of my booted feet rapping on the flagstones.

I was about half-way towards the altar when I heard voices whispering. I ducked down between the pews, and listened keenly. They seemed to be following my path from the main door towards the altar, but I dared not turn towards them. Far better to remain where I was, I reasoned, and, in any case, I recognised who was speaking.

It was Yevhen and Olexander.

'Should we be a little less brazen?' asked the old man, articulating a question that had occurred to me. (The other was even more simple: what was Olexander doing with Yevhen, of all people?)

'I *was* less brazen', replied Yevhen, 'and still a man died. In any event, I believe my actions have Vasil's approval.'

'He has told you this?'

'He has intimated as much. He is not interested in standing in the way of my plans – any more than I am interested in his. He is a fool. He thinks more of Constantinople than Kiev!'

'He would not be the first in our city to do so,' whispered Olexander. 'I'll warrant he may not be the last.'

They passed by me at this point, more interested in their whispered conversation than the man crouched to one side of the great aisle. They came so close I could have reached out to touch them.

Both carried torches, held at about waist height. Olexander, trapped now only in the hunched prison of his ancient body, was clearly recognisable, and Yevhen's haughty bearing was unmistakable. The adviser strolled through the cathedral as if he owned it. Even so, they continued to whisper – for all Yevhen's confidence, I surmised that he would prefer to go about his business undisturbed.

I tentatively followed the two men, carefully placing my feet on the cold stone floor, scarcely daring to breathe for fear of revealing my presence. I kept just close enough to hear any further dialogue between the men, but neither now said a word.

I was still shaken by Olexander's release from prison. Of course, after Dodo and Lesia's appearance, I had had every confidence that he would come with us, but I had come to respect his noble decision to stay. Was there another reason for this – was the old man perhaps in cahoots with Yevhen, and thus not inclined to join our hasty escape? Indeed, apart from Lesia's reaction at seeing him, which seemed genuine enough, I now had no reason to think that Olexander had ever been a prisoner at all. Perhaps it was a set-up. Yevhen, via his puppet Olexander, wanted me to come to the cathedral. In which case, both men might know I was behind them.

That thought sent a shiver down my spine.

They turned into a side corridor, and I followed. Though I could just perceive window shapes set high up on the walls, either the clouds outside had thickened or the 'panes' were illusory, for even the torchlight struggled to pierce the velvety darkness. I followed the twin points of light, not wanting to lose sight of them but not wishing to reveal myself inadvertently to the two men.

Yevhen and Olexander came to a halt at last. I stood, straining for their voices.

'You know what you must do?' queried Yevhen.

'I will try my best,' affirmed Olexander.

Yevhen said nothing else, but I heard the metallic rattle of a bunch of keys being removed from a pocket, examined and then harshly slotted home.

There was a sharp crack as a door, I surmised, was pulled open.

'I must return to the governor's residence,' said Yevhen. 'I will be missed.'

'The door?' queried Olexander.

'I will leave it open. You may return here… once you have completed your task.'

'It will not be easy.'

'I have every confidence in you.'

With that, one of the torchlights disappeared into the still deeper darkness of the doorway, and the other began to return towards me.

I panicked, not knowing what to do. I could turn round, but it was some way back to the door into the main chamber, and I would be vulnerable to Yevhen's torchlight. Now that he was facing in my direction even absolute silence might not save me. Indeed, the corridor was so narrow that I had no realistic hope of avoiding detection.

The corridor thus far had been lacking in any feature that might come to my aid, but, as I recollected seeing the two lanterns come to a halt, I did wonder if some sort of alcove had briefly been illuminated.

It was too late to turn back now. I had to take careful steps towards Yevhen, hoping against hope that I could find an alcove before the adviser's torchlight illuminated me. And that I could do so without making a sound.

The torch, illuminating Yevhen's waxy face and broad shoulders, bobbed closer, but still I could not find anywhere to hide. I felt sweat prickling between my shoulder blades as I continued to stare, with awful fascination, at the oncoming figure.

Just when I was about to give up, to admit to the futility of it all and let Yevhen know I was there, I found a large recess set into the stone wall.

It was, as I had hoped, the first in a series of alcoves that ran along one side of the corridor. Hardly believing my luck I ducked into it, taking a deep breath as Yevhen drew closer. All I could hear was his footfalls, sounding like heavy rain beating against concrete. All the while, my heart pounded like a piston – I almost came to wonder if Yevhen could hear *that*.

But no. He passed without a sideways glance, though I glimpsed a twisted smile on his face which quite chilled me.

Once Yevhen was out of sight I crept forward, my hands nervously outstretched like a man suddenly gone blind. I checked the opposite wall for the doorway, but could find nothing at first. I wondered if I had become disorientated in the dark, and had already come too far and somehow missed it.

Soon, however, my expectant hands found another space in the corridor wall. Yevhen had left the door open, and I could just make out one or two steps fading into the darkness.

I considered going back to try to find a torch or a candle, but I was wary of running into Yevhen – and letting Olexander proceed too far into the catacombs without me. There was nothing else for it. I was going to have to follow the old man down into the darkness.

I placed my feet carefully on the first step and began to descend, holding on to the central stone spine, around which the stairs rotated, for dear life. The masonry felt wet beneath my palms, though I could not tell if it was the result of condensation or merely the cold sweat on my hands. I wondered how far the stairs descended, but thought better of this unhelpful speculation and instead concentrated on my slow, careful descent.

I was soon in absolute darkness, unable even to see my hands in front of my face. I decided that, undignified though it might be, the only safe way to descend was on my bottom, shuffling with agonising slowness from one stair to another, arcing into the depths of the earth like a mote of dust. I kept a strong grip on each chiselled step as I made my way deeper into what I assumed were the catacombs under the cathedral.

I knew Olexander had come this way but, having seen him with Yevhen, I was no longer sure if I relished the prospect of running into him again. I was wondering what I would say to him when I heard a noise high above my head.

I looked up, gripping the clammy stonework even more tightly, and for a moment my vision reeled in the darkness. High over my head – I was surprised at how far I had already come – I could make out the faintest patch of light. It was a peaked rectangle, and I surmised it was torchlight reflected on one of the walls that surrounded the twisting stairway. Someone was standing in the doorway.

Whoever it was could not see me, nor I them. I remained motionless, however, wondering what would happen next.

The answer was not long in coming. The light blinked out and was followed by the sound of the door slamming back into its frame.

And, even where I was, I could hear a key being turned in the lock.

# VIII
# Lamenta

The Doctor crawled towards Mykola, his breathing shallow. He tugged the soldier's arm, and he awoke instantly, swinging round suddenly.

'Who's there?'

The Doctor put his fingers to his lips, hushing him. 'There are wolves,' he said, pointing. 'They're coming closer.'

'Curiosity, I'll warrant,' said Mykola, getting to his feet.

He roused a few nearby soldiers and ordered that lanterns be lit. He then unsheathed his sword and strode over to the knot of horses, who had sensed the pad-footed approach of the wolves and were fidgeting.

'Quickly,' snapped Mykola. 'Bring the lights!'

The Doctor stood at the young captain's side. He could see the creatures more clearly now, sleek and purposeful and the colour of ash. Their ears were flat against their heads, lips pulled back slightly to reveal their perfect ivory-white teeth.

Mykola grabbed a pair of burning torches from one of the men, and strode forward, waving them high above his head. The horses began to murmur and stamp their feet. One of the soldiers quickly went over and patted them, whispering soothing noises into their ears.

Mykola took another two steps towards the wolves, who had stopped in their tracks. He lowered the torches and began shouting, punctuating his words with whoops and flaming stabs in their direction.

The wolves – the Doctor could see four of them, though there might be others in the area – took another step forward. One began to growl deep in its throat.

Mykola whooped again, cutting arcs in the darkness with the torches.

At last, the wolves turned as one, and trotted elegantly away from the camp. The Doctor watched them until they faded into the night.

'You see?' said Mykola confidently. 'Show them no fear, and they will respect you. Make it plain to them that you are frightened, and they will feed on your doubt, moments before they feed on you.'

'Have you no fear, sir?' queried the Doctor.

'None that I would reveal to a pack of wolves,' said Mykola, with a bitter smile.

The sound of many footsteps running in the corridor roused Isaac from his sleep. There was no little commotion outside: raised voices, calling for lanterns; shouted instructions; hysterical inquiries.

Isaac turned. Rebekah was sleeping the sleep of the innocent, her peaceful expression utterly at odds with the commotion that had gripped the governor's residence. Isaac smiled. They often joked that she would sleep through the Tartar attack – and he supposed that being murdered in your bed was not too bad a way to go. Not when one considered the Mongols' reputation for torture and butchery.

Perhaps, indeed, this was the precursor to the attack. Isaac pondered this as he pulled on a simple linen gown then padded barefoot towards the door.

'What is going on?' he asked a passing servant.

'An attack, sir,' replied the woman and then, realising whom she was addressing: 'Your son.'

Isaac ran at once to Nahum's temporary quarters, passing all manner of serving folk and soldiers proceeding, it seemed, in random directions. It was as if a giant figure had disturbed an ant's nest, turning ordered discipline into chaotic anarchy in the blink of an eye.

A soldier was stationed outside Nahum's room and there were more inside. Nahum sat on the edge of his bed, dabbing at his cheek with a white cloth. Dmitri – fully dressed – was bending over him, alternating sympathetic noises with blunt questions.

Isaac ran over to embrace his son. 'Have you been injured?'

Nahum shook his head. 'Merely a scratch. Do not worry.'

He removed the cloth to reveal a small gash just in front of his ear, surrounded by tiny dots of bruised purple.

'Even so, it should be attended to.'

'It is fine. I am fine. Father, you should return to your bed!'

'What happened?'

Dmitri smoothly interjected. 'I rather suspect even your son is tiring of telling this story. He says that the cook, Elisabet, attacked him.'

'I swear she flew through the air towards me,' said Nahum. 'I could not believe her strength!'

'However did you repel her?' asked Isaac.

'That is the strangest thing,' said Nahum, still shaking his head in disbelief. 'She overpowered me in a moment. Her face lunged for my neck – I turned my head a little, and she bit my cheek. But you have never seen teeth so sharp, so narrow!'

Isaac nodded, taking this all in. 'Go on.'

'She stood, silently regarding me, and then, just as swiftly as she had come, she moved away. I was too frightened to follow,' he added apologetically.

Isaac turned to Dmitri. 'Elisabet, you say? Is she not the wife… widow… of…?'

Dmitri nodded. 'I have ordered a search of every room.'

'If she is hiding within this building', reasoned Isaac aloud, 'and her attack leaves marks not at all unlike those found on

Taras's body... then the Doctor is right. We have indeed imprisoned an innocent man.'

'That matters little,' snapped Dmitri.

Isaac shook his head. 'But Steven –'

'He has already found a way to leave our prison,' interrupted Dmitri. 'And, though I wish him well, we have other, more pressing, concerns.' He turned to one of the soldiers. 'Seek adviser Yevhen. Inform him that we must speak together.'

The soldier nodded and departed, just as another squeezed into the room. He was panting, clutching his chest, and the bright whites of his eyes spoke only of fear. He approached Dmitri respectfully.

'My lord,' he said between breaths. 'There is something you should see.'

'The cook?'

'No, my lord,' the soldier replied. 'We have found a body.'


He was little more than a lad, kitted out in a padded canvas jacket several sizes too large for him. A visored helmet had fallen away from his head, revealing boyish curls and an innocent, though now horribly blank, expression. A short dagger had also tumbled from his hands, part of a vain attempt to halt an unstoppable foe.

'I wish the Doctor were here,' muttered Isaac under his breath as he bent towards the dead soldier. 'I feel sure he would have some insight into this.'

'But you are also a man of great learning,' said Dmitri. 'A trusted adviser. What say you on this matter?'

Isaac glanced up, only too aware of the fearful symmetry of the scene: a corpse surrounded by soldiers and attended by two puzzled, fearful men. It had been the same with Taras.

The boy seemed to have been killed with a single savage blow to the throat, which had left two huge flaps of skin with darkness and blood where they met. The wound, however, had clearly not been caused by a sword or dagger, for the gash was ragged and rough. Thinking back to Taras's body, Isaac gently turned the soldier's face away from him. Sure enough, there were pinprick wounds about the neck and ear.

'Little learning is needed to see that this fellow died at the hands of the beast that attacked Taras,' announced Isaac. 'And my son.'

'But your son was attacked by a woman,' said Dmitri.

Thudding footsteps heralded the arrival of Yevhen. 'We know of creatures like this. The cook and the beast may be the same.' He turned to Isaac, an awful smirk etched on his face. 'Your son survived the attack. I wonder why.'

'Where have you been?' snapped the governor. 'The men have been trying to find you.'

Isaac was pleased to see a momentary look of guilt cross Yevhen's face, though unfortunately it was short-lived. Soon the self-satisfied grimace was back. 'I was... I was in the kitchens, my lord. I needed some water. I could not sleep.'

'While you were in the kitchens,' said Isaac, 'did you see Taras's widow? I believe she is a cook there.'

'But it is night. Why should she be there?' Yevhen looked evasive as he replied, but Isaac could not tell if this reflected a specific uncertainty or merely a naturally duplicitous nature.

'You heard that Nahum was attacked by Elisabet. And a beast has killed this boy.'

Yevhen laughed. 'Are there not monsters enough outside the city?'

'Answer the question,' snapped Dmitri, clearly tiring of Yevhen's theatrics.

'No, I did not see Taras's widow in the kitchens,' his adviser replied through gritted teeth. 'There was no one else there.'

Isaac nodded his head. Of course, if there was no one else

there, there was no one to prove or disprove that Yevhen had been getting himself some water. But where else could he have been?

Dmitri, however, seemed satisfied with Yevhen's words. 'Let us all return to sleep, if we can,' he said. 'There is nothing more to be gained here tonight. We shall resume our deliberations in the morning.'

With that, the governor and the majority of the guards swept away, leaving an uncomfortable Isaac standing shoulder to shoulder with Yevhen.

'Your son,' began Yevhen, adopting a more conciliatory tone. 'He is unharmed?'

'A few scratches, nothing more,' replied Isaac. 'Whatever really happened tonight, he will be shocked to hear of another death. I should return to him.'

As Isaac walked away, he glanced back over his shoulder at Yevhen, who was standing motionless, looking down at the dead soldier.

Yevhen's tight feature seemed to soften, his shoulders falling as if an invisible burden had been placed there.

Isaac wondered if the burden was guilt.

# IX
# Terra firma

With the door shut and locked, and even the faint light that had come through it extinguished, I was once again plunged into an inky darkness that left me utterly blind. Almost immediately, my eyes began playing tricks, flashing random shapes and patterns. I blinked a few times to clear them of the phantom images.

I resumed my slow and careful descent, all the while hoping I would soon hear the sound of Olexander's progress some distance below me. I decided I would far rather encounter him, even if he was plotting with Yevhen, than tumble to my death from a broken step or patch of mould that I could not see.

I seemed to spend an eternity shuffling down the column of steps. I wondered, fancifully, if I was descending into hell (though, if anything, it became colder the further I went) or if the stairs ended at all. Perhaps I was doomed to remain on the staircase for ever, stuck in some sort of loop, wondering always whether to head back for the door or carry on to a floor I had never seen.

A feeling of absolute relief washed over me when I noticed that I only had a few more steps to go.

It took a moment for me to realise the importance of this – not only was I nearing the floor, but I could see it. I stopped where I was, only five or six steps from the ground, and looked around. Some distance away a twisted column of stone plunged downwards from the invisible ceiling, illuminated by a blazing torch shoved into a metal bracket. I could just perceive a second light, as dim as a midnight star, deeper in the catacombs.

I couldn't help but grin. Thank goodness Olexander was better prepared for this expedition than I was! Of course, he had no idea that anyone was following him, but I imagined the torches he lit along the way would mark his path back to the stairs, and the door he still expected to be open. They formed a string of fiery beads, leading out of the labyrinth – and a chill gripped me as I remembered that every labyrinth must have a beast at its centre.

I finished my descent and examined my surroundings as keenly as the limited light allowed. It seemed that I was in a great, dark space, a void under the cathedral riddled with foundational columns and pillars. I hoped Olexander knew where he was going, and that there was a purpose to his exploration, for surely this was not a place well visited by travellers or guides. It would be easy to get lost in it, and wander in unwitting circles until overcome by exhaustion.

I walked towards the second torch as quickly as I could, my hands still outstretched in the area of oppressive darkness between the two shallow pools of brightness. I began to pass chambers and vaults, and areas with low ceilings and doors, but I concentrated on following Olexander. There was so much to explore here, but little, I imagined, would help to explain what had killed Taras the builder, or why I had been blamed for his death.

The second torch was much the same as the first, a sulphurous mass of licking flame set into a latticed holder of blackened metal. I was not sure if Olexander was carrying a supply of torches, or if some had been left down here in the catacombs. I suspected the latter.

When I came to the third torch I saw that it crackled and spat more loudly than the others. And I noticed for the first time a definite slant to the flame, which could only mean that some air was moving back into the catacombs. The slight wind – no more than a breath, the touch of which was icy on my skin – seemed to be coming from a point almost diametrically opposite the staircase and door behind me. All this, to my mind, implied a second exit, another way to leave this dark nightmare of stone and space. That prospect cheered me no end.

I couldn't believe how far, and how quickly, Olexander had come. For all the fact that I had come down the stairs some time after him, and doubtless descended more slowly, I had thought I would catch up with his bent frame within minutes. I had no idea how long I had been on the stairs, and in the tunnels under the cathedral, but I suspected it was beginning to run into hours.

It was as I reached the fifth or sixth torch that I began to sense that I was not alone. Occasionally I thought I heard a scuffed footfall, just out of step with my own. I had imagined it to be Olexander, but now I was less sure. There was a curious sliding undercurrent to the noise, which set my teeth on edge. I tried to tell myself it was only the harsh whisper of rats' feet, but I could not rid myself of the impression that I was being watched.

I turned sharply the next time the noise came, trying to pinpoint the source of the sound. Nothing, bar the flickering shadows on ancient stone walls. Even so, the hairs on the back of my neck began to rise: something was very, very wrong.

I headed towards the next torch, walking faster now despite the uneven surface beneath my feet. I suddenly felt cold, and hungry; it was all I could do to stop my teeth chattering.

Something caressed the side of my face; already on edge, I turned instinctively towards it before realising it was just another breath of wind.

I set my face forward again – towards Olexander, I hoped – but there was a niggle in my subconscious. I had seen something anomalous when I looked sideways, I was sure of it; I risked a longer glance, and immediately realised what it was. There was a bright, rounded object just on the edge of the light cast by the nearest torch; an object that was very much out of place in the drab angularity of the catacombs.

I changed direction and headed towards it, steeling myself to flee at the slightest motion. But the shape – a coloured, indistinct mass at first – was absolutely motionless, as unmoving as the great columns that supported the roof over my head. As I drew nearer, it resembled a random pile of rags; it was only when I came closer still that I realised it was a body.

I was making a habit of this.

It was a woman, dressed in what could best be described as medieval underwear. Her throat was in shreds as if some wild dog had killed her. On the peripheries of the main wound I noticed smaller rips and incisions that reminded me of my awful discovery of Taras's body. Her body felt as if had been cut from melting ice; I drew back when my fingertips inadvertently brushed her cheek.

I stood, staring down at the unfortunate woman. How had she come to be here? Her bare feet were clean, so she had not walked into the catacombs. The small pool of blood under her back seemed to indicate that she had been brought here soon after death.

As to what had killed her… Even the Doctor claimed not to know what creature we were dealing with. But I didn't think it was simple cynicism on my part to imagine that a second death implied many more to come.

'Lord Jesus have mercy.'

The words, half-whispered behind me, came out of nowhere.

Shocked, I turned to see Olexander. He had a look of resigned horror on his face.

I am sorry to say that my surprise at seeing him, mixed with my anger at what I believed was his treacherous liaison with Yevhen, drove me into a fury. I grabbed the old man by the throat, almost knocking his lantern from his grasp, and spat into his face: 'What the hell do you think you're doing?'

Or words to that effect.

Olexander struggled from my grip, as shocked I think by the venom of my words as by my actions.

'What do you mean?' he croaked.

'You said you were imprisoned by Yevhen,' I said.

'I was.'

'But I saw you talking to him!'

Olexander looked at me with blank incomprehension.

'You're colluding with him, aren't you?' I continued, not realising that my awful descent into the catacombs, and my discovery of the corpse, had probably pushed me to the verge of hysteria. 'Admit it!'

Olexander shook his head slowly. 'You do not understand,' he said. 'Yevhen came to offer me my freedom – my return to the society that I miss.'

'At a price?'

'Everything Yevhen does has a price.' The old man paused, looking around nervously. 'He will ensure my release from prison on condition that I reason with the dark angel.'

'The dark angel?'

'The creature he has liberated from the casket. The supposed protector of Kiev, defender of our people.'

I pointed at the corpse, to the face puffed up with death and the hair matted with dry blood. 'You want to reason with the thing that did that? The creature that killed Taras?' I snorted. 'I wish you luck!'

'Perhaps together we might succeed. Perhaps this creature is rational.'

'You've been sent down here to die,' I said. 'Don't you realise? We've been locked in.'

Olexander nodded, as if he expected something like this from Yevhen. 'Yevhen said I might succeed because of my knowledge of languages, of texts, of diplomacy and customs.'

'I very much doubt this thing speaks any language you've ever heard of,' I commented bitterly. 'I'll be surprised if it speaks any language at all!'

'But we must try,' continued Olexander. 'We must point the angel away from us, and towards the Tartars.'

'You really think it will listen? You really think it will apologise for what it's done, then go off after the Mongols for you?'

'I think we must try.'

I paused, trying to control my anger.

'Why does Yevhen think this creature is down here?' I asked in a quieter voice. 'I found Taras's body above ground.'

'He believes that Bishop Vasil's men took the corpse away. Yevhen himself saw Taras die. They opened the casket together, and some sort of monster emerged.'

'I overheard someone talking,' I said. 'It might have been Vasil. He said he'd allowed Yevhen to go ahead with his plan, but that it had failed.' I paused. 'He said also that he had a plan of his own. He mentioned a threat from the south.'

'The south?' Olexander paused. 'He must mean Islam.'

'I don't understand.' I shook my head, wondering if there might be some link to the cloaked man I had seen.

Olexander shrugged. 'Neither do I. But we have information that must be passed on to the governor. And I have a job to do. Do you trust me?' He sighed. 'Will you help me?'

I watched the old man closely as he spoke, and saw innate dignity behind his fear. I did trust him, I decided: the worst I could accuse him of was honest naivety. And, if he had looked small and crushed within the awful prison cell, he looked utterly lost here, a ragbag of skin and bones held together only by the desire to clear his name, to have a role in the salvation of his people.

'Do you have a map?' I asked.

'I have one that shows the way to the casket of the angel, but little else. And it shows but one way into the catacombs.'

I nodded in the direction of the dead woman. 'The fact that she's here means there may be another entrance. And there is a breeze coming from somewhere.' I sighed. 'I wouldn't trust Yevhen's map if my life depended on it!'

'It may, Steven. It may.' Olexander turned towards me. 'Do not think that I am suddenly enamoured of the man. I hate him, and all he stands for!' His pale features broke into a broad smile. 'But I have to tell you, Steven, it is nice to have even this measure of freedom.'

'We've got to find this other way out,' I said. 'Or this freedom we both enjoy might be short-lived.' I glanced away from the dead woman's staring eyes. 'Do you know her?'

Olexander bent closer, squinting furiously. 'Yes. Yes, I believe I do. How interesting! Her name is Elisabet, and she is a cook at the governor's residence.'

'That's interesting?'

Olexander nodded. 'She is… was… married to Taras the builder.'

'That's more than a coincidence,' I agreed. 'And, if she was killed elsewhere, why bring her body back here?'

Olexander nodded. 'Why indeed, my friend?' He walked away. 'Come. There is another torch some way ahead. I assume that is how you followed me?'

'Did you think I would?'

'I hoped that you *might*.'

I noticed for the first time that he was carrying a bag of some sort over his shoulders.

'Here, let me take that,' I said.

'Thank you,' said the old man. 'Am I forgiven for choosing to believe that adviser Yevhen might for once in his life be telling the truth?'

I laughed. 'I still don't understand why you chose to stay in the prison in the first place,' I said.

'There are ways of doing things,' muttered the old man. 'And there are two types of freedom. Freedom of the body, which any strong man can take from you, and freedom of the spirit, which is no one's to remove, or impart. Even so, I must clear my name. Physical freedom would mean nothing without it.'

I nodded. I can't pretend I truly understood, still less identified with, the man's reasoning. But I did respect it, and I felt a little ashamed of my overhasty dismissal of him as a traitor.

'We are not far from the casket,' Olexander said as we walked towards the next torch.

'And you're curious?'

'We have come very far,' he said gently, ducking my question somewhat.

'Why did you double back to find me?'

'I heard something,' said Olexander. 'I hoped it was you!'

'I thought I heard something as well. Perhaps we were both listening to the other!' It certainly seemed possible – or, perhaps, my optimism was simply the result of no longer being on my own, in the dark. I suddenly felt far better equipped to face the creature, or Yevhen, or whatever other dangers might exist within the tunnels.

We soon reached the last torch Olexander had lit. 'Not far now,' he said.

We found our way to an unlit torch and the old man ignited it with his lantern.

'We should be grateful,' he observed. 'I sense that no one has been down here for many decades – but these torches speak of a more recent visitation.'

'Yevhen and Taras?' I queried. 'Or Bishop Vasil's men?'

Olexander shrugged his shoulders, then pointed the way ahead with his outstretched, bony finger. 'Look. There it is.'

I saw some sort of covered tomb ahead, a small room within the larger chamber. The small door in the wall facing us was open.

'What now?' I queried.

Whatever response Olexander would have made never came. A mute fear gripped us both as something flickered in the doorway. It was a tall creature bent double by the frame. Then it stepped out before us, drawing itself up to its full height.

The beast turned its skull-like face in our direction, its eyes glowing like brands of fire. Its pale skin seemed somehow to be constantly moving and re-forming, never quite at rest. I noticed slender, almost skeletal limbs that terminated in stunted fingers and toes, each one tapering to a wicked talon. And, surrounding and filling its leech-like mouth, were row upon row of ivory-white barbs.

I don't know how long we stood watching the creature, and it us. My mind was screaming in panic, but every muscle in my body was frozen. I barely blinked; I was aware of an awful taste at the back of my mouth, but I could not swallow.

Mocking my own inaction, Olexander coughed politely and then stepped forward, bowing as if greeting a dignitary from a foreign land. 'We know of you only as the dark angel,' he said. 'I have been sent by the rulers of our city to plead for our lives. To talk to you, to communicate, if I may. I come in peace.'

The creature moved its head a little to one side, as if turning the sounds over in its mind. Then the great maw opened, and a tiny facsimile of a generic human voice emerged, completely at odds with the beast's awesome frame.

'Peace?' came the bland-sounding query. The creature turned its gaze from Olexander to me, and then back again. 'I am… I am… an instrument of war!'

It took one elegant step forward, its fingers flexing.

'The people of Kiev face a great threat,' continued Olexander, seemingly unfazed. 'There are those who believe you may save us. We ask only for your help.'

The creature came closer still, its eyes, like its skin, now flowing with colours and shades of light and dark. 'This bunker must be compromised,' it said, as if that explained everything.

'We beg you –' said Olexander.

They were his last words.

The creature leapt at him, its mouth gnawing at his neck and shoulder. Olexander screamed once as he fell and it held tight to him like a funeral shroud. There was just the slightest of pauses as they hit the ground, the creature's head swinging from side to side.

Then it raised one of its long arms and drew its claws across Olexander's throat.

My body finally came to life. Sickened by what I had seen, and without even thinking, I turned to flee, my feet flapping furiously against the damp catacomb floor.

Before I even had time to consider where to run, or what to do, there was a rushing weight on my back that knocked me flying. My face clattered into the cold stone ground, sending a shower of sparking stars before my eyes.

I could taste blood in my mouth.

With flailing arms I tried to right myself, though my entire body screamed an immediate protest.

I looked up to see two eyes flaming in the shadows.

And I screamed in terror as that great mouth swept down on me.

# X
# Laqueus

*Reloading archive 76-FG-92-SD…*
*Complete.*
*Resume archive 76-FG-92-SD…*

*Initial summary:*
*Command structure pathways to target BDR-997-XRF are being established. Ingress to the northern dome is confirmed as next priority.*

The assassin approaches one of the dome's smaller portals. It is wary of discovery, but knows that the success of its mission will depend on it hiding the caution it feels. As the mission proceeds, it will become even more important to maintain appearances.

Unclean soldiers stationed within the dome idly watch as the assassin rests a hand on the scanner. In tones laced with humour and resignation, they joke about having had the same food now for over a week. There is a click of recognition from the hardware, an appropriate comment is made in return, and then the assassin moves towards the service corridors. They are arranged like concentric circles around inner geometric rooms; the optimum path is plotted.

As the assassin walks through the tunnels soldiers pass, staring always forward, contemplating their own fate and not the enemy in their midst. At one junction a senior officer demands identification, but once this is given he loses interest, and sets off in a different direction.

The corridor branches into an unexpected junction – the

maps are in error. The assassin pauses, decides on one doorway, but it does not open. Security clearance is insufficient.

The assassin pauses, calculates a new route, then walks away. It is stopped moments later by a biomechanoid, hastily assembled from the scraps of flesh and metal recovered from a bombed-out bunker. The assassin wonders briefly if this thing can innately recognise its enemy. Perhaps a fury burns deep within its circuitry and sluggishly pumping hearts, fury at being denied the peace of death – and it adopts all protocols, with precise formality and an absence of humour.

The assassin tries to placate the mechanoid, to reason with it. But, somehow, suspicions have been aroused. An arm, blackened with the smoke of the original attack and now kept alive by a network of pulsing tubes, raises a simple percussive weapon.

The assassin pauses as if in meek surrender, and waits for the moment. The biomechanoid turns, about to call others to its aid.

The assassin strikes, completing the job left half-done. As the biomechanoid dies, there are no screams – the creatures that formed it welcome the silence of darkness.

The assassin continues towards its target. The dome will soon be on alert – but the target is close, so very close.

And then it will be over.


*Result of action:*
*Dome penetrated. Unassigned mechanoid destroyed. Mission success index: 59.1%.*


'It is as I predicted.' Mykola's face broke into a satisfied smile. 'The wolves did not threaten us.'

'Indeed, sir,' said the Doctor. 'We are all in your debt.' He dusted down his frock coat and trousers, breathing deeply in the fresh morning air.

'I am sure my men would have responded in a similar manner,' replied Mykola modestly. 'I was simply the first to wake. Your own actions should be commended.'

The Doctor looked at the young captain closely, aware that his respect for him was rising. The reality was proving rather different to the shallow villain or easily swayed weakling he, and perhaps Governor Dmitri, had expected. Whatever Mykola had done in the recent past – and that, at the very least, seemed to involve lying in order to incriminate Steven – his considered admissions to the Doctor spoke of a man still struggling to come to terms with other people's expectations of him and with the awful authority of command.

'We must move out now,' said Mykola, staring at the just-rising sun. 'I sense that the Tartars are not far away.'

'How will you know for sure?' queried the Doctor.

'I believe we will hear them plain enough.'

Within minutes they were back on their horses, provisions and equipment safely stowed away, and were heading implacably for the Mongol army.

The Doctor rode at the front of the group, alongside Mykola. He wasn't sure what, if anything, to say to the man. Subtle questioning had produced little by way of an honest response, but a straight question would probably get no answer at all. And so the Doctor lapsed into silence, mulling over Mykola's careful words, and his own fears for the safety of Dodo and Steven in Kiev.

It was the young captain who spoke first, about an hour into their journey. 'Do you think your friends will be safe in the city?' he asked, as if reading the Doctor's mind.

'Steven is a man of great character and resourcefulness,' said the Doctor. 'And Dodo is quite capable of looking after herself.'

Mykola glanced away from him, lowering his voice. 'I meant... Do you fear for them, if the Tartars attack?'

'I fear for us all,' said the Doctor.

'I had hoped', continued Mykola, 'that perhaps you had foreknowledge of the fate of our city.'

'What do you mean?'

'It is said by some that you know of the future, and of our fate at the hands of the Tartars. Perhaps Kiev will be safe after all, and that is why you are content to leave your friends there.' There was an honest desperation in the man's voice.

'What can anyone know of the future?' the Doctor asked with a dismissive chuckle as if the idea was, self-evidently, nonsensical.

'Any man can see into the future, if God Himself wills it so.'

The Doctor saw the fear behind the man's questions. Mykola only wanted his loved ones to be safe, and was thus likely to seize on even the slightest hint that they would be. The Doctor reflected that it would be a cold-hearted man who did otherwise.

He sighed. 'I'll be honest with you, young man,' he said at length. 'I have a vision of the future, and it is not pleasant.' He paused, his eyes scanning the lush grasslands and forests that surrounded them. 'But I would scarcely approach the Mongols if I did not think there was some chance that the city might be spared.'

'Is that your only reason for coming?'

'I do have other concerns,' admitted the Doctor. 'But all my concerns will be met if I am able to persuade the Mongol leaders to stay their hand.'

'Are you confident?'

'I am confident I can put a strong case,' smiled the Doctor. 'I cannot be confident that what I say will be received with open hearts and minds.'

Mykola nodded sagely. 'We must all do what we think is for the best,' he said in a quiet voice.

The Doctor was about to question him further when the captain sat bolt upright in his saddle, pointing into the middle distance. 'Look!' he exclaimed in a loud voice.

The men behind the Doctor murmured their interest. A light was glinting on the edge of the plain, the weak sun catching something metallic and shiny.

It was moving towards them.

'What is it?' queried the Doctor.

Mykola shaded his eyes, squinting further into the distance. 'I cannot tell. Someone on horseback, coming at speed towards us.'

'A Tartar?' asked one of the soldiers, nervously gripping the sword at his side.

'Perhaps,' said Mykola. 'I do not believe he has seen us – in any case, can one man defeat us all?' As he said this, he turned to the soldiers who flanked him, clearly hoping to instil enthusiasm and bravado with words alone.

'But they are devils. Their trickery is notorious,' said a soldier, fidgeting nervously in his saddle.

'If you think such things you should have stayed in the city, playing with the girls of the street!' exclaimed Mykola. 'We should capture this lone rider, and from him discover the location of the Tartar army.'

'Your friend may have a point,' said the Doctor. 'It could be a trap. He could intentionally have alerted us to his presence.'

'Nonsense!' said Mykola. 'He has made a mistake. We must use that mistake against our foe!' He jerked on the reins of his horse, altering direction and speed. 'You will all follow me. We do not wish to meet this Tartar head-on.'

The Doctor said nothing, for Mykola's mind was clearly made up. He spurred his horse clumsily, gripping the leather reins tightly as his mount caught up with the others.

They proceeded swiftly through the long grass, heading towards a small clump of bent trees that would offer them a vantage point from which to sweep down towards the Mongol scout. All eyes were trained on the rider who was coming closer all the time, now forming a bright brown speck against the yellowing plain.

The Doctor stared at the approaching figure, nodding his head slowly. Yes, it was a Mongol soldier, his horse galloping at full speed across the grasslands.

Even from a distance, the Mongol and his mount were very different from the soldiers and horses who surrounded the Doctor. The horse was only three-quarters of the size of the great beasts that had carried the men from the city; a stocky little thing, it was scarcely bigger than a pony, but blessed with powerful legs that propelled it forward at great speed. The Mongols were legendary horsemen, and it was in no small part down to the unique creatures they bred and utilised in their battles.

The soldier himself was small, and covered from head to foot in folds of light leather armour. The Doctor could just make out a conical helmet of metal – presumably it was this that flashed in the sunlight – as the man bent closer to the head of his horse, urging it to still greater speed.

The Doctor looked at the men from Kiev, and saw that their eyes were narrowed with contempt. They had clearly never seen a soldier of this ilk before, and he looked puny compared to the great clanking knights of Europe.

The Mongol was close to passing them by when Mykola cracked his reins again, and, as one, the horses crashed through the knotted trees and back on to the plain. The Russian soldiers let out whoops of joy, unsheathing their weapons in expectation of the battle to come.

The Mongol horseman seemed barely to look in their direction, concentrating instead on turning his horse around. In a moment, he was riding away from them.

'He's frightened, lads!' exclaimed one of the soldiers.

Mykola and the others, shouting in joyful abandon, pursued the fleeing figure across the plain.

The Doctor frowned. His mount seemed inclined to stay to the rear of the tight knot of soldiers, and he was grateful.

Without warning, there was a whispered whistle from one side; in the blink of an eye, four soldiers tumbled from their horses, screaming.

Panicked, the Doctor swung round in his saddle to look to the source of the sound – it came again, and three more men fell, blood arcing in the air – and saw two rows of Mongol bowmen standing proudly in the long grass.

The Doctor's mount clattered over a fallen horse, stumbled, and then began to rear up on its hind legs.

With a sickening thud, an arrow embedded itself in the creature's flank and it slid to the ground in a flurry of splayed limbs.

The Doctor was thrown free, and as he hit the ground hard the breath was knocked from him. His back exploded in agony and for a moment a kaleidoscope of colours sparkled before his eyes.

Then his lungs sucked in air again, and his vision cleared. He saw a finely chiselled, golden face looking down at him. The mouth below a delicately trimmed moustache broke into a surprised smile.

Then the archer raised his bow, aiming its notched arrow at the Doctor's chest.

# XI
# Libertas

I think I blacked out. Certainly, I remembered the awful skeletal thing launching itself at me; the next moment, I was on my own, and the creature was gone.

I shook my head. How long had I been lying on the floor? I couldn't tell, though my arms and legs were stiff and cold.

In a rush of awful memory, I remembered the attack on Olexander and I forced myself to my feet, hobbling over to where the old man had fallen.

His skin, stretched tightly across his face, was translucent; his throat and shoulders a mass of sodden clothing and ripped skin. One leg had buckled underneath him; his other foot had lost its shoe. The cracked leather boot rested some distance away, a pitiful detail.

I suddenly sensed I was not alone. I turned, and saw the 'angel' standing just within the doorway to the central tomb. It bent down and angled its face in my direction. It was blank, devoid of expression and meaning.

Even so, I was not prepared to abuse my good fortune, or whatever it was that had saved me from Olexander's fate. Pure fear gripped me again.

I turned, and ran deeper into the catacombs.

I didn't stop until I was in complete darkness, well away from Olexander's path of feeble torches. For once, the shadows were welcoming.

But I also knew that I was very, very lost.

I wandered for hours. My knees and face and hands became sore with constant stumbling into invisible walls and columns;

I couldn't find any of the prepared torches here, but, in any case, I had nothing to light them with.

The breeze from what I hoped was an open door seemed to have stopped, leaving me without any sense of geography or direction. I was on the verge of collapsing into a sobbing heap, of vowing to go no further and waiting for death itself to claim me, when I heard something moving through the dark behind me.

It was the same rattling, tapping sound I had detected earlier. This time I was sure it was the creature. I could do nothing to avoid the beast, nor defeat it if it chose to strike. I sat and waited for the attack – perhaps it would be swift, and would mark my final liberation from the catacombs.

Accompanied by the rattle of claws on stone, a whisper of cold wind caressed the side of my face. The 'angel', it seemed, had passed within centimetres of me, but it didn't attack, or speak, or in any way act as if it realised I was there.

I sat in the darkness, dumbfounded. If it wasn't just an organic killing machine, why had it butchered Taras, his wife and Olexander with such gruesome efficiency? After its initial attack on me, why did it now seem to behave as if I didn't exist?

As I pondered the beast's motives, I remembered my earlier conviction that there must be other exits. Perhaps that was where it was heading now.

I jumped to my feet, feeling positive for the first time in hours, but scarcely believing that so evil a being could, perhaps, lead me straight to that thing that I most desired: a way out of the awful tomb in which I was trapped.

My ears, thank goodness, seemed suited to this realm of sensory absence: keeping a sensible distance between us, I followed what I assumed was the creature.

Whatever it was that I was following, it made no attempt to

disguise its progress whereas before I would have sworn that it was keeping to a stealthy near-silence. The rattle of claws on the hard, stone surface set my teeth on edge, and also brought to mind the bodies I had seen. Three of them now, and each killed with a stomach-churning brutality. Olexander's poor, noble attempt to reason with the beast seemed always doomed to failure – and yet the creature *had* spoken. It was capable of some form of self-expression. How had it described itself? An instrument of war?

I turned the phrase over in my mind. Perhaps it meant only that it was a biological expression of someone else's hatred, no more or less morally responsible for its actions than one of the great horses that carried a knight into bloody battle.

Such speculation was pointless. I knew only that Yevhen had released something from a casket under the cathedral, and that, far from protecting the people of Kiev, the 'angel' seemed intent only on killing those it encountered. As if the city authorities did not have enough to deal with, with the Mongol hordes only a few days away!

I thought briefly of the Doctor, wondering if he was enjoying any sort of success within the Mongol camp. I somewhat wished he had changed his mind for nobler reasons than simply the preservation of the future we all knew, but, whatever the circumstances, I was glad that he had. I had the utmost faith in the old man – for all his incorrigibility, my belief in him burned in my heart like one of Olexander's torches.

And then I thought of Dodo, still, I guessed, in the governor's residence and thus at the mercy of Yevhen. I hurried my pace, impatient to be away from the catacombs.

I soon noticed the black nothingness of the tunnels becoming grey, the dim light hinting at walls and pillars and doors. In time I could see my own feet, the path before me –

and something tall moving through the remaining shadows.

And, ahead of that, there was a partly open door. Set into a wall, it burned like a beacon.

I could have wept for joy.

I watched as the disgusting creature made its way into the light, and then I waited. I did not want to emerge and find the dark angel waiting for me.

I fought a losing battle with my impatience – with my desperation to be out of these tunnels – and soon I found myself striding towards the doorway.

It was roughly hewn from what appeared to be oak, and probably about three-quarters of the size of a normal door. The great metal hinges were rusty, and a split towards the handle allowed light and wind into the tunnels. But, to me, this was like stumbling upon an entrance to heaven.

I emerged to find myself in what appeared to be a storeroom. Piles of barrels were covered with mildewed sheets and the room was rich with dust, though the floor near the door to the catacombs spoke of recent activity. I realised that the layout of the room would have obscured the entrance from any who did not already know it to be there.

From where I stood, I could see that there were two doors in the centre of opposing walls. One was still closed from the inside with a large plank of wood held in place by strong metal prongs. If this meant the creature had gone the other way, then this, clearly, was the door for me.

I removed the wooden plank, and pushed and pulled at the door. Eventually it opened, though with a graceless juddering that spoke of decades of neglect.

It was an outside door. Beyond was a square of some sort, hemmed in by imposing civic buildings. I breathed deeply, and emerged into the sunlight. At last, I was free!

I closed the door behind me and, in doing so, looked up at

the building from which I had emerged. Even from this unfamiliar angle, I recognised the dark peaked roof and slab-like towers. It was the governor's residence – and the creature was at large, somewhere within the maze of rooms and corridors.

It was time, I decided, to throw myself upon the mercy of Dmitri, to plead for my life and to tell him what I had learnt of the plots of adviser Yevhen and Bishop Vasil. Even more importantly, Dodo and many others were now virtual prisoners within that building – and Dmitri had unwittingly sealed the dark angel in along with them.

There was nothing else for it: I would have to march around to the front of the building and give myself up, risking death if the governor didn't accept my innocence.

'You asked to see me?'

Dmitri's courteous tones belied the fact that he was the governor of an entire city, and I a suspected murderer who had escaped from prison.

'Thank you,' I said. 'I want you to know that I'm not guilty of Taras's murder. I have proof now, and every reason –'

Dmitri interrupted me with a wave of the hand, as if this were a mere trifle, a pleasantry to be dispensed with at the start of a conversation. 'But of course.'

I was wrongfooted by this, and had to resist the temptation to launch into my prepared defence. 'Sorry?'

'We witnessed an attack last night, in this very building. It is clear no mortal man is responsible.'

'That's what I wanted to talk to you about. In private.'

Dmitri considered my request. 'Very well,' he said. Another wave of the hand, and he dismissed the soldiers that stood near the door. 'Even my advisers are not here. You are free to say whatever you wish, without fear of censure by anyone... other than myself,' he added with a smile.

'It seems…' I wondered where to start. 'It seems that adviser Yevhen has released some creature from its tomb under the cathedral. I believe that this "dark angel" killed Taras, and was responsible for whatever attack you suffered last night.' I paused. 'While in prison, I met with former adviser Olexander. I that I saw this creature kill him in cold blood.'

Dmitri nodded impassively. 'Go on.'

'Under the cathedral is a catacomb. A passageway leads directly to this building. I followed the beast through the tunnels. I believe everyone here must be in danger.'

I paused, watching as Dmitri turned this over in his mind. 'I have heard rumours of such tunnels,' he said. 'It was considered wise to link the ecclesiastical heart of Kiev to the civic – should a man from one wish to throw himself on the mercy of the men in the other. But the tunnels themselves are known, I am sure, to only a few souls. I have never seen them on any map or design of the city.'

'I can lead you to the doorway,' I said eagerly.

Dmitri nodded. 'Thank you. I will order a search, though I will not be able to commit many men to the task. It is said the tunnels are rat holes, and someone might find themselves walking them for weeks with no hope of escape.'

'I can vouch for that,' I said.

'More importantly,' continued Dmitri, 'you say that the "dark angel" is now at liberty within our city – worse still, within these very chambers?'

'I believe so.'

'Then my men must concentrate on flushing the creature out – here, above ground, where it can be captured or destroyed.'

'Forgive me,' I said. 'I'm not sure you'll easily succeed in killing it.'

Dmitri sighed, as if accepting what I had said.

I took heart from his ready acceptance of my story. 'What

will you do about Yevhen?' I asked boldly.

'For the moment, nothing,' said Dmitri. 'He may still be of some use. With the Tartar attack imminent…'

'Something else is going on,' I added quickly. 'I believe the bishop… Vasil? I believe he has come up with his own plan to save the city from the Mongols.'

Dmitri arched his eyebrows in surprise. 'Vasil? What plans has he to avert the attack?'

'At first Vasil and Yevhen were working together, though they seemed to fall out over this creature. In any event, Vasil is now planning a direct appeal to the Mongols.'

Dmitri looked surprised. 'An appeal, to those devils? On what grounds?'

'He mentioned a "southern problem".'

Dmitri's eyebrows arched, but he said nothing.

'Olexander reckoned it might refer to the Muslims,' I ventured.

'It is true that the Church would dearly love to rid the world of Islam,' said Dmitri. 'But even so…' He shook his head slowly.

I remembered the brown-cloaked man the clerics had been so keen to keep hidden. 'I think there is a Mongol emissary in Kiev, smuggled in by Vasil,' I said.

Dmitri nodded curtly. 'Then the rumours are not without substance,' he said. The boiling irritation he felt was obvious on his features. 'We are in no position to trade with the Tartars… Surely they will take whatever is not offered to them. Vasil is a fool!' He strode angrily towards the door, pulled it open, and barked instructions at one of the soldiers just beyond: 'Order a search of all Church properties in Kiev.'

I saw the soldier's eyes widen. Such an action was almost unthinkable.

'You will find a Tartar spy in our midst. You will find him, and bring him to me.'

The dazed man opened his mouth to speak, seemingly on

the verge of challenging the governor.

Dmitri paused just long enough to draw breath, and continued before the soldier could utter a sound. 'Bring Bishop Vasil to me as well. While we are preparing to die for our city, this traitor is colluding with the enemy!' He spat his words through gritted teeth. 'Tell this "man of God" that, unless he convinces me otherwise, I shall soon send him to his true lord and master!'

He turned and slammed the door shut, breathing deeply as his irritation subsided. 'Thank you, Steven, for bringing this information to me. I am sorry this knowledge has come via such suffering – in prison, and in these tunnels you speak of.'

'That's OK,' I said. 'Though, I must say… I'm amazed you accept everything I have said. During my travels… Well, let's just say, I'm not often believed!'

'I hear many rumours, suspect many plots. It could be said that I am only effective if I am able to sift all gossip, all tittle-tattle, looking for evil, suspecting always the worst of those who surround me. What you have said this morning ties many threads together for the first time!'

'I could be lying,' I blurted out, before remembering that this was probably not the time or the place to play devil's advocate.

'And, as a traveller, you would hope to gain what, exactly? Your freedom is the one thing you crave, and yet you know by now that I am not willing to let you go until after the Tartars have been defeated.' He paused. 'In any event, I trust you, Steven. I always have. I am saddened, however, that it has been so difficult to assure you of that trust.' Dmitri looked keenly about the empty debating room, tapping his fingers to his lips. 'Do not let Yevhen know that we are aware of this beast he has liberated,' he whispered. 'There is still more duplicity and treachery in the man that only time will draw out.'

I got to my feet. 'Thank you for believing me,' I said. 'And now, with your leave, I would very much like to have a wash, find some clean clothes – and then be reunited with Dodo.'

Dmitri smiled. 'You will find her with Yevhen's daughter, I daresay. Since my order that those closest to me remain at my side, I have barely seen either of them.'

'You have many things to consider,' I said, thinking of how Dodo and Lesia had rescued me, and wondering if they had indeed managed to return without being apprehended.

'I do,' said Dmitri, as the great burden of responsibility settled around him again. 'There is so much –'

The door flew open, and Yevhen strode into the debating chamber. 'Forgive me, my lord, I have grave news,' he said, bowing his head humbly.

It was only when he looked up that he saw me standing there. He blinked in surprise.

'What is this man doing here?'

'He is a free man, who can come and go as he pleases,' said Dmitri.

'But the murder… The prison…'

'Steven is no more capable of these despicable acts than you or I,' said Dmitri. I saw him stare at his adviser keenly, his rhetorical statement concealing a growing suspicion. 'And, surely, a man cannot be blamed for wanting to escape from prison if he is truly innocent?'

I must admit, I did enjoy watching Yevhen squirming in anger. 'This is Isaac's doing!' he finally exploded.

'Nonsense,' said Dmitri. 'I have not seen my other adviser all day, though I expect him to be here soon. I must inform you both that Bishop Vasil will be arrested and tried for treason.'

'Treason?'

'Far from joining us in our struggle against the Tartars, it seems that Vasil is planning to appease them.'

Yevhen shook his head sadly, although I wondered if this

was, to him, an entirely bewildering turn of events.

'You said you had bad news?' prompted Dmitri.

Yevhen nodded gravely. 'Our physicians are attending the bodies now…'

'Bodies?'

'A great illness is sweeping through the city.'

'What sort of illness?'

'We are not yet sure.'

'How will we recognise it?'

'Vomiting, an aged appearance to the skin, a fevered but cold brow, an inclination to sleep. Death seems surely to follow.'

Dmitri sighed in anguish. 'Why must the people of Kiev be bludgeoned in this way?' he asked desperately. I could see the frustration etched on his face – how much more was he expected to cope with?

'How many have died?' I asked Yevhen.

'A handful,' he replied, still staring at Dmitri. 'But disease can spread like fire through a city that is preparing for siege.' He glanced at me momentarily, his eyes cold and grey. 'Perhaps, if it takes hold, there will be no one left by the time the Tartars invade.'

# XII

## Sors immanis et inanis, rota tu volubilis, status malus

Dodo banged heartily on the door. 'Lesia? Lesia? Come on, you can't stay in there all day!'

There was no response, and Dodo tugged on the handle of twisted metal. The door was unlocked and she pulled it open, the treated wooden planks grating across the rough stone floor. She turned to the guard behind her.

'You stay here. We ladies need our privacy.'

The soldier snorted, but made no move to follow her in.

Dodo shut the door on him with a broad grin. 'Come on, sleepyhead,' she said as she approached the comatose body in the bed. She shook her friend's sleeping form vigorously. 'Time to get up! If I can make the effort, so can you.'

The mass beneath the sheets offered little resistance to Dodo's prods and pushes; she made her way to the top of the bed, and pulled back the covers.

Lesia was still asleep, a blank, dreaming look on her face. Her dark hair fanned out across the pillow like a ragged halo.

'Stop mucking about!' said Dodo. 'Your father will not approve!' she added in a haughty tone, before walking over to the window and opening the rough wooden shutters.

Sunlight, filtered through grey rain-clouds, painted the room with repressed watercolour light. 'Doesn't look very good out,' Dodo observed. 'Anyway, I expect you and lover boy would prefer to stay in. We'll have to see what we can arrange, eh?'

She was back at the top of the bed again, prodding the sleeping body with growing irritation.

'Lesia, will you get up!'

A dark look crossed Dodo's face.

'Stop it, Lesia. You're frightening me.'

Still there was not the slightest movement from the sleeping woman. Even her chest seemed motionless beneath her pale bedclothes.

'Lesia!'

Worried now, Dodo reached down to touch her friend's face. She noticed that Lesia's eyes were fluttering a little, as if she was dreaming – but her skin was deathly cold to the touch.

'Oh my God…'

Dodo ran from the room.


Yevhen swept into the room, agitated. 'Is it the disease?' he queried.

Isaac, who had only just arrived, looked up from his cursory inspection of the sleeping girl. 'I do not think so,' he said. 'Physicians have been called, and we shall of course rely on their expertise in the stars and the humours…' He puffed his cheeks. 'But I must admit this is a malaise the like of which I have never seen.'

'She's just as I found her,' offered Dodo, wary of Yevhen's wrath, but he seemed to ignore her words. Instead, he strode to the bed and gathered his daughter to him, first gently and with concern etching his features, then more strongly. He whispered into her ear, but the young woman remained little more than a doll in his arms.

'You might decide it best to leave her be,' suggested Isaac. 'Some conditions –'

'I will decide how best to protect my own family!' Yevhen spat, glaring at the older man. 'I know where my priorities lie. I wish that were true of all the city leaders,' he added, his words ripe with implied threat.

'What do you mean by that, sir?'

'Do not play the fool with me, Jew,' spat Yevhen. 'The

governor may be ignorant of your alliance with the travellers, but I am not.'

'What are you on about?' asked Dodo, who could stand in silence no more.

'Isaac has engineered the release of your friend,' said Yevhen through gritted teeth. 'Have you not heard?'

Isaac smiled sweetly. 'I am naturally pleased to hear the governor has decided that Steven is innocent of murder. But I am afraid to say that I had nothing to do with the governor's change of heart.' He stared levelly at his fellow adviser, refusing to be intimidated by him. 'Your daughter is ill, sir,' he continued in a voice so quiet Dodo had to strain to hear it. 'I humbly suggest we keep our thoughts and our prayers focused on that.'

Yevhen nodded, as if shamed by Isaac's words, but Dodo could see there was still a fire burning behind his eyes.

'How much longer are these doctors of yours going to be?' she queried.

'I imagine they are dealing with those poor souls who have fallen victim to this vile disease,' said Isaac. 'The numbers are growing by the moment.'

Yevhen straightened, and turned away from his daughter. It was clear he had made a decision. 'Is it not plain what is wrong with the girl?' he asked grandly. He turned to Isaac. 'You are so wise, and yet you do not see the evidence of your own eyes?'

'What are you talking about?' asked Dodo.

'A night-time visitation,' Yevhen announced grandly. 'I can feel it in her fever, smell it on her skin. She has been corrupted.' His voice lowered to a near whisper. 'An incubus.'

Isaac reached out to his fellow adviser, as if he were about to put a comforting arm around him. 'You have been working too hard,' he said lightly.

'The evidence is clear enough!' snapped Yevhen, striding

towards the door. 'My very own daughter has not been able to resist temptation. She has given in to lust, and an incubus has her soul.' He glanced back towards the bed. 'She now sleeps the sleep of the damned.'

'An incubus!' Isaac spluttered. 'Were this malady not so serious, sir, I would laugh!'

Yevhen turned, pointing an angry finger towards Isaac. 'You do not believe in God, sir! Of course you do not believe in demons!'

'We believe in the same God,' offered Isaac with as much dignity as he could muster. 'Different expressions of Him, perhaps, but the same creator.' He held a hand over his heart. 'The only monsters I believe in are here.'

'You will burn in hell for your blasphemy!' snapped Yevhen, marching through the doorway.

Isaac watched him go, and Dodo saw the unease that creased his features. 'It will, perhaps, be heaven to be away from you,' the old man whispered.

Still boiling with contempt, and knotted with worry about his daughter, Yevhen marched down the corridor towards his rooms. He hated being away from his usual dwellings, and the madness of Dmitri's decree only inflamed his irritation further.

A soldier passed by, his eyes turned away from the adviser. For a moment Yevhen watched him go, then he snapped 'Boy?'

The lad paused, then turned. 'My lord?' he queried nervously.

Yevhen shook his head sadly. A broadsword hung from the boy's belt, a reminder that the defence of Kiev rested with such as him – but his voice had barely broken!

'Come with me,' said Yevhen.

'But I have been ordered to search for a beast, at liberty within these walls.'

'You will have time enough to complete your search when you have performed an errand for me.'

'And the tunnels, sir. We must look out for secret passageways.'

Yevhen's eyebrows arched, but he made no comment on the young soldier's revelation. 'There are enough dark monsters and tunnels in Kiev to last you a lifetime, boy. I merely wish you to deliver a letter.'

The soldier nodded curtly, and followed Yevhen into his room. The adviser strode over to a desk, rummaged for a small scrap of parchment and a quill, and began to write.

After a few minutes, he looked up. 'Have you ever wondered what the holy scriptures truly say, boy? Or imagined how they would sound in our own tongue?'

The soldier's eyes widened, and he stammered as he searched for an appropriate response. 'I am content', he said, 'with... with what I hear. What I know. What I am allowed to know.'

'But of course,' smiled Yevhen. 'I was like you once. But I had a desire to learn, to realise for myself. I had to teach myself Latin.' He watched as the ink dried on the parchment. 'Let me be honest with you. I am not sure the reward was worthy of the effort.'

'No, sir?'

Yevhen shook his head. 'We only want an illusion of freedom, do we not, boy?'

'I do not know, sir. You may be right.'

Yevhen handed over the sheet of parchment. 'Give this to Bishop Vasil.' He paused for a moment, thinking. 'I suppose he may already be... busy. In which case, give it to the most senior cleric you can find. They will know what to do.'

'My lord.' The boy bowed quickly, and headed for the door.

'One last thing,' said Yevhen, stopping him in his tracks.

The boy turned.

'The instructs that, once read, it is to be burnt in flame. See that this is done.'

The soldier nodded.

'Soon there will be flames enough to burn all the vile libraries of Kiev,' said Yevhen quietly as he watched the boy go.

Dodo was escorted into the debating chamber. Steven and Dmitri looked up from their discussion, the former breaking immediately into a broad smile.

'Dodo!' he exclaimed. 'I'm so glad to see you!'

She hugged him, squealing in delight. 'You're a free man now!'

'Was it ever in doubt?' Steven laughed.

'Come, sit with us,' said Dmitri, his grave tones cutting through their celebration. 'We were discussing the Doctor.'

'Have you heard from him?' asked Dodo, unable to contain her excitement.

Dmitri shook his head. 'No, and neither would I expect to. Even if the Doctor is, in time, victorious, I must assume for the moment that he fails. We may not see him again until the Tartars are at our very doors.'

'Or we just may not see him again,' said Dodo, copying his deflated tone.

'Try to understand why I must speak in this way,' said Dmitri. Dodo instantly felt ashamed of her irritation. 'The Doctor has told me…' The governor struggled to articulate his thoughts. 'You come from a time that has yet to happen, a world that has yet to be – yet it is our world, our earth, and we people are to you the corpses of history.'

'The Doctor said that?' queried Steven.

'Not in his words,' said Dmitri, 'but in the pauses between his words.' He sighed. 'I am beginning to wonder if we should just sit here, in sackcloth and ashes, and wait patiently for our executioners.'

'You can't do that,' exclaimed Dodo. 'We're trying to help you as much as we can. And, if things were different, maybe…'

'The Tartars sweep towards us, illness grips our people, it seems a monster roams this very building which I have sought to make a secure fortress…' Dmitri managed an ironic laugh. 'Even adviser Yevhen's daughter is in the grip of some awful trance that separates her from us. I wish I could travel to that land of safety and sleep as easily as her!'

'Look,' said Steven, resting a hand on Dmitri's arm. 'The Doctor is the most incredible person I've ever met. He will do everything he possibly can to help you.'

'And one or two things that are impossible,' added Dodo, trying to lighten the mood.

Dmitri smiled. 'I am sure you are right,' he said, though his words carried little weight of conviction. 'How is Lesia?'

'I really don't know,' said Dodo. 'I just hope your medical people can work out what's wrong with her.'

'It is a worrying development,' agreed Dmitri. He lowered his voice. 'And we must be wary. All creatures will endeavour to protect their young – but sometimes they only succeed in injuring those they most want to help.' He stared at Dodo, his grave eyes underlining the allusion he was making. 'Do you understand?'

Dodo nodded. 'I'll stay with Lesia.'

'Excellent,' said Dmitri, striding towards the door. 'Come with me, Steven. There is still much to do.'

The robed man stared imperiously down at the soldier, who had remained on one bended knee at the bottom of the altar steps.

'And this note came from adviser Yevhen?'

The soldier nodded. 'I saw him write it with his own hand.'

The cleric turned the letter over between delicate fingers, as if the very words carried poison. 'And the letter speaks nothing but truth?'

'Forgive me, my lord. I do not know the contents of the note.'

'You believe in God?'

'Of course.'

'In the glory of Christ, his saints and the virgin?'

The soldier nodded furiously.

'And in the evils of apostasy, heresy and unholy ignorance?'

'I am loyal to my Lord and my country.'

The robed man approached a candle that burned pitifully to one side of the great altar. 'Bishop Vasil is not able to see to this matter himself, but he has made clear what should happen.' He applied the parchment to the flame, which expanded and brightened greedily. 'Adviser Yevhen suggests much the same thing. Listen carefully. This is what you must do.'

When Dodo returned to Lesia's room Nahum was sitting quietly on a stool at the sleeping woman's bedside. He immediately jumped to his feet, his face red with embarrassment – and his eyes wide with fear.

'It's OK,' said Dodo.

'OK?' repeated Nahum, clearly not reassured in the slightest.

'It's all right,' explained Dodo. 'I know.'

The young man stared at her blankly, though this time Dodo sensed the ignorance was less than entirely genuine.

'Lesia told me. About you and her.' She stepped over to Nahum's side, and extended a gentle hand to touch his arm. 'You must be very concerned.'

Nahum glanced around the room, as if seeking reassurance that this was not a plot of Yevhen's hatching. After a moment, he averted his eyes – shyness or fear, Dodo could not tell which – and simply nodded his head.

Dodo perched herself on the end of the bed, and looked down at her friend. She seemed not to have changed, though that awful deathly look – as if the real Lesia had departed, leaving only an empty shell behind – remained as strong as before.

Dodo didn't know what to say: she had barely even spoken to Isaac's son before, let alone engaged him in discussions of life, love and death. So she sat in silence, glancing between Nahum's downcast face, the swirling cloud patterns through the windows and Lesia's unchangeable, empty expression.

'Lesia and I grew up together,' said Nahum after some minutes.

The interjection into the all-consuming silence was such that Dodo nearly jumped in surprise.

'Really?' she said.

'Because of our fathers we played together, were taught together. She was the sister I never had, and I her brother.' He paused, a distant look on his face. 'I truly believe Lesia knows more about me than anyone, save God. There have been times when she has proved she knows me better than I.'

Dodo nodded. 'She never has anything but praise for you.'

Nahum looked troubled. 'She is full of virtue... and forgiveness,' he said vaguely. 'But the one thing that surprised her was when we became more than friends.'

'I don't blame you for keeping it quiet,' said Dodo. 'Yevhen isn't exactly my favourite person round here either.'

'We will tell him... one day, when the season is right. I believe my father knows, though he keeps quiet and gentle counsel. But Lesia's father...'

'He'd go ballistic!'

Dodo wet a square of linen with water from a pitcher that

had been left at the side of the bed, and dabbed Lesia's forehead with it. She wasn't sure this was terribly helpful, but it seemed to be the height of medical intervention as far as she could perceive. That, and leeches.

'I do think he cares for Lesia,' said Dodo. 'He just doesn't know how to show it.'

Nahum nodded. 'We all express our deep feelings in ways that are true to our inner character,' he said.

'Sorry?'

'A phrase of my father's. We are all consistent, in line with our virtue, our measure of received and expressible love.'

'I asked Yevhen for permission to sit with Lesia,' said Dodo. 'Actually, I ran into him in a corridor and I didn't want to do anything to cause him further irritation. You know, he seemed genuinely happy that I was so concerned. He told me what a fine girl she was, how like her mother, and how proud he was of her.'

'She died in childbirth.'

'Who?'

'Lesia's mother. She died bringing Lesia into the world.'

Dodo paused. 'Is that why Yevhen is so awful to everyone?'

Nahum shook his head. 'He has always been self-seeking,' he said, with remarkably little malice in his voice. 'But now he has another reason to rail against the iniquities of the world.'

'That's one thing I don't understand,' said Dodo. 'Ever since we arrived, you can feel the fear in the air. Most people are just waiting for the Mongols to show up and kill them.' She got to her feet, drawn to the window and the grey vista beyond. 'And yet you carry on as if nothing is the matter. You joke, and you laugh... You fall in love.'

Nahum did not reply instantly. When she turned to look at him, his face showed only puzzlement. 'But that is how this world is.' He shrugged his shoulders. 'I do not understand what you are saying.'

'I suppose…' Dodo sighed. 'I suppose I'm just saying that where I come from, life is pretty much a doddle. Women rarely die in childbirth, diseases don't wipe out entire cities – Mongol hordes aren't forever waiting around the next corner for the right time to invade.'

'Then you and your people must be truly blessed, and the streets must resound with singing!'

'Hardly,' said Dodo. 'If anything, it makes people worse.'

'Then it is as I said,' concluded Nahum. 'By our actions, and not by our circumstances, do you see the true colour of our hearts.'

Dodo smiled. 'Do you say this sort of thing to Lesia?'

'If she allows me.'

'No wonder she fancies you something rotten.'

The room was a mess with papers, books and writing materials covering every possible surface: the floor, chairs, a low table set just in front of the window. But despite this, it was opulent: one wall was dominated by a great tapestry showing a hunting scene, and gold-coloured cloth hung in costly cascades from the canopy over the bed. The man could not believe how quickly the chamber's new occupant had brought it down into a mire of untidiness and dirt. It only confirmed his worst suspicions.

The man glanced down at some of the parchments, and saw arcane symbols and satanic language captured in ink. He averted his eyes, lest the meaningless written languages of Babel corrupt him, then strode towards the window and pulled the shutters together.

Without warning, the door on the far side of the room opened. The old Jewish adviser stepped in, his eyes flashing with shock when he saw the soldier.

'Can I help you?' he asked, masking his surprise with politeness.

'I am…' The soldier struggled to find the words. 'I am patrolling the corridors and rooms. On Yevhen's instructions.'

'Yevhen?' Isaac arched his eyebrows. 'Even Yevhen should respect the privacy of those around him.' He smiled good-naturedly. 'Still, orders are there to be obeyed, no?'

The soldier found himself nodding curtly.

'I am looking for my wife,' continued Isaac, looking vaguely around the room, as if she were hiding in the shadows. 'You have not seen her?'

'No, sir, I have not.' The soldier stepped towards Isaac.

'Hmm.'

The man watched Isaac's gaze rest on the shuttered windows.

'It is dark in here,' the old man said. 'I thought I had opened the shutters, but am clearly in error. If you permit me to do so, my friend, then you will have little need for the torch you carry.'

'I have every need for it,' said the soldier, bringing his mail-covered fist on to the back of the adviser's head.

Isaac slumped to the floor with a throttled groan.

The man turned, taking one last look at the room – the room of the heretic.

Then he dropped the torch on to a pile of papers, and made for the door.

# XIII
# Dies irae, dies illa, solvet saeclum in favilla

Dmitri asked me to accompany a small group of soldiers in their search for the disgraced Archbishop Vasil. I couldn't believe how quickly things had changed: less than twenty-four hours before I had been a fugitive, wanted for murder, hiding in the darkness under the cathedral. Now, it seemed, I was known to be innocent and was trusted by the governor – so much so, in fact, that he seemed to have a role for me in his plans.

Of course, I am sure the trust only went so far. Doubtless I would not be allowed to enter the TARDIS, and I had the lingering suspicion that the men who searched so diligently for Vasil had also been instructed to watch over me. However, I did feel that some sort of bond existed between Dmitri and myself – and, if I had felt for him in the past, my overwhelming sadness at the impossibility of his position was now complete.

A thorough examination of Vasil's quarters indicated that he had expected trouble of some sort. Servants in the residential quarters attached to the great cathedral indicated that the bishop had not been seen for some hours, and that he had neglected his ecclesiastical duties that morning. The last person to see him had observed a desperate attempt to pack a few possessions. You don't have to be Sherlock Holmes to work out that he was either in hiding, or had fled the city – it was unlikely, in either case, that we would find him easily.

We emerged from the semidarkness of the church buildings, and knew at once that something was very wrong. The air was rich with the awful aroma of fire, and a column of grey smoke hung over some nearby buildings.

'We are indeed doomed,' muttered one soldier with awful gallows humour. 'It seems they are burning the victims of disease now.'

I wasn't so sure. I pointed in the direction of the smoke, still unfamiliar with the geography of this vast city. 'Where is that?' I queried.

Sudden panic registered on the faces of many of the guards. 'Governor Dmitri!' exclaimed one.

We set off as one across the square and towards the great, dark building that housed the debating chambers, civil offices and residential quarters of the rulers of Kiev. We ran through narrow streets, hemmed in by buildings and overflowing with people who were either scurrying away in pointless panic or standing rock solid in the road, rooted to the spot in impotent terror.

The picture was much the same once we entered the building. Soldiers and servants rushed everywhere, or stood mutely in the shadows, but no one could tells us exactly where the fire was, and what was being done about it.

It was impossible to see the focus of the blaze from the front of the building, so we moved instinctively through the passageways towards the rear. All the while, the stench of burning grew stronger, prickling our lungs and making our throats raw. Although it was a high-status building, and thus largely constructed of stone, I had seen for myself that wood was a vital construction material. I feared that, unless checked, the flames would soon consume the governor's quarters completely.

At last we came to a knot of minor officials talking earnestly. Beyond them, blocking a corridor from floor to ceiling, was a wall of fire.

'What's going on?' I asked, and the group immediately opened to reveal Isaac's wife and son at its heart. Both were weak with fear, and each had to support the other.

'Isaac!' exclaimed the woman. 'He is trapped in the inferno!'

'And where is Dmitri?' I asked.

'He is trying to find another way round,' explained Nahum. 'But I am sure this is the only way to get to my father's chambers.'

'No one has seen him!' exclaimed Rebekah, collapsing into wails of anguish.

'I have tried to approach the rooms from here', continued Nahum, 'but the fire is too strong. It would devour me in moments.'

I remembered the storeroom I had discovered after my escape from tunnels – with one door leading outside and another leading further into the building.

I turned quickly to the soldiers who had accompanied me on the fruitless search for Vasil. 'You know that there are secret tunnels that run through this building and back to the cathedral?' I asked.

One or two nodded in response.

'Were any of you ordered to search the underground passageways?'

One man nodded.

'Did you find a way through to that corridor down there?'

The man looked back at me blankly.

'Think, man!'

He shrugged his shoulders languidly. 'I cannot remember.'

'How do we get to the storeroom?' I queried. 'The one with the doors to the catacombs?'

Again, the man looked at me vacantly.

I could wait no longer. I hurried back through the corridors, not caring if the soldiers were following me or not. I would find the storeroom on my own if I had to.

I burst out of the building, pushing my way through the ragged crowd that had gathered there. I ran as fast as I could towards the small square surrounded by civic buildings that I remembered so keenly from my escape from the labyrinth.

I found the door easily enough, and was grateful beyond words that it hadn't been bolted shut. Beyond was the storeroom, much as I remembered it from before, although some items had been moved, and the floor was further disturbed, which was consistent with the cursory exploration Dmitri had ordered.

The secret entrance to the labyrinth was to my left; the other door, which I had never opened, faced me. I ran to it, then turned at a noise behind me: two of the soldiers had followed me and were nervously stepping down into the chamber.

I reached for the door handle, then withdrew my hand. The metal was hot. This at least meant we were in the right part of the building – but it also meant it would not be easy to open the door.

'Quick!' I snapped to the men. 'Bring some rags!'

They rummaged around, sending great plumes of dust spiralling into the air, while I tried desperately to pull my sleeves down over my hands as I scrabbled at the red-hot handle. I was frustrated to be so close and yet so powerless to intervene.

One of the soldiers offered a bundle of linen strips; I wrapped them quickly over my fingers and thumbs, and pulled again at the door.

It seemed not to shift at all; I suspected that the wood had expanded with the heat, and that there was now precious little gap between the big oak planks and the unforgiving flagstones.

I readjusted my makeshift protection against the heat – my fingers were screaming in protest, but I gritted my teeth to block the pain – and pulled again, bringing my full weight to bear, both hands straining at the handle with as much force as I could muster.

With a shriek, the door opened a crack and one of the guards forced his fingers into the gap, pulling hard.

Another harsh sound of protest, and the gap grew wider, admitting smoke and heat from whatever was beyond.

The gap between the door and wall was now sufficiently large for us to force our way through; I pushed forward, without a word, and found myself in a plain corridor that probably linked the servants' quarters with the kitchens. The stones that formed the floor and walls seemed to glow with heat, for the timbers of the ceiling were ablaze. Great chunks of wood fell like scarlet and orange rain; all the while the conflagration, somewhere over our heads, popped and crackled like animal fat falling into flame.

Through the heat haze I saw a twisted structure at the far end of the corridor, stretching up into the ceiling. I ran to the staircase and ascended it quickly, using my arms for balance but keeping my hands as far from the glowing stone blocks as possible.

As I climbed, I glanced down to see one of the soldiers diligently following me. Though less than three metres in height, the staircase became noticeably cooler as we ascended. It terminated in a simple peaked archway with a heavy curtain of stained brown fabric suspended over it, and I pushed my way through.

I was in a much grander corridor – the curtain that covered the archway matched a number of other tapestries and drapes along the walls. One doorway was open, the door itself having caught fire and fallen to the floor. It seemed that a spark had ignited the tinder-dry wooden beams at the far end of the corridor; these flames, in turn, had spread through the floor to the ceiling of the lower passageway we had been in moments ago.

The fire had also spread to the opposite end of the corridor, where rugs and drapes had created a solid wall of fire. I sensed, rather than heard, voices beyond the flames, and guessed that Nahum and the others were there, trying desperately to peer through the billowing smoke and fire.

The soldier and I ran through the open doorway into the room beyond; I was moving instinctively, and I wondered if the man knew where he was. I pulled the rags from my hands and held them over my mouth, for the air was thick with debris and sparks.

There had once been a table or desk in the room, but this was now little more than a framework of blackened spindles. Everything else was either invisible beneath tongues of fire, or had already burnt out, surrendering to the heat. Even the window shutters were ablaze. Scraps of burning parchment, lifted by the heat of the flames, drifted around the room like vengeful spirits.

There was a second doorway, a smaller one near the window, and in it I noticed something dark, just extending into the main chamber. I ran towards it, dodging the flames as best I could.

It was the slumped body of a man. I wondered if, in blind panic, he had sought refuge in the smaller room which was less affected by the fire. However, the fumes seemed finally to have got the better of him.

I reached for his clothing and found it warm, but not hot, to touch. The soldier and I turned the man over. It was, as we had hoped, Isaac, his face blackened with smoke and a little dried blood on his lips.

We began to haul him from the room and into the main chamber just as one of the great wooden timbers that supported the ceiling gave way. It fell to the floor, shattering in a shower of golden sparks.

# XIV
## Quid sum miser tunc dicturus, quem patronum rogaturus, cum vix justus sit securus?

The Doctor was saddle-sore, thirsty and bored by the unchanging terrain, but most of all he was grateful to be alive.

The Mongol archers had killed the soldiers in seconds, and without compunction. Only Mykola's status as leader of the men and the Doctor's distinctiveness had saved them. The Doctor's expressions of outrage had fallen on deaf ears. The dead men were left where they had fallen, without ceremony or second glance.

The Mongols had indicated that the Doctor and Mykola should remount their horses, and had tethered the ones the men from Kiev had been riding to their own, much smaller mounts. As soldiers, they cared little for human life, but as horsemen they were not about to abandon any creature.

Soon the archers were joined by other riders wearing tough, folded leather armour and carrying great spears adorned with tribal flags. The trap – for that is what it surely was – had been efficiently put in place, and now they were returning to the main army with their prisoners. The Doctor wondered how long the expedition from Kiev had been under observation – and, indeed, whether the ever-diminishing gap between the Mongol army and Kiev itself was filled with scouts and spies, alert to every individual who came and went.

It was a sobering thought.

They travelled in silence, any attempt at communication being met with a threat of violence. The Doctor tried to watch the path of the sun behind the clouded skies but, even so, he had little idea of when they were captured, or for how long they had travelled.

They heard the Mongol army long before they saw it.

The senior Mongol soldier raised a hand, and the entire group slowed to a halt. They were atop a lush hillside, looking down over the dry, wide valley through which the Mongol army was moving.

The Doctor had seen many great and terrifying sights in his time, but this massed movement of men was amongst the most awesome.

It was impossible to even estimate the number of men and horses that moved implacably across the terrain. There were thousands of soldiers, their horses throwing up a cloud of smoke that obscured still more. It was, from this distance, an army of ants in a haze of its own creation – and, though the Doctor could just make out the start of the massed procession far over to his left, to his right the Mongols simply faded into the horizon.

At the head of the great horde he could just perceive soldiers riding in orderly ranks, the flags of the various clans visible as intermittent splashes of blue and red amongst the massed brown of armour and horse. Then came great swathes of packhorses, weighed down by equipment and spare weaponry, and then the artillery – literally hundreds of enormous, wheeled catapults and ballista. The great wooden machines rumbled forward like tanks, and were followed by a secondary army of reserve soldiers – boys in training and foreign conscripts, the Doctor suspected.

Towards the rear were numerous wagons and camels carrying further supplies and supporting equipment. And, on the periphery of even the Doctor's keen vision, came hundreds of flocks of goats and sheep. Truly this was an army prepared for everything, including the longest of campaigns. It was as if an entire country had upped sticks and moved *en masse* to invade another. The Doctor knew from his reading of Earth history that this wasn't too far from the truth.

If the intention of this first sight of the Mongol army was to intimidate, it certainly succeeded. The Doctor glanced sideways at Mykola, and saw that he was pale and very nearly shaking with fear.

The leader of their Mongol captors flicked the reins of his horse, and as one the group swept down into the valley. The Doctor wondered how anyone was expected to find their way through the various groups and subgroupings of the army, but the man seemed to know exactly where he was heading. The Doctor also wondered about the chain of command – when was the order to stop issued, and how long would it take to reach the herdsmen many miles to the rear?

The massed ranks of soldiers were as impressive close up as they were from a distance, each face a picture of studied discipline and concentration. The noise, however, was almost deafening, and the Doctor was amazed that the Mongols put up with it.

Barely a word passed between the scouting party and the surrounding men. Instead, the group's horses soon settled into the brisk trot of those that surrounded them. It was as if the Doctor and Mykola had been swallowed whole by the Mongol army.

Again the Doctor tried to establish dialogue with the Mongols, pleading for an audience with their leader, but his words continued to fall on deaf ears. There was nothing for it but to settle once again into the rhythm of the horses, to think longingly of whatever food and drink might be offered to them when they finally stopped – and to remember the casual slaughter of the Russian soldiers.

When the sun touched the horizon the great army at last

came to rest. A Mongol soldier offered a hand to help the Doctor dismount, for which he was grateful. He spent a few moments walking up and down, trying to ease a multitude of aches and pains from his body. 'I'm far too old for this sort of thing,' he muttered, catching the soldier's eye.

The Mongol said nothing in reply, but grinned happily.

'I do not believe what I am seeing.'

The Doctor turned to find Mykola at his side. The young captain looked only a little less pale than when they had first seen the Mongol hordes stretched out like a blanket over the valley floor.

The Doctor was silent, unable to come up with any words that would not compound Mykola's pessimism.

Moments later, the air rang to the sound of a single horseman galloping at speed towards them. The dust cleared to reveal a tall, slender man atop a great white horse. His robes, and the turban of sorts that he wore, were pale cream and a curved sword rested in his lap.

He did not dismount, but nodded respectfully towards the Doctor and Mykola. When he spoke his voice was dignified but bland, seeming to contain every accent in the world, and none at all.

'Prince Mongke – cousin of Batu Khan, leader of the Mongol army on behalf of the Great Khan Ogedei, the power of God on Earth and Emperor of Mankind – wishes to see you.'

After another ride across the valley, the Doctor found himself standing before an enormous tent of such grace and beauty it was difficult to believe that, somehow, it was portable. Great swathes of silk and cotton formed porticoes, doorways and myriad chambers; flags fluttered from spike-topped spears; rugs and carpets covered the ground. Mongol soldiers stood at each entrance; women went in and out with bowls and pitchers.

The Doctor turned to their escort, extending a hand in greeting. 'I am the Doctor,' he said. 'We haven't been properly introduced.'

'I am Abd N-Nun Ayyub,' said the man, gripping his hand tightly. 'I am an interpreter in the court of Ogedei Khan.'

'You speak many languages?' queried the Doctor.

'All that are known to the Mongol Empire.' He turned an inquiring eye towards Mykola.

'Mykola, a brave soldier of Kiev,' said the Doctor, for Mykola himself seemed barely able to speak.

'You are a traveller?' queried Abd N-Nun Ayyub.

The Doctor nodded. 'My home is very far away.'

'Then we have one thing in common,' said Abd N-Nun Ayyub with a smile. 'Come, let us meet the lord Mongke.'

The Doctor stepped into a tented corridor, with Mykola following nervously behind. The fabric walls billowed gently in the wind, glowing an organic orange with the light of the setting sun. Tiny lanterns hung like twinkling fruit from the poles that formed the structure.

Beyond the corridor was a great room, brightly lit and pleasantly warm. Tapestries from myriad cultures hung on the walls, trophies won in battle and offered in meek surrender. The entire floor was covered with layer upon layer of fine carpets and rugs held down by fine gilt-encrusted statues of gods and monsters. It was, the Doctor considered, at least the equal of anything he had seen in Kiev – and they were thousands of miles from the Mongol capital.

At the far end of the room, on a commander's stool that better resembled a kingly throne, sat Mongke Khan. In common with most of his people, he was not a tall man, but his broad features, dominated by piercing dark eyes, exuded a haughty authority. His moustache was neatly trimmed, but his thin beard spread in disarray over his white kimono-like robes.

He held his hands in his lap, like some religious thinker, though his strong leather boots and the sheathed and curved sword at his side spoke eloquently of his true nature.

'Mongke greets you on behalf of the Great Khan of God,' Mongke said in a surprisingly quiet voice.

The Doctor bowed. 'I stand before you as a friend and servant of the people of Kiev.'

Mongke turned his attention to Mykola. 'And you?'

'A soldier,' the young man said simply.

'The captain of the Russian party,' interjected Abd N-Nun Ayyub.

'The Russians fought bravely?' queried Mongke.

'I believe it was over in the blink of an eye,' said Abd N-Nun Ayyub.

'The Mongol army is truly one of the most awesome military units I have ever witnessed,' said the Doctor. 'The legacy of Genghis lives on.'

Mongke's thin lips twisted into a smile. 'The punishment of God continues to roll out of the east. There is still much work to do.' For a moment, his hand rested on the banners of yak hair that surrounded the throne. 'We shall not rest until the nine tails stand proud over every city of Europe.'

'Every city quakes before your might,' said the Doctor.

'Then perhaps we will have little need for battle,' said Mongke.

'That is the hope of millions,' the Doctor agreed.

'I notice', said Mongke, cutting through any attempt on the Doctor's part to build on these encouraging words, 'that you call us Mongols. I had thought that the people of Europe abuse us as "Tartars".'

'My knowledge is sketchy', said the Doctor, 'but I know that there were once two tribes, the Tartars and the Mongols. And that you wiped out the Tartars.'

'But the name persists,' said Mongke. 'Though some call us the *Mogogoli*, the sons of the great giant Magog.'

'You are well informed.'

'I know also that chroniclers state that we have the faces of dogs, and that we tear off the breasts of white women to eat as fine delicacies. I am even told that our grotesque faces adorn the outside of churches like little stone monsters.' Mongke's handsome face broke into another bitter smile. 'If you wish to crush an enemy, it is often useful to find out first what he thinks you are,' he said, by way of explanation.

'You are greatly feared,' stated the Doctor.

'If you can exceed those fears, then so much the better.' Mongke's chest puffed proudly. 'We *are* greatly feared, but in the flesh the armies of the Great Khan are still worse! Even when we are outnumbered, we outthink our opponents. Even when a battle seems lost, we outfight our enemies. The so-called great knights of Christendom – it would take a hundred of those lumbering fools to defeat even a handful of my fine warriors!'

'News of your victories has reached Kiev,' observed the Doctor.

'A city to which you have no allegiance, and no ties, I am told,' said Mongke. 'Tell me about your land, your people.'

'My people are beyond even the influence of the Great Khan,' said the Doctor. 'My land could not be reached if you rode for a thousand years.'

'You speak in riddles.'

The Doctor's eyes glinted. 'I am old, sir. I know much, but it tends to come by riddle and by rhyme.'

'But the people of Kiev respect you…'

The Doctor nodded. 'They have asked me to beg for mercy.'

'And now you speak nonsense!' said Mongke. 'We are deaf to all pleas and begging words.' He paused. 'However, sometimes

165

we tire of bloodshed. Perhaps I shall hear your entreaties, when I need entertainment.'

The Doctor nodded. 'I hope I will entertain, on behalf of those I am pledged to protect.'

'More nonsense! How can one man protect a city?'

'An intention, an idea, a spark of genius', the Doctor replied slowly, 'can be worth more than all the armies under the sun.'

Mongke laughed at this. 'Well said, old man!' he exclaimed. 'I will talk with you further.'

'Very good, my lord,' said the Doctor, bowing. Abd N-Nun Ayyub appeared at his side to escort him away. 'And Mykola?'

'The soldier will stay here. I need to learn of the defence of Kiev: the number of soldiers, the likely strength of opposition, the weak points in any fortifications.'

'I shall tell you nothing!' exclaimed Mykola.

'Within minutes I shall know everything I need,' countered Mongke, gripping his sword tightly. He turned to the Doctor and Abd N-Nun Ayyub, his eyes dark and unfathomable. 'You may leave us now.'

'You are no fool,' said Abd N-Nun Ayyub later. 'But there were moments during our audience with Mongke Khan when you *played* at foolishness.'

The Doctor said nothing, not sure that he could trust the Arab interpreter.

Abd N-Nun Ayyub stared back at the Doctor from the other side of the crackling fire, and seemed to sense his indecision. He raised his palms to the flames to warm them, but it seemed, equally, a symbolic gesture. 'I am employed by the khans, but am not blind to their acts of evil,' he said, by way of reassurance. 'You have my word that I am not here to spy on you.'

The Doctor sighed. 'There are things I must achieve', he said, 'but I cannot allow Mongke to become too interested in me.'

'Are you truly from the heavens, as you implied?'

'I am but a traveller,' said the Doctor simply. 'I would be a stranger in all the lands of this world.'

'You are from paradise, then. You are an angel, and you cannot allow Mongke to see that.'

The Doctor shook his head. 'No, but I have something about me of value. Knowledge.'

'Knowledge of what?'

'Of the future. I know that a future khan – Kbubilai – will rule over an empire yet more vast than that of Genghis, the first Great Khan.'

'I could predict such a turn of events.'

'But I know how it will be achieved. I have met him!'

Abd N-Nun Ayyub was about to press the Doctor for more details when a third figure approached the fire. He bowed low to both men. 'I am Ling,' he said by way of introduction. 'You are called the Doctor, no?'

The Doctor nodded.

'Then we have much in common,' the man continued. 'I, too, am a physician – something of an expert in my field. And I too am a stranger here.'

'We are a long way from Chung-tu and the former Chin Empire,' said the Doctor.

'What do you know of the city of Chung-tu?' queried Ling, excited.

'I recognised your accent,' said the Doctor. 'And I know that the Chin were attacked by Genghis some thirty years ago.'

'I told you this old man was wise,' said Abd N-Nun Ayyub with a smile.

'May I sit with you?' asked Ling.

'Actually', said the Doctor, 'I was about to ask Abd N-Nun Ayyub if he wouldn't mind accompanying me on a short walk.

My legs are a little stiff. Will you join us?'

'I would be honoured.'

Abd N-Nun Ayyub helped the Doctor to his feet. 'Is there anything I can show you? Mongke has instructed me to allow you whatever liberty you desire within the area occupied by his army.'

'But not beyond it?' queried the Doctor with a smile.

'You would not get far!' interjected Ling brightly. 'Only a fool would try.'

'Then I shall not,' said the Doctor. 'In any case, for the moment, I belong here.' He turned to the interpreter. 'I would very much like to see the siege engines.'

'It will be a long walk,' said Abd N-Nun Ayyub.

'It would be preferable to even another moment in the saddle,' said the Doctor.

They set off across the valley floor, making their way through the numerous rows of rounded tents that housed the sleeping army. Abd N-Nun Ayyub explained that these were similar to the *gers* of the original Mongol nomads, portable yet comfortable dwellings ideally suited to a life on the steppes. They were made from woollen felt, stretched tightly across a wooden frame, and both Abd N-Nun Ayyub and Ling had become so accustomed to sleeping in them that they felt almost uncomfortable now in buildings of stone.

'Your very presence here', said the Doctor to the two men, thinking aloud, 'says so much about the Mongol mentality. They are not invaders in the usual sense. They are not interested in foisting their culture on others, but in acquiring, learning, utilising all that they find.'

Ling nodded. 'Their invasions are bloody,' he whispered, 'but once they have appointed overseers, life continues much as before.'

The Doctor thought of Kiev, of the city's pretence at normal life, and – if the history books were to be believed – of its sure and certain fate.

'In my homeland, the people enjoy many freedoms,' continued Ling. 'The Mongols do not change our way of life or prohibit our religions. Only the severest of crimes evokes the penalty of death, and all civil institutions run smoothly and without corruption.'

'But, as you say, this comes at a great price.'

Ling nodded. 'Before the Mongols came, there were some fifty million people living within the Chin Empire.' The Doctor heard his voice crackle with emotion. 'After their conquest, less than nine million were left.'

The Doctor could scarcely believe what he was hearing. 'Nine million?'

Ling nodded. Only a few scant decades separated him from the slaughter he was describing and it was clear that, in his own mind, an eternity would not lessen the pain. 'We have given the khans much,' he said. 'Not least our bodies and souls... but also our skills, our knowledge. You have noticed, perhaps, that all Mongol soldiers wear an undershirt of silk?'

'I can't say I have, but please, carry on.'

'Long ago in our history we realised that when a man is struck by an arrow, clumsy removal of the head can only make the wound bigger and more prone to infection.'

'And the silk shirt?'

'Even the fine arrowheads of the Mongols are unlikely to pierce silk,' explained Ling. 'Instead, the material will be pulled into the wound. From there, it can be tugged out, bringing the arrowhead with it.'

'Ingenious!' said the Doctor. 'Quite ingenious!'

'I have performed the procedure many times,' continued Ling. 'Even better, the soldier in the field can remove the arrow himself. I have seen men return to the heat of battle mere seconds after being struck.' He paused, then let out a high-pitched giggle. 'Of course, they often die of blood loss within the hour…'

'You have a strong sense of the absurd, sir,' said the Doctor.

Ling smiled. 'I am a physician, surrounded on all sides by the instruments of war and torture,' he said. 'I cannot help but laugh in bitter sadness every morning I awake.'

'And, of course, the Chinese have given the world gunpowder,' said the Doctor.

'Yes,' said Ling, 'and the Mongols delight in finding ever more destructive uses for it. They have rockets to startle enemy cavalry, clay grenades for close combat…'

The Doctor stopped in his tracks. He thought of the alien creature in Kiev, and the TARDIS in the governor's residence, and could barely suppress a shudder.

'I feel weary now,' he announced. 'Perhaps, if there is time, I will inspect the siege engines tomorrow. Forgive me for my change of heart.'

Abd N-Nun Ayyub smiled indulgently. 'Then let us return to the warmth of the fire,' he said.

As they turned back a shrill noise came across the basin of the valley. At first the Doctor thought it was the cry of a wolf, but it was too piercing, too close at hand. Then he realised what it was, and his legs felt weaker than ever.

Abd N-Nun Ayyub extended a steadying arm.

'Are you well, sir?' he queried, but the Doctor was not listening. Instead, his ears were attentive to every awful nuance of the sound, the great rending cries of a man being tortured.

'Mykola,' he whispered.

# XV
# In flagrante delicto

The room was an inferno, a shrieking vortex of flame and collapsing, twisted wood. I could see the panic in the soldier's eyes – and the tongues of fire, reflected back at me – but concentrated instead on bringing Isaac through the doorway into the main room, and then into the corridor.

For all the old man's frailty, it took both me and the soldier, pulling with all our might, to haul him on to my shoulders. Just as I was tensing to receive the weight of the unconscious man, a burning chunk of masonry tumbled down towards us from the ceiling. I saw it just in time and dodged it, but almost fell over in the process.

The soldier helped to steady me, and then led me through the smoke and the devastation. In these conditions it was very much the blind leading the blind, and we both stumbled into stools and unrecognisable items of furniture that now blazed like braziers.

We staggered into the corridor, the soldier now taking even more of the old man's weight, just as something substantial gave way within the chamber. There was a rending crash as tortured woodwork finally resigned itself to the inferno and a rush of hot, sparking air nearly knocked us over. Somehow we remained on our feet, which was just as well – in front of us the floor had collapsed completely, leaving only a gaping maw that led straight down into the lower corridor.

We looked around wildly, hoping that perhaps the edge of the hole would take our weight, but flames were licking through the splits between the great planks that remained. They did not inspire confidence – especially with the weight of a man across my back.

'You'll have to jump down,' I said to the soldier. 'I'll try to lower Isaac to you.'

'It is too far,' he said.

'Look around,' I said. 'There's no other way out!'

With both ends of the corridor now impassable, and Isaac's chamber itself disintegrating behind us, we had little alternative. Perhaps we should have investigated the windows – though I remember that the shutters were both closed and on fire – but we had been in such haste to drag Isaac away from the flames that it had not occurred to us to do this.

The soldier peered into the lower corridor, then lowered himself down with as much dignity as he could muster. I heard, rather than saw, him fall and tumble untidily. He cursed, got to his feet and reached up for Isaac.

I laid the old man on the floor, manoeuvred him into a sitting position, then pushed him into the darkness.

It was a soft landing for Isaac, if not for the soldier. When I dropped down myself – my ankles crunched with the impact but otherwise complained little – the man had Isaac half in his arms, half on his shoulders piggy-back style.

Isaac had revived a little and we supported him between us, his feet dragging over the stone floor as we rushed towards the storeroom and then through the door to the square outside.

As we emerged we saw a group of soldiers barking orders to civilians who were carrying what looked like urns of water. 'It's a bit late for that,' I commented in frustration as another plume of fire flashed out of the building.

'Your bravery is to be commended, Steven,' said Dmitri some hours later. We sat, as we had earlier in the day, in the debating chamber, a sanctuary of calm in a world gone mad.

'Is Isaac all right?' I asked.

Yevhen shook his head. 'I am afraid not.' He turned to me, and I thought I saw his features soften. 'Your friend, Dodo, is proving an excellent and diligent nurse. Her affection for Lesia has touched me.'

I didn't know what to say, but was saved from making any response by Dmitri's impatient query. 'This building contains the Tartar?'

'Indeed, my lord,' said Yevhen. 'Let us go in.'

After all the build-up, our first contact with the Mongol Empire was something of a disappointment – to me, at least. Within the building – a poor family's dwelling that smelt of the animals that slept there – stood a small, brown-skinned man. A dark moustache drooped under his nose, giving him an almost comical air, but his eyes were bright with intelligence and determination. His robes were simple and brown – almost monk-like – but I recognised the tassels at their lower edge. I confirmed to the others that this was the man I had seen under ecclesiastical escort.

'I am Dmitri, appointed by Prince Michael as the one governor of Kiev. I greet you with respect and, I hope, in peace.'

The small man nodded politely, but said nothing.

'May we talk as representatives of our people?' asked Dmitri.

The Mongol again gave no verbal response.

Dmitri turned to his advisers. 'Does he speak?'

'Let us assume that he did with the bishops', said Isaac, 'but chooses not to do so now.'

'You will be kept well and in safety,' said Dmitri. 'I hope that, soon, we will talk. I do not wish to use force against you.'

I was reminded of his polite intransigence when the Doctor had been here, but wondered how long his dignified refusal to use violence would last.

'Bring him back with us,' Dmitri ordered, turning for the door.

* * *

When we emerged the twilight had become the soulless dark of night. Torches were lit, casting fingers of light and dark against the city walls. I saw the soldiers on the battlements huddling around a sort of brazier. The autumn nights were bitter.

As I glanced up I noticed them becoming agitated, lighting lanterns and calling to their fellows further along the wall. Soon they were shouting, one even going as far as to put a cow horn to his lips to blow a shrill note of alarm.

'What is going on?' cried Yevhen.

Within moments, we could hear the soldiers' exclamations for ourselves.

'Torches, on the hillside!' cried one.

A pause, and then: 'The Tartars! They are here!'

# XVI
## Somnus ex sanitas

*Reloading archive 76-FG-92-SD...*
*Complete.*
*Resume archive 76-FG-92-SD...*

*Initial summary:*
*Access to target BDR-997-XRF is still blocked. Other*
*strategies are being formulated.*

The hospital has the stench of a charnel house. Antiseptic-
suited figures run from one operating theatre to another,
striving to save lives or reuse the dead; their footsteps form
the constant beat against which all other activities are
monitored. Drills whine in distant rooms; the injured groan in
nearby beds.

The spy feigns unconsciousness. Eyes closed in a parody of
sleep, it listens to the innuendo and gossip of the medical
staff, and pieces together plans and counterattacks best left
unspoken. Occasional hands roll the spy on to its side, or
reattach it to the sedative. The drug must be filtered out of its
blood stream, a process that requires concentration. Usually,
however, the spy is left alone.

A day passes, every nonvisual sense straining for nuance and
information. As expected, the spy's target is due to inspect
the wards, a feeble exercise in morale-building amongst the
dead and the damned, the impure and the unclean. A hush
falls over the rooms as he approaches, mouthing tired
soliloquies of victory and perseverance.

Curtains are pulled back. The target approaches, places a

comforting hand on the spy's chest. Optimum times are calculated and recalculated.

And then the spy attacks.

There is a flurry of activity, cries of alarm and calls for help. But by the time the first weapon is used, the spy has fled for the corridors, leaving madness and guilt in its wake.

The mission is almost over.

*Result of action:*
*Target BDR-997-XRF attacked and compromised. Dome compromised. Mission success index: 98.7%.*

After the fire and the other terrible events of the day, sweet silence gripped the governor's residence and the city beyond its walls. Dodo was in Lesia's room with another pitcher of water but, having seen no change in her friend's condition, was drifting off to sleep.

Suddenly the city was alive.

Dodo snapped into wakefulness in a moment. The oppressive fear that gripped the people was as palpable as a coming storm. She ran to the window.

She could see little through the translucent horn strips, but could hear the cries of confusion and alarm well enough. The streets rang with booted feet; women sobbed and cried in shrill hysteria.

Dodo moved towards the door, hoping to find out what was going on. As she did so, she noticed for the first time that Lesia was moving. Her arms and legs were sweeping in gentle arcs beneath the heavy blankets.

'Thank goodness!' Dodo cried, running to her friend's bed. She held her slender hand tightly. 'It's all right, Lesia. You're going to be OK.'

As she poured some cool, fresh water into a tankard, she

saw the young woman's eyes flicker open.

Steven sat on the edge of the bed reflecting, as Dodo had done, on the change of atmosphere within the city. Kiev had rarely been a place of laughter and love, but now the mood had darkened still further. On their return journey to the governor's residence he had sensed an almost overwhelming sense of resignation; even Isaac seemed less than his usual cheerful self. Given that only a few hours earlier the old man had been in very real danger of losing his life, it seemed more than likely that he was still suffering from shock.

Steven's thoughts were interrupted by a polite knock at the door.

'Is that you, Dodo?' He opened the door, and was surprised to see that it was Yevhen.

Paradoxically, the adviser looked less agitated than Steven had seen him look for some time; perhaps he was admitting to himself that he was out of ideas.

'I thought you should know,' said Yevhen. 'It is as we imagined: the Tartars on the hillside are scouts ahead of the main army.'

Steven nodded, remembering the Mongols' torches. 'I'm not surprised,' he said. 'At least they're not planning a surprise attack. How far behind do you think the main army is?'

'Less than a day's ride,' said Yevhen. 'The scouts seem happy to remain within sight. It seems they wish to observe and intimidate.'

'They've succeeded with the latter,' said Steven.

'We still have faith in our protector,' said Yevhen.

'Is that enough?' queried Steven.

Yevhen paused. 'Our people are frightened for their very lives,' he said. 'We do not want to die – and I have done everything within my power to see that that does not happen.' He took a few paces further into the room, as if appealing to Steven. 'But even if we die, do not think we have failed.'

'No?'

'People die of old age – or worse – with every day that passes. It is the true nature of this fallen world. The people of God are not immune from death.' Yevhen paused for a moment. 'You do not believe in heaven, do you?' he queried directly.

'I... I'm not sure. I have seen little evidence for it.'

'Until tonight, my own eyes had seen no evidence of the Tartars that threaten us. But now they are here!'

'So what are you saying?'

'We pass through this world in the twinkling of an eye on our way elsewhere. Even if our lives here are bitter and full of pain, this will soon be forgotten in the glorious eternity of paradise.'

Steven didn't know what to say, surprised by Yevhen's sudden calm. The Russian adviser's tone was almost defeatist; Steven wondered for a moment if he had misjudged the man.

'I wanted you to know', said Yevhen, 'that whatever I have done in the past, the pain I have caused – it has been with a greater purpose in mind.'

Steven might have responded sympathetically, had not he remembered the awful sound of the door into the catacombs being locked, and the beast's brutal attack on Olexander. He felt his heart hardening against Yevhen. 'You can't just explain away everything you've done,' he said. 'You have murdered, imprisoned, manipulated... Dmitri might be too occupied with the Mongol threat to see you for the man that you are, but I know only too well.'

Stung, Yevhen turned for the door. 'I only oppose those who oppose me.'

'Perhaps you should take the hint,' said Steven. 'That's just about everyone.'

Yevhen paused in the doorway. 'I meant what I said about your friend. Her generosity has touched me.'

'Get out!' shouted Steven.

His anger continued to burn long after the door had slammed shut.

They made camp in the moon's silvered light. The clouds that had seemed so prevalent since their arrival had for once lifted, but the unblemished starscape brought little cheer to the Doctor.

He turned to Abd N-Nun Ayyub, who stood, polishing his meal knife with a wetted cloth.

'I need to speak to Mongke,' said the Doctor. 'Urgently.'

'It will be difficult,' said Abd N-Nun Ayyub. 'He has much to prepare. Kiev is within sight.'

'Which is why I must speak with him.'

'You know he respects you as a man of knowledge. He is entertained by your tales.'

'If only I could come up with enough to distract him from the destruction of Kiev!' exclaimed the Doctor bitterly. 'But I suspect he would be bored with such fancies eventually, hmm?'

'I will see what the khan says,' said Abd N-Nun Ayyub. 'Just do not ask again that he spare the Russian city. Your presence here is tolerated, but is less than vital.'

The Doctor considered the Arab's warnings when, some time later, he found himself riding alongside Mongke as the khan inspected his resting army. 'Tomorrow is the great day, Doctor!' Mongke exclaimed. 'Kiev will topple, like a horse caught by a concealed trap. Its legs will break, and it will be good only for carrion!'

'Kiev is a mother,' said the Doctor, adopting the Mongol's fanciful language. 'In beauty, in poise, in strength, it is more than a match for any stallion you have ever seen. She carries in her belly the hopes and fears of an entire nation.'

'No Mongol would ever kill a horse still carrying its young,' said Mongke. 'And I have indeed heard this city called the mother of Russian cities. Do you suggest to me that I capture it undamaged?'

'I make no suggestion to the khan,' said the Doctor. 'As you know, I tell stories and riddles. It is not for me to prescribe their meaning.'

Mongke laughed. 'Well said, old man! Well said.' He paused for a moment, patting the neck of his horse as if it, too, had contributed to the conversation. 'Of course, we Mongols are the wrath of the Creator, the bringers of Apocalypse. However, we would like to conquer without unnecessary fighting. There are always more battles to be fought, no? Why tire oneself without good cause!'

'I have heard your soldiers talk of a spy within Kiev.'

'An emissary exists,' said Mongke. 'Invited there by the men of God. We have not had a report for some time. I think I shall send Abd N-Nun Ayyub to the city ahead of us. He is a man of great learning and wisdom, much like yourself. They will trust him, no? It will be as if I send my own son – and then, perhaps, they will meekly surrender, and we can be on our way!'

'Let us hope the light will shine on Abd N-Nun Ayyub's endeavours.'

'We shall see, old man.'

With that, Mongke cracked his reins hard, and his horse galloped towards the front of the army. The audience was at an end.

Yevhen slept.

Yevhen slept, and dreamed.

He dreamed of hillsides in spring, of skies without cloud, of people dressed in clothes so fine they could not be bought. He saw a city of gold and silver, with towers and minarets that scratched the very underbelly of heaven.

But this was heaven, and it was in his heart. It was in human form at his side – his true love, long dead, now radiant with the breath of life. Her slender fingers caressed his cheek, her lips grazed against his ears whispering songs and poems that stirred his soul.

They were naked on the hillside – he saw that now – and her body was pressed down on his. They were naked, and without shame. Her legs were tight against his own, her breasts flat against his chest.

Her mouth hovered over his.

The sky darkened, and everything changed. For the first time Yevhen felt fear. Over his lover's shoulders he could see storm clouds gathering.

Lightning sparkled in the sudden shadows and the woman's lips, once red, became as black as midnight blood.

Yevhen screamed and, as he did so, he became aware of a different environment, a more mundane one. His temporary quarters in darkness, his sheets in disarray – oh, the shamelessness of his thoughts! – and something… someone… pressing down on him.

Unblemished skin, smooth and strong, holding him down – but the eyes glowed like a cat's caught in torchlight.

Yevhen screamed again. He heard the clatter of soldiers' feet in the corridor, then felt the nightmarish attacker ease its grip. It slithered from the bed, the door crashed open – and he was alone again with his guilt and confusion.

Dmitri was poring over the plans of the city defences when

a light knock at the door disturbed his thoughts.

'Who is it?' he asked.

'Lesia.'

'Lesia? Come in, come in.' Dmitri looked up. Indeed it was Yevhen's daughter, looking tired and drained but evidently better than before. Her dark, unbrushed hair fell around her neck and chest; he couldn't help but notice that her nightshirt had fallen away from one shoulder. Yevhen's girl was very much a woman now; Dmitri returned his attention to the maps.

'You are better, then?'

'Yes.' He felt, rather than saw, her come alongside him.

'I am glad. As your father must be. Now, if you would excuse me…'

'Yevhen is full of bitterness,' said Lesia in a strange singsong voice. Dmitri thought it odd that she referred to her father by name, and wondered if she was still suffering from whatever catatonia had earlier seized her.

'Well,' he said, wondering what to say. 'Your father has many excellent qualities.'

'He has not forgiven his wife for dying in childbirth. He blames his daughter.'

'But still he loves you.'

'Love?' Lesia rested a gentle hand on Dmitri's shoulder.

There was a commotion outside and, embarrassed by Lesia's behaviour, Dmitri shrugged away from her touch. 'What is that noise?' he asked.

'Yevhen thinks he has been attacked by a succubus. The guards are searching for the beast.' Lesia's hand rested again on Dmitri, more heavily this time. 'They should search more diligently.'

Dmitri turned, and saw that Lesia's eyes glowed like hot coals.

'Lesia…'

Her lips nuzzled the governor's neck, then Dmitri tensed as he felt teeth on his skin.

His terrified screams laced the night air with a deeper madness.

# XVII
# Insania

My sleep was only dimly interrupted by disturbances from the corridors. I remember cries for help and the stamp of soldiers' boots: although I was very tired, and no one hammered on my door, I did investigate once or twice but by the time I pulled my door open there was no one there.

Soon after daybreak, however, I was summoned to the great debating chamber. Dmitri asked me to join him and his advisers at the head of the table. I was shocked to see that his face and neck were swollen and bloody.

'You are late,' he said with unusual bluntness.

'I came as fast as I could.'

Dmitri became aware of my interest in his wounds. 'I was attacked,' he said by way of explanation. 'This creature still roams the corridors. It attacked your friend, and seems to have taken Yevhen's daughter from us.'

'Is Dodo all right?' I asked.

'A bump to the head, nothing more,' said Isaac.

'Why was I not told?'

'She insisted that you not be disturbed. She will join us presently.'

I glanced at Yevhen, and saw that the fragility he had shown yesterday was long gone. 'The creature came for me also,' he said. 'I was saved by the soldiers. But I fear my daughter is dead.'

'It's interesting, isn't it?' I said, thinking out loud. 'First the creature seemed to attack anyone it came into contact with; now it seems to concentrate on the leaders of Kiev, and those under their protection.'

Isaac nodded. 'I have been puzzling over its behaviour myself. Why does it hide for so long? Why does it allow some to live, kill others, and merely attack still more?' He rubbed his chin. 'Perhaps it has reason to –'

'It matters not!' interjected Dmitri. 'What matters now is that the devils are at our door. The attack could begin within hours!'

I nodded, accepting his prioritisation. Even so, I found his manner less stately than usual. I saw what I thought was tiredness clouding his eyes – after his attack, it was quite possible that he had not slept.

The governor turned to one of the soldiers who stood at his side. 'You may bring them in now.'

Moments later the door opened to admit two very different men: the Mongol spy I had already seen, now surrounded by guards, and a tall, dignified man who seemed of Middle Eastern origin. The Mongol stood at the bottom of the table between two soldiers; the taller man swept towards Dmitri.

He stopped, bowing low. 'I am Abd N-Nun Ayyub. I bring greetings from Prince Mongke – cousin of Batu Khan, leader of the Mongol army on behalf of the Great Khan Ogedei who rules the world.'

I imagined that courtesy demanded a response from Dmitri, but none was forthcoming. Instead, he stared coldly at the envoy. 'You do not resemble this spy.'

Abd N-Nun Ayyub smiled. 'We are both emissaries,' he said. 'This fellow is a true Mongol. I, on the other hand, hail from a land now ruled over by Ogedei Khan.'

'Why are you here?' Dmitri asked.

'Mongke Khan is mindful not to crush this city – as he surely will if you resist the power of the Mongol army.'

'I believe our defences are strong,' countered Dmitri.

Abd N-Nun Ayyub did not rise to the challenge. 'A complete

surrender will save much bloodshed. Once you have sworn allegiance to the Great Khan things can continue much as before.'

Dmitri shook his head furiously. 'I know the barbarism of the Tartars!' he exclaimed. 'I have heard such tales…'

'Heard, not seen with your own eyes,' said Abd N-Nun Ayyub gently.

'You feast on the still-beating hearts of young children; you rape virgins until they die of exhaustion and shame.'

Abd N-Nun Ayyub shook his head. 'I am no defender of Mongol atrocity,' he said. 'But this is not how the great army that sweeps towards you will behave – if you surrender.'

'We cannot surrender.'

'The offer is a genuine one,' said Abd N-Nun Ayyub. 'The Doctor, who I believe is known to you, recommends that you accept, and agree to disarm.'

I could not hide my delight at hearing the Doctor's name. 'You've seen the Doctor?' I asked. 'Is he all right?'

'The Doctor is being treated with great honour, as will all the leaders of this city when they throw open the gates of Kiev!'

'We cannot trust the Tartars to honour any agreement,' said Dmitri with a chilling edge to his voice.

I could not believe what I was hearing. 'But this is everything you've wanted – the chance of survival!'

'I had a dream last night,' said Dmitri suddenly. 'A vision. Things that seem full of grace and virtue can be riddled with rottenness and deceit.'

'But, my lord,' said Isaac. 'I must recommend that we at least hear what the envoy has to say. To do otherwise –'

'Would you recommend that we sit here while the devils inch ever closer?' shouted Dmitri. 'That we welcome with open arms the army that weeks ago was feasting on the bones of Russian children?'

I noticed that he looked pale. His forehead prickled with sweat. 'Are you all right?' I asked, suspecting that the great burden he had been carrying had finally proved too much for him.

'My thinking has never been more clear!' said Dmitri. 'I see what we must do. For the first time, I see that our salvation is at hand.'

Even Yevhen seemed a little disturbed by his words. 'What do you mean?' he asked.

'Route the men,' Dmitri replied. 'Issue arms, encourage them with words of our forthcoming victory.' He turned his attention to Abd N-Nun Ayyub and the silent Mongol soldier at the foot of the table. 'And take these devils from my sight and have them executed.'

'But, my lord!' exclaimed Isaac. 'You will only magnify the Tartar fury against us!'

The governor smiled. 'So be it.'

'You'll be condemning your people to death!' I exclaimed. 'Think about what you're doing,' I added in a quieter voice, desperate to appeal to the person I had come to respect, even admire.

It was clear that person was gone. Dmitri gestured to one of the soldiers. 'Do it now, or I shall kill them myself.'

I took one look at the absolute terror that gripped the Arab's noble face, and could stand no more. I knew further argument was pointless. I got to my feet, and walked from the room.

I found Isaac's son, Nahum, waiting just outside. 'Is the governor well?' he asked.

I shook my head.

'I had heard as much,' he continued. 'The attack seems to have disturbed him greatly.'

I led Nahum away from the room. I did not even want to

think about what was going on in there. 'Have you seen Dodo?' I asked.

'No – but I was about to see her. I am concerned by the abduction of Lesia.'

We walked to Dodo's room, and banged on the door. She had just finished getting dressed. She complained of feeling a little dizzy, but other than that she seemed well. Both Nahum and I were keen to hear what had happened.

'I was in Lesia's room – I'd been there all day. I heard voices outside the window – they sounded anxious.'

'The Mongols are close,' I said. 'We saw their advance scouts on the hillside last night. The city was in uproar.'

'Anyway, I'd just gone back to Lesia when I noticed that she was starting to wake up. I went to get help.' Dodo shook her head, as if trying to re-establish a faulty connection. 'The next thing I remember is someone helping me up from the floor. Lesia was gone.'

'Are you sure you're all right now?' I asked.

'I'm fine,' she said. 'I don't think I was hit so much as… pushed.'

'Did you hear anyone enter the room?' asked Nahum.

Dodo shook her head. 'I reckon whoever went off with Lesia had been hiding in the room.'

I thought such concealment unlikely, if only for the simple fact that most of the rooms in the governor's residence were spartan at best, but said nothing.

'We must find Lesia!' exclaimed Nahum.

'If we find her, talk to her, we might understand more about the creature,' I agreed. 'Maybe there's still some way of turning this thing against the Mongols.'

'Where shall we begin?' asked Nahum.

'The governor's men still patrol these buildings regularly,' I said. 'Perhaps the creature has fled back into the catacombs.'

Nahum looked concerned. 'But the fire… That part of the building is no longer safe.'

'The perfect place to hide, then,' observed Dodo. 'Come on, let's go!' Her excitement was infectious.

I nodded. 'Right now, I want to be as far from Dmitri as possible.'

I was more familiar with the layout of the governor's residence now and, with Nahum's help, we proceeded swiftly through the building towards the fire-damaged corridors and rooms at the rear. No soldiers followed. I was not quite sure when our *de facto* liberty had been granted to us, but it was welcome all the same. With the Mongols so close, I imagine Dmitri had decided that the soldiers assigned to observe us could be better used elsewhere.

The corridors were blackened shells now, stretching around us like the bones of some great cremated animal. The air was still rich with the aroma of fire damage, and our feet scuffed up ash and cloying dust as we walked. We approached the storeroom in silence; there was little light there, and we concentrated instead on moving forward without injury or mishap.

I recognised the door – or what was left of it – that led into the chamber which concealed the entrance to the tunnels under Kiev. It was hanging in shattered pieces, and we pushed our way through with ease.

I was surprised to find that the storeroom was not in darkness. The opposite door, leading out to the square, had been left open – or perhaps it had buckled in the heat and would not close. The room, though blackened by the spreading fire, seemed otherwise undamaged.

There was but one change to the room: an enormous bundle of rags lying near the door. Intrigued, I went over to the mound, and was about to examine it further when Nahum noticed my intent. 'No!' he snapped. 'Don't touch it.'

I watched, puzzled, as he edged closer to the mound. His wary movements resembled those of a man approaching an unexploded bomb. It was only when I looked back at the rags that I realised that I was looking at a human body, wrapped in torn clothes and the remains of some sort of shroud. It was lying face down on the floor; I could just about make out strands of dirty-looking hair trailing over the shoulders.

Dodo seemed to realise what it was at about the same time; I heard her stifle a scream, but I didn't turn. I was intrigued by Nahum's behaviour; he removed his outer jerkin, wrapped his hands in it as best he could, and then turned the body over.

'Did the creature do this?' asked Dodo.

Nahum shook his head. 'Disease,' he said simply.

I looked down and saw a boyish face made grey and weather-beaten by death. 'Did he die here?'

'No. This fellow died somewhere in the city and was dragged here. With the Tartars so close, our people do not have time to bury their dead.'

'Why bring him here?' asked Dodo, quite clearly shocked.

'All the city folk saw the fire. They will have guessed that this part of the building is not in use. Why not make it a temporary morgue?' Nahum pointed towards the outer door. I saw that there were further bodies there, half-hidden beneath a large woollen shroud.

I didn't know how to identify the disease, or what precautions to advise to minimise the outbreak. Nahum seemed to have assumed that it spread by direct contact, but I suspected the insanitary conditions were to blame. Whatever the illness was, the governor needed to be informed that bodies carrying the infection were being left in the building.

I turned to Dodo. 'Go to Dmitri,' I said. 'Tell him what we've seen.'

'But I want to stay with you!'

'He needs to know,' I reasoned. 'And we also need to keep an eye on Dmitri and Yevhen. Please.'

'Oh, all right,' said Dodo. With a shrug of resignation, she made for the door.

Nahum watched her go. 'Where is the entrance to the tunnels?' he asked, carefully removing the jerkin from his hands. He dropped the garment to the floor then kicked it away into the shadows, clearly not wanting to risk any contamination.

'Over here.' I led him past some barrels thick with dust, to the door. Even though I knew it was there, I was surprised again by how well hidden it was. Its wooden slats seemed to have taken on the same dark grey hue as the stonework.

'Torches,' I said suddenly. 'I don't suppose you thought to bring a torch or something?'

Nahum shrugged his shoulders.

'We'll have to go back,' I said. 'There's no way –'

The door to the tunnels creaked suddenly. I turned in alarm. Someone or something was coming through.

We ducked for cover without a word. I found myself behind some broken pieces of furniture and a split mattress with straw that had started to rot spilling out of it. I glanced back towards the secret door, and saw it open further.

I could just make out a dark head and pale shoulders emerging into the room; I could not tell who it was. Nahum, from his position, obviously could.

Before I could do or say anything, I saw him leap to his feet and run towards the figure. 'Lesia!' he cried.

I jumped up and followed Nahum. The figure was turned slightly away from us, but I recognised her as Yevhen's daughter, with her distinctive long, dark hair tumbling down her back.

'Lesia,' said Nahum again. 'We've been so worried about you.'

Lesia turned to look at us, and Nahum screamed.

Her face was a bleached-white skull.

# XVIII
## Via lata gradior

The Doctor stood beside Mongke at the head of the great army, and looked down on the city. The walls and fortifications looked pitifully weak. People scurried in the streets and clambered over walls and buildings as if they were ants tending their nest.

The Doctor wondered if any of the black specks he could see were Steven or Dodo. He did not like leaving them at the mercy of men such as Yevhen, but his life was a series of such heart-rending decisions. Every word, every action, every desire to keep his companions safe was balanced against the unimaginable consequence of failure, and the safety of millions.

Mongke turned to him, his handsome face glowing in the crisp morning air. 'It helps to see things from here, does it not?' he queried. 'The whole picture of what might happen can play out before my mind's eye.'

The Doctor nodded stiffly. 'And mine also.'

Mongke glanced at him. 'You have people you care about? Down there, in the city?'

'Yes.' The Doctor sighed. 'That is the problem with the bigger picture. You cannot rid yourself of the smaller details… the people you care about.'

'We live in violent times,' said Mongke.

'I hope you are not trying to justify your butchery to me!' The Doctor's voice rose sharply, strength of conviction belying his ancient frame.

'You are too concerned with the heavens to accept what I say,' said Mongke. 'I am telling you of the world that surrounds us. I wish, sometimes, it were different. But it is not.' He pointed towards the city. 'If things were reversed... If the Russians were invading our fair land... Would they show us any mercy?' He paused, waiting for his point to strike home. 'Would they?'

The Doctor said nothing. He knew mere words could not change the heart of a man. People altered, he supposed, because of bitter experiences and liberating events, not intellectual argument or the power of rhetoric. But the stories... Perhaps there was something he could say, some rambling tale that Mongke would think of as truth filtered by dementia...

No, it would not work. It was not a question of changing Mongke's heart, but the heart of an entire nation – an entire world. When civilisations arise, the Doctor reminded himself, it happens over decades, not moments.

In any event, his role here was to prevent disruption, not exacerbate it. If you're in a hole, he remembered Dodo once saying, the first thing to do is stop digging.

'Cousin Batu will join us shortly. Together we will oversee the destruction of Kiev.'

'Destruction?' asked the Doctor, aghast. 'Must it come to that?'

'What is dead is no longer your enemy.'

The Doctor opened his mouth to speak, but became aware of a rush of activity behind them. He turned, and saw a small knot of Mongol soldiers pushing their way towards Mongke. They dragged a silver-bearded man between them, a slender form beneath heaped robes. 'A spy!' exclaimed one of the soldiers, bowing low before Mongke. 'He was wandering in the forests. He says he is looking for the Tartars!' Despite his leader's presence, the soldier could barely conceal a belly laugh.

Mongke smiled in grim amusement. 'Tartars, eh?'

The Doctor looked closely at the robed figure. He did not recognise him, but the quality of his robes and his clear complexion spoke of a certain status.

The robed man was thrown at Mongke's feet, and the Mongol leader stared down at him. 'A cleric? From Kiev?'

The man looked up, his hands held together in an abject form of supplication. 'Archbishop Vasil, my lord.'

Despite the prisoner's status compared to that of the Mongol warlord, the Doctor heard the deferential words stick slightly in the bishop's throat. He did not seem comfortable addressing anyone as 'lord'.

'Bishop Vasil, eh?' murmured the Doctor. 'We were not introduced before I left the city.'

Vasil looked at the Doctor, his eyes narrowing. 'The traveller?'

'I am with the Mongol army to plead the cause of Kiev,' said the Doctor. 'Why are you here?'

Vasil directed his answer at Mongke. 'I am here to negotiate an alliance – an alliance between our people, and yours.'

'Your people?' spluttered the Doctor, not understanding what he was hearing. 'The people of Kiev?'

Vasil shook his head imperiously. 'The people of God,' he said.

The skull-faced thing that so resembled Lesia took an involuntary step back. Steven and Nahum watched, dumbstruck, as the mouth gaped open, revealing row upon row of narrow teeth.

Steven grabbed Nahum, hoping to pull him to safety, but the young man did not move, overcome by the shock of seeing Lesia, or the thing that resembled Lesia. 'Come on!' Steven urged, looking from Nahum's pale eyes to the dark sockets of the creature, and expecting with every moment that the needle-filled jaws would lunge down on them.

But the creature did not move. Steven could see it moving its head from him to Nahum and back again. Despite its inhuman features, something like recognition flickered across its face.

It took another step back, its skull-face still grotesquely surrounded by Lesia's hair. Something flowed from the nostrils and from behind its dark eyes, strands and teardrops of mercury and water. They changed colour, knitting themselves into muscle and cartilage, flowing over the face like a grotesque mask. Skin followed, pouring itself on to the fleshy strands and into the now reddening mouth. Within a moment, and as the black orbs of the eyes lightened, the transformation was complete.

'Lesia!' exclaimed Nahum again.

The creature, now to all intents and purposes a young woman, stared down at the cowering forms of Steven and Nahum. Then it turned and dashed across the room. The door into the house slammed shut behind it, leaving the two young men to exchange terrified glances.

Once again the creature had spared their lives.

'I cannot eat this!' exclaimed Dmitri. Like a child he pushed the plate across the table top, his lips curling petulantly.

Dodo looked at the food spread across the table: blood puddings, an array of coloured and shaped cheeses, marinaded pigeon with stodgy-looking dumplings. There were fresh vegetables and even a pair of cooked hares, arranged on an ornate silver plate as if still fleeing across the fields. It wasn't what Dodo thought of as a fine meal, but she knew this was the pinnacle of cuisine at a time when the poor stole scraps from their neighbours' cattle.

She shook her head. She could not comprehend the change in Dmitri's character. The news that the people of Kiev had been dumping infected bodies inside his residence seemed to upset him greatly, but even that did not entirely explain his mood.

'You should be ashamed of yourself!' Dodo admonished.

Dmitri raised a warning finger. 'Do not lecture me, little girl.'

'You should eat,' continued Dodo, in a more conciliatory tone, 'if only to keep your strength up.'

'We shall eat and drink, for tomorrow we die, eh?' Dmitri nudged her, as if he were making some bawdy joke.

She looked across the banqueting table at Isaac and Yevhen, imploring with her eyes that they do something. Isaac shrugged his shoulders diffidently, as if to suggest that he was powerless. Yevhen simply stared at the ceiling, his mind elsewhere.

Dmitri noticed none of this. 'In any case', he said, 'you expect me to eat, when the stench of death fills my nostrils?' He turned to his advisers. 'Does the disease still rage?'

'My lord, it is like a fire in the forest that cannot be controlled,' said Isaac. 'I am not sure how many have died – but their bodies number in the hundreds.'

Dmitri sighed, his head dropping, his hands in his hair, a picture of absolute despair. 'Soon there will be no one left to defend our fine city,' he whispered. 'How long until the disease takes hold here, in this sanctuary I have tried to create?'

'No one here has even the first sign of disease,' said Yevhen suddenly.

Isaac cleared his throat, as if hoping to change the subject. 'There is still much to be done,' he said. 'With the emissaries dead...'

'Spies,' corrected Dmitri, still staring down at the table.

'... there is no hope of a political settlement,' concluded Isaac.

Dmitri clamped his hands over his ears, as if he no longer

wanted to hear any of it. 'Take this food away,' he said. 'Feed it to the swine!'

'You can't throw something away just because you don't like it!' exclaimed Dodo, irritated again.

'I can do whatever…' Dmitri's voice trailed away, and he looked up suddenly. Dodo shrank back from his bloodshot stare, his fixed expression. 'Why, of course!' he exclaimed, a strange delight gripping his features.

'My lord?' queried Isaac, wary of this sudden change of mood.

'The siege engines,' Dmitri continued, his eyes blazing. 'How many are ready?'

'A handful,' said Yevhen.

'They will suffice. And the bodies of the Tartar spies?'

'Where you left them, I imagine,' said Isaac bitterly.

'Good, good! This is what we shall do.' Dmitri spread his hands over the table top as if unfurling a grand and mapped-out plan. 'We shall load the corpses of the dog-faced Tartars into a trebuchet, and hurl them over the city walls. Their shattered bodies will be a testimony to our intent – our intent to fight to the last man!'

'Do not compound your folly,' warned Isaac with a gravity that was rare before the governor. 'This action will only inspire the Tartars to greater fury!'

'And that will not be the end of it,' Dmitri continued, not listening. 'Order the soldiers to search the streets, the church yards, the room young Dodo has told us of. Find every corpse riddled with the illness. Catapult the refuse over the walls!'

'That's monstrous!' said Dodo.

'It is war,' said Dmitri simply. 'With the corpses disposed of, we may yet survive this disease. And it is possible that the illness will grip the Tartars as surely as it has decimated our own people.' For a moment, he sounded as if he was extolling some golden age, some sure way of escape. Then he sighed again, and the bitterness returned to his voice. 'Perhaps the disease will consume us all, and death will welcome Russian and Tartar with equal delight!'

Steven was the first to get to his feet. 'We've got to tell Isaac and the others,' he said.

'Tell them what?' asked Nahum.

'Well…' Steven paused, trying to unravel what they had witnessed. 'That we saw the monster, or whatever it is.'

'We saw Lesia,' said Nahum abjectly. 'The beast has swallowed her whole.'

'Nonsense,' said Steven. 'That thing looked like Lesia but it wasn't really her. When you first saw the beast it resembled the cook, remember.'

'Whatever it is, it has been hiding in the catacombs, but has now returned.'

'I'm not so sure about that,' said Steven.

'But you saw it with your own eyes!'

'What I mean is', Steven said, 'I'm not sure it *has* been in the catacombs all this time. We've assumed it has because there have been no further attacks.'

Nahum shook his head, not following Steven's argument. 'Then where has it been?'

'Isn't it obvious?' said Steven. 'As you said, we saw it with our eyes. That thing looks like Lesia – it might have been under our noses all this time!'

Comprehension began to dawn on Nahum's face. 'It was not Lesia asleep on the bed.'

'Perhaps not.'

'So she might still be alive – and elsewhere!' Nahum made as if to begin the search immediately.

Steven put a calming hand on his arm. 'First we should tell

the others what we've seen – that this monster can impersonate Lesia and, for all we know, other people. Then perhaps we will have time to search for her.'

The Doctor's discussion with Mongke and Bishop Vasil was interrupted by a strange whistling sound, carried to them by the strong autumn winds. It originated in the city and, as the three men turned, it came again.

They watched as a flurry of black dots seemed to hurl themselves over the walls of Kiev, landing near the group of Mongol soldiers stationed in the valley. A pause, as some machine was reset and refilled with its seemingly human cargo, and then the flurry resumed.

'What are they doing?' asked Mongke. For once, it seemed, something had taken him by surprise.

The Doctor said nothing, knowing only too well the desperate measures that otherwise rational men are sometimes forced to take.

Mongke sent one of the nearby soldiers to establish what was happening – and find out why, seemingly, the people of Kiev were catapulting themselves over the walls rather than risk the Mongol attack.

As they waited patiently for the reply, another sound carried across the Russian landscape, this time from the east. A great pounding noise came from somewhere in the bulk of the army behind them. It was like an army of devils stamping their feet on the earth; in fact, it was drumming to herald the arrival of Batu Khan.

The Doctor turned to watch in awe. First came row upon row of camels, each carrying a huge *naqara* drum. Then came a unit of riders, sweeping across the landscape with awful precision. Then came Batu and his entourage.

The Khan, resplendent in robes of gold, swept up to Mongke

on a horse the colour of snow, and dismounted expertly before the animal had halted. The two men embraced each other warmly and, finally, the drums ceased their pounding.

Batu's face seemed crueller than Mongke's and an aura of perpetual bloodshed surrounded him. He was clearly the senior tactician here and, the Doctor swiftly surmised, even less likely to show mercy than his cousin.

And yet Batu's first words surprised the Doctor. 'Have we decided the fate of this miserable city?'

Mongke shook his head. 'There may still be reason to save it,' he said, shooting the Doctor a glance before indicating Vasil. 'This man is the senior cleric. He has come with word of a treaty, a pact. The Church wishes to introduce us to a common enemy.'

Batu nodded, taking this in. 'And the civilian authorities? Have they made entreaties? Have they grovelled at the feet of the Great Khan?'

'I have a trusted man there,' said Mongke, 'though it is clear that they still prepare for battle, for siege.'

Batu nodded, almost appreciative. 'It is wise that they do so,' he said.

Mongke indicated the Doctor. 'And they have sent this man, a practitioner and scientist called Doctor. He is no Russian… '

'I can see that,' interjected Batu with a smile.

'… but still he pleads for Kiev.'

'I am merely a traveller,' said the Doctor. 'I hope only to save the lives of the citizens.'

'He also tells a good tale, and his words are full of symbols and hidden meaning,' continued Mongke. 'I am convinced he walks among the stars!'

'Then he shall entertain us when the work is done,' said Batu. He turned to Vasil. 'Whatever form that work might take.'

Vasil bowed, and for the first time the Doctor sensed his fear.

The bishop had recognised the darkness of his heart mirrored in the form of Batu, and it seemed to disturb him. 'My lord, the enemy of which I speak –'

Suddenly a soldier pushed through into the circle of talking men, leaving Vasil unable to complete his entreaty. It was the soldier Mongke had sent to investigate the strange activity down below.

'Dead bodies, my lords,' said the man, bowing low. 'They are hurling corpses over the city walls – corpses riddled with some infection.'

'They hope to spread the sickness of their sin to us?' exclaimed Batu. 'How dare they slight the holiness of our endeavour!'

'It is worse,' continued the soldier. 'Among the bodies we saw the emissary sent to the Church, and the Arab interpreter. They have both been executed.'

The Doctor shook his head slowly, remembering Abd N-Nun Ayyub's honesty and integrity. He watched as Batu snarled in fury.

'They shall pay!' the khan exclaimed. 'They shall pay for this insult with the blood of their virgins and children and mothers!'

Even Mongke's face had hardened at this insult. 'The khans are not used to such poor treatment,' he added quietly.

'Please, my lords,' said the Doctor. 'The men and women, the children… they are not responsible for the actions of their leaders.' His face clouded; he could not imagine the sane and sensible governor he had left behind ordering so brutal an action as this. Perhaps Yevhen was now in charge.

Batu made no reply, but turned instead to the still-cowering bishop. 'You were about to tell me of a pact… And yet your people have killed the very representative sent to investigate such a possibility.'

'But, my lord…' Vasil wiped the sweat from his brow. 'It is as the traveller has said. The secular leaders are blind fools. But the people of God still wish to welcome you with open arms, as an ally.'

'You lie!' spat Batu. 'Any treaty you wish to make with us is prompted by fear, not respect!' He grabbed the bishop by the shoulders, almost dragging him to his feet. 'Is there anything you can say that will stop me from stamping this city into the dust?'

Vasil shook his head, desperate – then suddenly exclaimed: 'There is a weapon that might be used against you!'

'Be quiet, man!' snapped the Doctor.

Batu raised a hand and a nearby soldier drew his sword, moving towards the Doctor to ensure his silence. Then the Khan turned back to Vasil, an awful smile on his lips.

'A weapon?' Batu asked, his eyes bright. 'Tell me more.'

'It is rumoured, my lord, that something resides in the catacombs under the cathedral. A weapon or a beast, the tales are unclear.'

'And it resides there still?'

'What little I know of the angel comes from one of the governor's advisers. He may already have already unleashed the weapon. Indeed, I… I may have encouraged him to do so.' Vasil glanced at the Khan, expecting a furious response.

Instead, Batu threw back his head and laughed. 'There is no weapon that can stop us! Instead, we shall use this creature to our own ends.'

Mongke nodded. 'Kiev will be destroyed – but perhaps we should spare the cathedral, in case there is some truth in this.'

The Doctor was about to interject, but he resisted the temptation. The more he said, the more he risked intriguing Batu further.

'Please, my lord,' he said quietly. 'I beg for mercy on behalf of the people of Kiev.'

'They are already dead,' said Batu with grim finality. 'It is a noble thing, to plead for those who are not your own people. But I cannot show them mercy, or we would be the laughing stock of the civilised world. I cannot let this insult go unpunished.'

'Then please', said the Doctor, knowing his mission to the Mongols had failed, 'let me return to the city, where I might die, with dignity, with the people I have tried to save.'

Batu nodded. 'Of course. You are a man of honour. Were that all in this awful land were so!'

He turned, and strode towards Vasil. 'But you… a supposed man of God! Is there a single reason why I should not cut you in two here and now?' He drew his sword, hefting it from hand to hand.

'Don't kill me,' Vasil whimpered, throwing himself at the khan's feet.

Batu shook his head. 'You are a dog – I should have you executed for cowardice, if nothing else!'

'Please,' cried Vasil in alarm. 'I'll do anything you want! Anything!'

'You fear death?' asked Batu. 'But does it not say in your scriptures…' He paused, trying to recollect. 'That you men of God count life a loss, and death a great gain when you are reunited with your Christ?'

Vasil, sobbing, said nothing. He raised his pitifully weak hands against the expected execution.

'Run,' said Batu in a low whisper. 'Run away from me. Run away to Hungary, or wherever your flight takes you. Run to the cities and churches we have not yet conquered. Run, and tell them of the coming apocalypse, and tell them not to insult us as this governor of Kiev has done. And tell them that there will be no pacts – not yet, not until it is right for the Mongol Empire, for the Great Khan who rules the world.' Batu pushed the disgraced cleric on to his back with a boot. 'And if I ever see you again, I shall kill you with my own bare hands. Remember that.'

Still crying with fear, Vasil got to his feet and ran, stumbling, into the distance.

Batu did not watch him go. Instead, he sheathed his weapon and turned his eyes back to the city. The catapulting had long since stopped, and units of Mongol soldiers were beginning to assemble around the city walls.

'Now, let us destroy this place,' he said.

# XIX
# Pestilentia

Dmitri was mad.

We had left a man struggling in the midst of a barbaric dilemma, and seemingly on the verge of barbarism himself, and returned to find a drooling idiot with every last vestige of sanity gone.

I watched the poor man as he sat in the corner, brooding, dribbling, spouting rubbish. 'How long has he been like this?' I asked, hardly believing that his decline could have been so sudden.

'Only a few minutes,' said Dodo.

I turned to Yevhen, who was preening himself at the head of the great table. 'Long enough for you to take charge?'

'Naturally,' said Yevhen with a lopsided smile. 'We need strong leadership at a time like this.'

'And Isaac agreed?'

Isaac shuffled uncomfortably. 'My lord Yevhen has been an adviser for longer than I.'

I turned my attention back to Yevhen. 'I notice you did not intercede until after the execution of the Mongol envoys.'

'That was perhaps the governor's last sane act. It was certainly one I did not disagree with.'

I stooped in front of Dmitri, staring into his eyes. He barely seemed to know I was there.

'The pressure of authority is a terrible thing to behold,' said Isaac softly at my shoulder. 'The burden has proved too great for this poor fellow.'

'Unless it's a side effect of the monster's attack,' I noted, observing the cuts and lacerations still visible on the former governor's face.

'We have seen it!' Nahum blurted out, reminding me why we had returned so swiftly to the others.

'Is that so?' queried Isaac. I saw that we also had Yevhen's undivided attention now.

'We were searching for…' I noticed Nahum's warning look, a look I was sure Isaac shared. 'We were searching for someone. We thought we had found them, but it was a creature, a beast.'

'What did it look like?' asked Dodo nervously, doubtless remembering the attack she had suffered.

'It looked like a human, but not quite finished,' said Nahum. 'A golem, father?'

'I have read of such things,' said Isaac. 'But my thoughts on legends and fables are, I think, known to all.' He shot Yevhen a glance, but the new governor was looking the other way.

'It can impersonate people,' I said, remembering what had happened to its face. I shivered at the memory – it had been like watching an invisible child creating a face from clay. I turned to Dodo. 'All that time you were tending Lesia… I'm not sure it was her at all.'

'Then where is my daughter?' asked Yevhen.

'We don't know,' I said.

'But why impersonate her, and then do nothing but attack this poor child?' asked Isaac, looking at Dodo. 'And why kill some, but leave others untouched?' He turned to Nahum. 'Did the beast make an attempt to attack you?'

'No, father. None at all.'

'It seems travellers and Jews are safe from this succubus,' muttered Yevhen.

I rounded on him. 'So much for this dark angel of yours! So much for the defender of Kiev!'

'What do you know of the dark angel?'

'Enough,' I said simply. 'Enough to know that you've released some monster, and you don't have the slightest idea how to control it!'

'Bickering will not help us,' interjected Isaac. 'We must prepare for the Tartar attack – and deal with this creature, if it attacks again.' He turned to Nahum. 'Where is the beast now?'

'It came back into the building,' he replied.

'It could be anywhere,' I added. I looked around the room. Oppressive under Dmitri's attempted curfew, it felt darker still now. 'It could be here, with us.' I couldn't help but look at the soldiers stationed at the doorway – but what was to stop the beast, if it had more than one face, from being in our midst? It could be Yevhen, or Isaac – or even Dodo. Or even the poor, muttering fool that had once been Dmitri.

'We should hunt the creature,' said Nahum.

'We have more important considerations,' Yevhen said. 'If this thing does not trouble us, it shall be ignored.'

'But what is it trying to achieve?' I asked. 'One minute it seems to attack indiscriminately, the next it goes into hiding.'

'I do not know,' said Isaac.

'The Doctor would know,' I muttered under my breath.

It was as if I had uttered a mystic mantra. I looked up to see a confusion of soldiers at the door to the great chamber – and then the Doctor striding imperiously through them.

'Doctor!' exclaimed Dodo, running to him and hugging him tightly.

'Now, now, my child,' said the Doctor, at once embarrassed but touched by this display of affection. 'I have only been gone a few days!'

'It is good to see you,' I agreed.

The Doctor smiled. 'It is good to see you all.'

Dodo hugged him again. 'Are you all right?'

'Yes, my child. I am quite well. I only wish I brought better news from the Mongol army.'

'Oh?' queried Yevhen, though I expected he guessed what the Doctor was about to say.

The Doctor turned on him angrily. 'Whose idea was it to execute the envoys? What fool ordered the catapulting of their bodies and the other corpses over the walls?'

'My lord the governor,' said Yevhen obsequiously. He pointed to the wretch in the corner. 'I am afraid the burdens of his position have driven him mad. I am the new governor.'

'Why did you not stop him?' asked the Doctor. 'With the envoys alive there was a chance – a slender chance, yes, but a chance all the same!' He put an awkward, fatherly arm around Dodo. 'But now I am afraid that nothing but destruction awaits Kiev. The attack is as certain as night following day.'

'Your mission was unsuccessful,' commented Yevhen.

'My mission was compromised by rash stupidity, calculated only to inflame the hatred of the Mongol warlords!'

'Don't be too hard on Dmitri,' I said. 'He was attacked by the creature. I think it may have sent him mad.'

'I heard something of what you said from the corridor,' said the Doctor. 'It is a sleeping foe, is it not? Its aggression is matched only by its periodic inactivity.'

I tried to fill him in on what had happened since the start of his trek to the Mongol army – my liberation from prison, my flight through the catacombs, the strange attack on Lesia and the plot hatched by the Church authorities to appease the Mongols.

'Yes, I met Archbishop Vasil,' said the Doctor. 'The execution of the emissary rather put paid to the Church's attempted appeasement – for the moment at least.' He paused, rubbing his chin. 'I am interested, my boy. You mentioned the cook's body in the catacombs?'

'That's who Olexander said it was. She was married to the builder…'

'A pattern emerges, does it not? From a lowly builder, to a cook with access to these chambers, then finally attacks on the leaders of Kiev…' The Doctor turned back to Yevhen, and his voice was clouded with remorse. 'The cook was killed, and taken away, to ensure that the creature could move about with impunity. I am afraid, sir, that it does not bode well for your daughter.'

Yevhen said nothing, but turned away sharply.

'It is clearly a creature of great ferocity, and yet… Insidiously… it has climbed social structures to find itself at the very heart of command. Fascinating, hmm?'

'That is as may be,' said Yevhen, his back still turned. 'But we have more important foes to concern ourselves with.'

'My concerns are not your concerns,' the Doctor said quietly.

'At last, a true word passes your lips!' exclaimed Yevhen.

'What are we going to do?' asked Dodo.

'Well,' said the Doctor. 'The illness you describe… It sounds to me like an acute bacterial infection, perhaps even cholera.' He turned to Yevhen. 'I will advise how to treat the afflicted with clean water and salt, given orally. But I will need antibiotics…' He seemed at last to notice the blank looks the others were giving him. 'I have medicinal preparations in the TARDIS,' he said. 'We should be able to prevent the spread of this disease.'

I could scarcely believe what I was hearing. 'After all this time, you're finally prepared to return to the TARDIS!'

'Only now that is there something I can help with,' said the Doctor. 'With acting governor Yevhen's permission, of course.'

Yevhen turned. 'You think I am a fool? Of course I will not allow you access to your "ship". You have clearly concluded that our opposition to the Mongols is futile. You will be away from here in the twinkling of an eye.'

'You have my word,' said the Doctor gravely.

'I would rather trust a whore's expression of undying love!'

Isaac spoke up, a rational and calm voice amid the charged atmosphere. 'But, my lord, if the Doctor has access to compounds that will rid the city –'

'No,' said Yevhen, determined. 'Our physicians are working on treatments that will restore the balance of the humours. We must trust them.'

'This disease is not an imbalance!' exclaimed the Doctor, furious. 'It is an infection that enters the body through contaminated food and water.'

'Your words are meaningless,' said Yevhen. 'We do not need your "help".'

'Then you sentence us all to death!' said Nahum, always more headstrong than his father. 'By disease, or at the hands of the Tartars, it matters not to you!'

'We have been doomed from the beginning,' said Yevhen. 'Is that not so, Doctor?'

The Doctor said nothing. It was clear that what Yevhen said was true enough.

Yevhen soon swept away on some business or other. The rest of us remained in the great chamber.

'The disease,' said Isaac gently. 'Is it too much to hope… that it might affect the Mongols… At least to delay their attacks?' He too had been appalled by what had happened, but his outrage was tempered by a desperate hope that perhaps Dmitri's plan had worked.

The Doctor shook his head. 'I doubt very much that the disease will have any impact on the Mongol army,' he said. He paused for a moment, deep in thought. 'Though I suppose… Well, yes, there is a precedent for this.'

'What do you mean?' I asked.

'Well, a future precedent, if you will.' He lowered his voice. 'In 1346 an army serving Janibeg Khan besieges the city of Kaffa. A dreadful pestilence sweeps through the Mongols, killing many of the soldiers. The commander... I forget the fellow's name now... He orders that the diseased corpses be catapulted over the walls and into the city. He simply waits for the illness to take hold.' He paused, his voice funereal. 'It is widely regarded as mankind's first attempt at biological warfare.'

'You're joking!' I exclaimed without thinking.

'This is no laughing matter, young man,' said the Doctor, and I immediately felt foolish. 'The effects on the besieged citizens of Kaffa was bad enough. Even worse was the long-term impact of the pestilence. Genoese merchants took the disease to the Mediterranean ports of southern Europe, from where it spread through Spain, France, Germany and Britain. Eventually it reached Scandinavia and Greenland.' He paused again, seemingly mindful of Dodo's presence. 'But you do not want to hear of this,' he said suddenly.

'What happened?' I asked.

'Please, Doctor,' added Dodo.

'Very well.' The Doctor's eyes were faraway. 'The ensuing plague was the most awful catastrophe of European history. A third of the population of the entire continent was killed. Nothing ever perpetrated by Genghis or the other khans compared to this.'

'The Black Death,' I said quietly.

The Doctor nodded. 'Bubonic plague. Little wonder that historians sometimes call this period the Dark Ages.' He turned to me, angry perhaps at the awfulness of his tale – angry, perhaps, at the impotence he still felt. 'You both come from a time of such great privilege! You, Dodo... an era when a plane falling from the sky is front page news! You, Steven... a period when illness and premature death has been conquered. My children, it is little wonder that you do not understand. Death is the neighbour of these poor people!' He indicated Isaac and Nahum, and I wondered what on earth they were making of the Doctor's prophecies, his tales of futures they could not comprehend. 'They are as intimate with death as we are with our families, our friends.' The Doctor turned on me, resuming an argument from days or weeks before – a common trait of his, I had noted. It was as if he played out his life, again and again, behind his eyes, and old events were as fresh as yesterday's. 'And you dare to lecture me on involvement in history, on making a stand!'

I did not know what to say in response. I was saved from doing so by a most unlikely event – without prompting, Dodo burst into tears.

The Doctor immediately held her close. 'My child, I am sorry. I should not have said such things. It is a gruesome tale, to be sure –'

'It's all my fault!' she exclaimed through her tears.

'Come, come,' said the Doctor. 'What are you talking about?'

'I… I said something to Dmitri.' It was almost impossible to hear her words through her sobbing. 'I said something, and it gave him the idea. It gave him the idea to throw the bodies over the walls.'

'Oh, my dear, I wish I had said nothing.'

'But… What Dmitri did… Might it have inspired this attack on Kaffa?' Dodo's desperation was clear on her face.

'It is by no means certain. No, not at all – though the Mongols are nothing if not great storytellers and military tacticians, always looking for new strategies.'

'But Dmitri was mad,' I interjected, seeing how upset Dodo had become. 'Who's to say this wouldn't have happened anyway?'

'Quite, quite,' agreed the Doctor hastily. 'It's quite improbable that the events we have witnessed here – a deranged governor in Kiev, sent mad by some sort of monster – will go on to be remembered by a Mongol leader a hundred years in the future. Yes, quite improbable.'

I could see that Dodo was less than entirely convinced. The Doctor said nothing more, but instead walked over to Dmitri who was slumped in a chair in the corner. The former governor's chin was moist, and his eyes were untroubled by blinking or movement. 'Yes, this creature brings madness in its wake,' the Doctor said. 'It chose not to kill Dmitri, but instead...' He stamped his feet in irritation. 'There is something obvious here, something we are not seeing! Why attack some, and not others? Why kill soldiers, but infect Dmitri only with madness?'

'Why are you so concerned with this creature?' asked Isaac.

'I have my reasons,' said the Doctor – and I had more than an inkling what they might be.

Before the Doctor could say anything else, Yevhen swept back into the room. 'I have some news for you,' he announced grandly.

'Later, man, later,' said the Doctor, clearly irritated. 'We need to know about the prophecies, the legends. They speak of the salvation of the city of Kiev, do they not?'

'I do not know,' said Yevhen, for the moment forgetting his announcement. 'I believe so.'

'Come, come,' said the Doctor, frustrated. 'Let us lay our cards on the table, so to speak. We have precious little to lose, and this creature could still be the salvation of Kiev. Now, acting governor Yevhen – what do you know of the legends of the dark angel?'

Still Yevhen seemed not inclined to speak.

'Come on, man!' I exclaimed. 'It's obvious you released the

thing from the catacombs under the cathedral. At least tell us what you know!'

Yevhen turned towards the window, hiding his face from us. 'Very well,' he said, his voice the whisper of decades. 'I shall tell you what I know.'

I listened attentively as Yevhen spoke in a still voice, his hands writhing nervously behind his back.

'A manuscript speaks of an angel, a protector. The document, passed down from eldest son to eldest son, tells of a potter, who lived in the countryside beyond our city. He was one of many who discovered the coffin of the angel. But he, uniquely, was blessed with an insight into the war in heaven – the war that saw the angel come to earth. He saw the angel fighting the forces of evil. It is a dark angel only because it is forced to use the instruments of evil to defeat the enemies of state and God. The potter came to believe that the angel's casket would protect the city of Kiev. In my folly, I too believed this.' He glanced at us momentarily. 'I believe the potter was my great-great-great-great-grandfather. Perhaps, as some would say, peasant stupidity does run in my family!'

This was quite an admission from Yevhen, and for a moment I almost felt sorry for the man. But when he turned I saw the cold darkness of his face, and my sympathy drained away. 'I tire of this. I order you all into the catacombs,' he said suddenly, his casual gesture encompassing the Doctor, Dodo and I, as well as Isaac and Nahum.

'Are you mad?' Nahum exclaimed. 'The creature lives there!'

Yevhen shook his head. 'You said yourself: the creature came into this building. You will be quite safe – safe, perhaps, even from the Mongols.'

'But…' stammered Isaac, 'I cannot leave Rebekah behind. And … I am needed here.'

'You are needed here if the rest of us perish,' said Yevhen.

'You want us out of the way!' I shouted. 'You've always had designs on the governor's position.'

'Perhaps you are right,' said Yevhen. 'But what do I govern? A terrified city, riddled with pestilence and soon to be attacked by a great army. This is not what I had in mind!' He raised a hand to summon the soldiers, underlining his intentions. 'Go,' he said. 'Go down into the depths. It will be a more comfortable domain than this.'

'Yes,' said the Doctor. 'I think a trip to these catacombs is long overdue. Let us do what the acting governor says.'

He moved as if to lead me away, but I was having none of it.

'But, Doctor!' I hissed. 'Yevhen must have an ulterior motive!'

'It is no use arguing,' said the Doctor. 'Come along, now. Come along. We will need your help in the tunnels.'

'You may take the madman with you,' said Yevhen, pointing at Dmitri. 'He is of no use to us here.'

And with that, and with the soldiers at our heels to ensure our compliance, we took up torches and lanterns, and bags of food, and went back into the tunnels that lead to the cathedral.

And I heard the door being locked firmly behind us.

# Codex II
# Est hic finis fabulae?

*A lithe trapper led our group through the thick darkness of the trees, along ancient trails invisible to untrained eyes. As we followed, we were wary, every sense straining against the silence and the gathering twilight. The trapper, though, was confident in his own abilities, and he forged on remorselessly, leaving some of us floundering in his wake.*

*The smell of scorched wood and earth grew stronger, and in time the first of the fire-damaged trees became visible, dark fingers of twig standing out amongst the vibrant pines that covered much of the slope. I watched the trapper drop to his knees and examine the outer edge of the conflagration, crumbling a small plant between his fingers. Once lush and green and full of sap, it was now little more than a desiccated stick of soft charcoal.*

*The trapper grunted, but said nothing. He waited for the group to assemble, and then, as one, we stepped through the blackened trees and into the clearing.*

*The firestorm had burnt a precise circle, obliterating everything from the soil up to the treetops. Now all that was left was a covering of ash and a dark emptiness where the heart of the forest had been. The blackened trees at the edge gave an impression of solidity, and it seemed to me that we were within some strange arboreal building, its roof open to the shifting sky.*

*The air was heavy and oppressive within this church of blackened trees, the effects of the last whispers of smoke and the cloying warmth of extinguished fire made worse by the fear we all felt. And, at the centre of this chamber, resting on an untidy plinth of scorched branch, lay a metal casket.*

*We approached the metal object cautiously, Petrov's brow was furrowed in puzzlement.*

*It was about the size of a burial casket, though this was no simple metal box. Like a smooth quicksilver seed, it lacked any trace of edge or line that might imply human construction, though there were areas pockmarked with shallow depressions and grooves. It was an almost uniform grey, with occasional splashes of red as if to remind us of its fiery arrival.*

*Petrov reached out a hand to touch the object.*

*'Is it hot?' asked someone at his side.*

*Petrov brushed his fingtertips against the metal, then pressed down more firmly. He shook his head. 'No, though it is metal. Some sort of fine iron, I'll warrant.'*

*Others now touched the casket, emboldened by the blacksmith's actions.*

*'It is like a tear, from God Himself,' said one man, almost overcome with emotion.*

*But I could not bring myself to touch the fallen object. Every time I looked at it a shiver moved up and down my spine.*

*Petrov turned to me, glowering. 'What is the matter? Are your hands too fine for this piece of heaven?'*

*Some of the men at his side chuckled, revelling in the big man's bravado.*

*'No hands are too fine, nor too coarse, for heaven,' I said. Goaded by the accusing eyes of the others, I stretched out my hands and touched the casket.*

*Suddenly I was transported elsewhere, a dream more real than life itself. Before I could even begin to puzzle over what was happening to me, I became aware that I was falling, fast. Wind tore at my eyes and face and fragile limbs. My stomach surged, my mouth was ready to scream – but any sound was ripped away by the awful descent.*

*Clouds flew past, then dark skies, and moons and planets and suns, then heavens and lands undreamed of. Then heat, then impact – then my eyes opened again to see hell itself. Creatures of war set about each other with grim determination – settlements uprooted like flowers, soldiers crushed in a moment. Everything was defiled, everything was teetering on the brink of the endless abyss.*

*I turned, and saw angels of light, saw salvation and security and the promise of protection. I ran towards the calm and implacable face of God, and away from the grinning visage of the Evil One.*

*Then I stumbled, fell, dream unfolding on to dream, and fell once more into the night sky, fell through noonday suns and the celestial spheres, through constellations and arcs and the very machinery of the universe.*

*I fell, but now I fell with the angels, and saw testaments of salvation, of the destruction of all evil things.*

*I found myself back in the clearing. Less than a moment had passed.*

*I withdrew my hand swiftly, as if scalded by the casket.*

*'Still hot?' asked Petrov, with genuine concern.*

*I shook my head, trying to find the words. 'A vision… A prophecy!' I wanted to say more, much more, but my voice was parched, as if from a long journey.*

*The trapper passed me a skin of water, and I drank greedily.*

*'What did you see?' asked Petrov impatiently.*

*'I saw…' I paused, striving to gather my turbulent thoughts. 'I saw a war in heaven. Yes, I fell to earth with Lucifer himself – the war was everywhere. Heaven, earth, hell. It mattered not. Only the battle mattered.' I took another*

swig. 'But the creatures I saw, the angels... They promised protection. They spoke of the end of the battle, the end of war.'

Petrov smiled. 'It is a good omen, as I thought.'

A man nodded. 'We must consult Alexander. His wisdom will help us understand this sign.'

Petrov laughed. 'Of course... But is it not clear to any man with a clean soul and a hardy spirit? This casket contains an angel, released to us to give us hope!'

'The cathedral,' added the trapper quietly. 'We must take this to the cathedral.'

Petrov nodded. 'A holy creature belongs in the house of the holy.' He turned to me, mindful of my vision, my insight into this great and awful gift from God. 'What say you?'

I could not help but turn away from the casket, disturbed by what I had seen. 'If Alexander agrees, then, of course. I am sure the city authorities can arrange transportation.'

'Nonsense!' growled Petrov. 'We will all play our part, and deliver the angel ourselves. But first, we will celebrate, and thank our Maker.' He clapped me on the shoulders. 'We do not find the coffin of an angel every day – still less are we blessed with an insight into the very heart of God.'

I nodded mutely.

We began to drift away, to make plans to transport the casket to the cathedral. I allowed myself one last glance back into the clearing. As I did so, a shadow fell across the sun, and the coffin fell into darkness.

# XX
# Deus absconditus

The siege of Kiev was swift and brutal.

The great Mongol army swept down and around the city, encircling it with grim precision. The cavalry moved in ordered units, ensuring that no Russian would escape the carnage. Behind them came the lumbering siege engines – the catapults, trebuchets and crossbow-like ballistas. Teams of soldiers scurried over the wheeled machines, preparing them for use.

Although arrows rained down from the walls in optimistic defiance, in truth the battle of the mind was long lost. The reputation of the Mongols travelled far ahead of them, inspiring only hopelessness and resignation. It was well known that they had a seemingly limitless supply of well-trained soldiers, devastating machinery, and the patience of God saddled with the savagery of Satan. Worse still was the noise of the great army. The hooves of ten thousand horses and the thundering rattle of wooden wagons, the bone-curdling war cries, mixed in with the lowing of distant livestock on the move – all made speech within the city near impossible. Women hugged their children tightly, whispering desperate assurances made mute by the evil monster beyond. Soldiers and civilians assembled diligently, holding their weapons and the hopes of their families high.

Some chose to banish their fear and prayed to the hidden god, who had himself felt utterly rejected – *Eli, Eli lema sabachthani* – and whose triumph had only come through death. Some controlled their fears, and prayed to the god of miracles, who had parted seas and killed the unworthy. Some succumbed utterly to their fears, and in doing so found the serenity of a thief who wants only to awake next day in paradise. Some prayed to themselves, and saw little but the emptiness of their souls, and feared for the true judgement to come.

The sky was red with the dust thrown up by the horses that pawed the earth beyond the walls. Many of the citizens had seen paintings of the apocalypse; now they were destined to experience their own.

And still the arrows and tar came down in waves from the fortified walls, and still the Mongol army worked diligently beneath them, preparing their great instruments of war. One or two soldiers fell, but they were quickly carried away for treatment or burial.

Within the city, acting governor Yevhen patrolled the makeshift defences. Never before had he felt so lonely, never before had he felt so driven. He bellowed orders, encouraged vigilance, reassured as best he could. He heard the noise outside abate momentarily, and steeled himself for the worst.

The attack began.

The Mongols had chosen to concentrate their attentions on the Polish Gate to the west of the city. There the battlements were made of wood – an obvious weak point, and one that Yevhen had tried hard to strengthen. But the leaders of the Great Khan's army were no fools.

A mass of shaped boulders began a relentless pounding of the wall. Smaller projectiles, seemingly of clay, showered down like rain, exploding on impact. Yevhen could not disguise his fear as flames licked the ramparts and soldiers scurried for safety. 'What devilry is this?' he exclaimed.

He ordered a unit of well-trained men to the area, to bolster the citizens who had been stationed there. From his vantage point he could see that the overall structure was standing firm, but the great doors of the gate were beginning to crack and, worse, the battlements were now ablaze. Water was being ferried to the site, but the amounts were pitiful.

Yevhen glanced back at the governor's residence, itself blackened with soot, and for a moment he remembered familial stories of the flame that fell from heaven to herald the arrival of the angel. He had always hated fire.

Then the first masonry began to fall from the gateway, and the thought was lost in the panic Yevhen had anticipated for weeks. 'To the Church of the Virgin!' he ordered. It was the one building in Kiev that could, the tacticians felt, be well defended, its natural shapes and battlements having been bolstered by weeks of tireless work. Yevhen remembered that the young traveller had been keen to help out. It all seemed so long ago now.

The general order was issued: families were to seek refuge in the church itself, and all men of fighting age were to assemble there for the final pitched battle. Yevhen wondered idly how much of the population had already succumbed to the disease. A quarter? A third? It was so difficult to tell. Certainly, he recognised that the army he had at his disposal was slight compared to that which threatened, with every moment, to spill through the walls of the city.

At last the Polish Gate began to buckle. A large explosive device found a natural weakness, and exploited it in a deafening, blinding crash of light. An entire corner section came away and, as it fell, it brought the remains of the wooden walkways and fortifications with it. Another pounding, and one of the great doors toppled over completely. A number of soldiers were trapped beneath it, but their cries were drowned by the awful shrieks of the populace. Most had fled to the church, but some were standing motionless, slack with fear, their minds gone.

A wall of Mongol archers advanced swiftly through the breach, each man notching, aiming and releasing arrow after arrow. Their march was implacable and barely a Mongol fell, though towards the peripheries some hand-to-hand fighting broke out.

Then the archers parted at the centre and the cavalry flowed through, a torrent of dark men on small brown horses. The steeds proved nimble, even over the rubble, and the great lances the riders carried efficiently dispatched any soldier they encountered. One brave defender of Kiev managed to dismount a horseman with his spear; when the man tumbled to the ground the Russian was at him with a sword in one hand and a dagger in the other. He hacked at the Mongol's face until there was nothing left; then he turned, too late, to see three further horsemen bearing down on him. Two lances hit him, one just below the shoulder, the other just above the groin. The points pressed on through armour, weak flesh and bone. The soldier was lifted bodily from the ground, like a trophy.

The Mongol archers fanned out further and, in desperation, more and more people took to the roof of the church: soldiers who had deserted their posts, women with screaming children still clinging to them. Though vulnerable to arrows, at least they were safe from the cavalry. Some men, driven to stupidity by the inevitability of their fate, even taunted the Mongols from the roof.

Such defiance was short-lived. Too many people had gathered on the roof; it had never been designed for such a great weight. Perhaps the hasty constructions around the building had only weakened its integrity; perhaps sheer weight of numbers would anyway have been enough. Whatever the cause, the roof began to shudder and sway, then, in the blink of an eye, it fell to the ground in a cloud of dust and wood splinters. Hundreds were killed by the falling masonry or by their fall; hundreds more were trampled to death in the panic that ensued.

The collapse of the Church of the Virgin effectively saw the end of any resistance to the Mongols. The sacking of Kiev began.

The destruction of the church was audible even within the governor's residence. Two soldiers, already pale with fear, exchanged terrified glances.

'What was that?' asked one, crossing himself.

'I do not know.'

'We should see.'

'We have been ordered to stay here.' The second soldier indicated the doorway that led to the catacombs.

'We could hide in the tunnels. Under the cathedral. St Sophia will protect us!'

'We must do as we are ordered.'

Yevhen was dragged before Batu Khan, and thrown unceremoniously at his feet.

'Get up,' said Batu. 'Are you the governor? I wish to know why the envoys were killed.'

Yevhen got to his feet, gingerly. He shook his head, finding the words lodged at the back of his throat. 'I have only assumed that role. I have sent the governor into the catacombs.'

'Why did you do that?'

'I hope he will be safe there.' The lie came easily to Yevhen, for he had built his life on such mistruths.

Batu glanced at Mongke, who was standing just behind him. 'Is there not a weapon under your cathedral?' he asked the Russian. 'Is that why you have sent him there?'

Yevhen could only shake his head mutely, shocked that the Mongol warlord was closer to the truth than he probably realised.

'Why else would you send a man into hiding, then reveal his location to us?' Batu paused. 'Unless you are a coward…'

'I am not a coward!' cried Yevhen.

'I have not seen you in battle.'

Yevhen snorted in derision. 'I have been in battle since news first reached us of your approach – battling Dmitri and the others. They are weak fools, all of them. They would happily have offered no resistance. They stood in the way of my plans, and so deserve to die.'

'As do you,' said Batu. 'You say too much to be a man of honour and worth.'

And with that, he drew his huge sword from its scabbard. The metal sang through the air like an arc of lightning.

The headless body of Yevhen collapsed to its knees in a parody of supplication.

Batu turned to Mongke. 'How many have survived?'

'What with the disease, the collapse of the church… Our own noble actions. A few thousand, perhaps.'

'Let them live. And let news of our great victory go forth, to the cities we are yet to conquer!'

Unnoticed by everyone, a Mongol soldier standing some distance away nodded almost imperceptibly at these words. Then he turned on his heels and disappeared into the shadows of Kiev.


'It is very quiet,' observed one of the Russian soldiers, still watching the locked door to the tunnels.

'Perhaps we have won,' said the other. 'Perhaps it is all over.'

'So quickly?' pondered the other. 'After all this time…' He paused, and for a moment his face was filled with joy. What if they had won? What if, somehow, they had defeated the devilish Tartars – done what no city had done before? Then he shook his head, his features becoming hard. 'No,' he said firmly. 'They would have sent word by now. We would have heard the sounds of rejoicing!'

'But it is all over,' came a quiet voice from the other side of the room. 'I am very nearly finished.'

The men turned and, to their horror, saw a short Mongol soldier step into the room. In truth, they did not recognise him as 'Mongol' or 'Tartar' – so alien was his face, so extraordinary was his clothing.

They drew their swords. 'Devil!' one spat.

'Put down your weapons,' said the man. 'I am tired of this.'

The soldiers gripped their swords ever more tightly, but did not advance on the Mongol.

'Very well,' he said. He paused, straightened up – and, incredibly, became slimmer, taller, before the amazed eyes of the soldiers. His skin lightened in colour – ruddy hues swirling into nothingness like distant clouds – and, under the skin, bones became mobile, disjointed, fluid. Eventually they too settled.

'Witchcraft!' cried one of the soldiers.

'Yevhen!' blurted out the other, recognising the now-solid visage in front of them.

'Yevhen is dead. All your people are dead. This bunker has been destroyed. My mission is over.' The figure twitched, uncomfortable in clothing that was now ill-fitting, for what he had been wearing had not changed.

'Bunker? Mission? What words are these?' The soldier raised his sword and made as if to advance.

The creature that wore Yevhen's face flew at them in a blur, spines extending from its fists and lips. Moments later it held the two corpses almost tenderly in its arms. 'I have followed my orders. It is over.' Then it dropped the bodies to the floor, and advanced on the locked door.

It found a key, and pushed it into place. 'I am so tired,' it said. 'I must rest now.'

The door opened, and the creature disappeared into the darkness.

# XXI
## Oblationes et holocausta

We were soon deep within the tunnels that linked the catacombs under the cathedral with the governor's residence. The Doctor was impatient to find the crypt that contained the tomb of the 'angel': I, on the other hand, was more interested in trying to find our way through the cold stone passageways and out again.

In any event, my sketchy geography reminded me that the crypt was between us and the cathedral. Behind us was only a locked door, so both our objectives could be met if we found our way through the darkness.

Dodo was quiet – still pondering the Doctor's awful story about the Black Death, I suspected – but Isaac and Nahum were talking animatedly, as if we were on some sort of fact-finding expedition. Both, it seemed, had long suspected the existence of a whole range of tunnels under the city, and were intrigued to finally find themselves exploring the subterranean corridors.

Dmitri brought up the rear, alternately mute and muttering, but able at least to walk unaided. He didn't know where he was, but seemed content enough just to be walking somewhere, to have something to do.

The Doctor was chattering away – to himself, if no one else – about labyrinths and mazes, and infallible ways of conquering them that involved paint or beads. '...and if a doorway is without a mark, you may go down that, making two marks on it. And if you proceed through a doorway with but one mark on it... Is it one or two more marks? Two, I think. Yes. Two. I'm certain. And if you arrive at a junction with no marks at all…'

I ignored him, and concentrated on my dim memories of my time in the catacombs, trying desperately to recognise patterns on the walls, bends in the tunnels, particular configurations of archways or doors.

In actual fact, we came upon the crypt soon enough, though I am sure it was more by accident than by design. It was much as I remembered it – a small structure beneath the great arches of the cathedral catacombs, punctured by a small open door. The Doctor, ever inquisitive, wanted to lead the way, but I overruled him. For all we knew, the skull-faced thing could have returned, and was waiting for us. I remembered my own encounter with the creature, and the way it had remained within the crypt watching me with great malevolence, and I suppressed a shudder.

I stepped into the arch of the doorway, and saw at once two things: the great, ruptured coffin within the centre, and a pale and near-naked body on the far side of the room. I recognised who it was, and darted outside again.

'Dodo!' I exclaimed.

'Steven?'

'I need your help. Don't worry, the creature's not here.' I turned to the others. 'I don't suppose we have a spare cloak?'

They looked at me blankly, but Nahum volunteered the rough cape he had been wearing. I listened, almost amused, to the conversation within the crypt – which had been preceded, no doubt, by some vigorous shaking, for the person was clearly comatose.

'Wake up!' I could hear Dodo saying. 'Come on!'

A muffled moan, a stifled cry of terror, then: 'Dodo!'

'Hello, sleepyhead.'

'Where am I?'

'You don't want to know.'

238

'And… And where are my clothes?'

'I'm not sure you want to know that either. Here, put this on.'

Moments later, Lesia – embarrassed and groggy – stepped through the doorway, pulling the cloak tightly around her with as much dignity as she could muster. Nahum let out a whoop of delight and ran to embrace her.

'Fascinating!' said the Doctor. 'The creature can change its face, but not its clothing.' He stifled a chuckle.

'I remember Steven's account of the discovery of the cook's body,' said Isaac. 'It all fits together.'

'But unfortunately she was killed', said the Doctor, 'and yet this girl was allowed to live… for which I am, of course, grateful. But why do you think that is, hmm?' Without thinking, he had turned to address Dmitri, but the former governor's face was blank and, whatever he was looking at, it was not at us.

'My son was not killed when there were opportunities to do so,' added Isaac. 'Steven also. There is no consistency in the creature's actions!'

'I believe there is!' said the Doctor. 'We're just not seeing it.' He stepped into the small room and Isaac and I followed him. He stepped up to the casket.

'I might not know much, Doctor', I observed, 'but that's no coffin!'

'Quite right, my boy. A life-support capsule of some sort, hmm?' He ran his fingers over the surface. 'Clearly capable of travelling great distances through space, all the while keeping its occupant in suspended animation.'

There was a sudden cry from outside. 'Doctor! Steven!' It was Dodo's voice.

I was nearest the door, and ducked through.

I saw the creature stepping into the circle of light created by our torches. It was angular and pale now, and had made no attempt to mimic the human form. Its head scanned from side to side, but it did not move – until it saw Dmitri.

Then the beast sprang through the air, barbs extending from its face.

Without thinking, Nahum ran to Dmitri's aid. The creature landed athletically, its clawed fists raised – but made no further forward movement. Nahum was effectively between the creature and the former governor.

'The leader must be terminated,' said the creature in a quiet singsong voice. 'The bunker is already compromised. Most of the unclean have been destroyed. When the leader is terminated, the mission is over.'

I went to stand by Nahum, further blocking Dmitri from view. 'Why don't you attack?' I asked.

The skull-face bobbed from side to side, taking us both in. 'The pure must not be damaged,' it said simply, as if this explained everything.

'Fascinating,' said the Doctor. 'This is beginning to make sense.' He took another step towards the monster, even going so far as to extend a hand towards its barbed face.

'Doctor!' I warned.

'It's quite all right, my boy,' said the Doctor. He ran a hand down the beast's face, as if stroking a pet. 'It only wants to attack Dmitri. The rest of us are safe.'

'But why?'

'Oh, my boy, please do use that fine mind of yours! What do we all have in common? Or, rather, in what vital way are all of us different from Dmitri?'

I paused, thinking. 'Well, Dodo and you and I don't belong here. Perhaps it's as simple as that.'

'And what of Isaac and Nahum, hmm? What of them?'

I shook my head.

The Doctor refused to elaborate, but instead turned on his

heel. 'Steven, my boy, come with me.'

'But what about Dmitri?'

'Oh, one of the others can stand there. They will be quite safe. Now, come along, come along.'

The Doctor was right: Dodo, Lesia, Nahum and Isaac stood in a small semicircle in front of the governor, and the creature was thus rendered motionless. Its claws twitched, as if reflecting its desire to attack, but otherwise it didn't move.

I followed the Doctor back into the crypt. He crouched by the casket, and ran his hands over its smooth metal sides. 'I have seen something similar to this before. Yes. And somewhere there should be…' He let out a gasp of delight, and removed a small panel from the side of the 'coffin'. It came away, resting in his hands like a computer pad. I could see a small recessed screen, and an array of nodules that I assumed were controls, and, at the base, a series of tiny holes.

'What's that?'

'The controlling device.' The Doctor pointed to the indentations, and I saw that they matched a random sequence of tiny metal needles in the casket. 'I think we can use this. I must get it back to the TARDIS.'

'The TARDIS!' I exclaimed. 'But it will still be guarded.'

The Doctor paused solemnly. 'Any Russian soldier who still lives will have concerns other than our access to the ship.'

We left the others behind, still locked in their motionless impasse and facing the beast. Again, I tried as best I could to follow my instincts and my memories of the tunnels. We had discussed heading back towards the great stairs that had so terrified me, but I reminded the Doctor that Yevhen had locked the door at the top some time ago. And, in any case, we wanted to go back to the governor's residence, to find the TARDIS.

It was then the Doctor's turn to remind me that Yevhen had also ordered *that* door to be locked. 'But the creature has come down here,' he added. 'Perhaps the it has been opened again.'

It seemed at the time a vague and forlorn hope, but I said nothing, and was pleasantly surprised when we found our way back to the entrance. The door was, indeed, open – and the reason became obvious as we stepped through it. Two Russian soldiers, doubtless attacked by the beast, lay in an awful pile on the floor, their faces in ribbons.

As I entered the room I felt the small metal panel become warm in my hands. The Doctor had entrusted it to me, and I turned to speak to him, slightly alarmed.

Before I could say a word I was transported – there is no other word for it – to a different place and time entirely. There was a knot in my stomach, and wind whipped my eyes. It was as if I was on some awful fairground ride – or, worse, one of those dreams where you fall from a great height, only to awake as you hit the ground.

But this was far worse – more real, it seemed in a moment, than reality itself. I tried to scream, but the sound was ripped away by my rushing descent.

I fell past moons and planets and suns, then dark skies, then clouds. The air around me began to burn, but before I could see what – if anything – I was travelling in, I landed. There was no thud of impact, no awful rending of bone and muscle: one moment I was falling like a missile, the next I was on my feet, walking about as if I had casually stepped off a footstool.

My vision settled and I saw a planet of red and brown rock, dominated by a circle of distant volcanoes that poured a constant stream of ash and flame into the air. Worse still, a battle was being played out in front of me. Great tanks that walked on insect legs over the uncertain terrain loosed off laser weapons; human-sized creatures in glorified spacesuits buzzed around them like insects. Another group of armour-clad humanoids were marching towards a dome-like structure only a mile or so from where I stood; without warning, the ground beneath them shattered, revealing a vast craft like a battle-green trapdoor spider. The entire platoon was wiped out in a moment, and the 'spider' settled back beneath the ground.

An aircraft flew low overhead, strafing the area with some sort of cluster bomb. I realised, then, that I was borrowing someone's eyes, someone's perceptions – I could no more control my body (whatever it was!) than I could run in one of those awful, powerless nightmares. I knew only that I was moving – at speed – and that my destination seemed to be the dome.

Above me, I realised, were more of the creatures in their pale spacesuits, and they were protecting me (us?) from attack. I soon came to the outside of the dome – all the while protected by the covering fire of the flying humanoids – and a blue-brown, three-digited hand extended towards some sort of control panel. I realised with a shock that this was 'my' hand, or the hand of whatever creature's experiences I seemed to be sharing. It flickered over the controls, and the door opened.

I/we stepped inside, into the darkness, to find the Doctor staring at me in concern. I was back in the governor's residence, and less than a moment had passed.

'Doctor, I… ' I paused, not knowing what to say. 'I've seen something. An alien war.'

The Doctor nodded. 'Perhaps I should have warned you. It seems likely that the creature can communicate with its capsule on some sort of mental plane. The control device was clearly seeking to establish a psychic communications protocol with you!'

'But the images…'

'Random bits and pieces, as interpreted by your mind. Still, they may be useful.' The Doctor looked closely at me, and for a moment I almost expected him to pull a great watch from the pocket of his frock coat and swing it before my eyes. 'Tell me everything you saw,' he said earnestly.

The words came out in a tumble – I was still struggling to make sense of what I had seen. 'It was so real,' I concluded. 'Just as real as what I see now.'

'Fascinating, quite fascinating!' said the Doctor with a chuckle. 'It confirms some details of my hypothesis, but we need more information. Come along, my boy. We must find the TARDIS!'

And, in case of another 'attack', he took the control panel from me, then set off through the seemingly deserted corridors of the residence. I glanced at the two corpses as we left the room, but even I could sense that the city was overflowing with the dead.

'What is this hypothesis of yours?' I called, struggling to keep up with the Doctor's unexpected burst of speed.

'Oh, that's not important,' he said. 'I have an idea of what drives this creature. But the important thing is to find a way of destroying it, and the technology that came with it.'

'But, Doctor,' I said, 'I doubt even I could make head or tail of that capsule. And there doesn't seem to be a weapon in it, or…'

'We cannot be sure the capsule is benign, or that the Mongols will not stumble upon some nugget of information they should not have.' The Doctor snorted. 'Unlike our friend the Monk, I must strive to keep the waters of time clear, not make them still muddier!'

The Doctor, of course, knew the route into the cellars very well. I almost expected to see a path worn into the cold flagstones, given the frequency of his trips to the TARDIS over the preceding weeks and months. He paused on the threshold of the great chamber that contained his ship, in case there were still guards within, but, as we had expected, they had long since been called elsewhere. The room was even darker than I remembered it and, after the unsuccessful attempt to set fire to the ship, the air was thick with the bitter stench of smoke and burnt wood.

The TARDIS stood implacably in the centre of the chamber, and the Doctor clapped his hands in delight when he saw that it was undamaged.

'You always said the TARDIS was indestructible,' I reminded the old man.

'Did I?' blustered the Doctor. 'Well, shall we say, ninety per cent indestructible, hmm?'

I didn't question his nonsensical words, but instead stood behind him as he fumbled his key into the lock. He pushed open the door, and we stepped into the control room. It might have been my imagination, but I thought I heard the usual hum of the room become louder, and the white, circle-covered walls brighten, as if it welcomed our attention after all this time.

'My boy,' said the Doctor, 'would you mind looking under this panel for a concealed switch? It is shaped like a "T", and it needs pulling towards you.' He indicated one part of the hexagonal control desk at the heart of the room.

I rooted about under the panel and finally found what he had described. It was tiny, little bigger than a finger, but although I was worried that it would snap it was incredibly strong. I tugged it, and heard a precise 'click' over my head.

I got to my feet to find that a subsection of the panel had rotated to reveal a host of connectors and sockets that I'd never seen before. Some wires were more like high-voltage cables, and terminated in a bewildering array of connectors; others were little thicker than strands of hair and pulsed with light. The Doctor, his face a picture of concentration, was furiously inserting a handful of these threads into pores on the underside of the alien panel. I looked up at the scanner on the wall, which showed static then, gradually, shapes.

'Like so much of the TARDIS,' announced the Doctor at last, patting his machine lovingly, 'it may not be pretty, but it works!' He inserted the final wire. 'There!'

The monochrome picture on the scanner stabilised. After a little more fiddling the picture took on colours, and I saw red volcanic mountains and myriad suited aliens and brown vehicles in the midst of battle.

'That's what I saw,' I said.

'This planet is doubtless many light years from Earth,' said the Doctor, his voice sounding as cold as the great voids of space. 'It might no longer support life, or it may even have been destroyed. Or perhaps other races live there now.' He turned to me gravely. 'Our enemy is a soldier, still fighting a war that ended centuries ago.'

# XXII
## Lux aeterna luceat eis

Dodo was bored.

At first she had stared at the skeletal creature with wide-eyed loathing, remembering the horrific tales of its attacks and her own encounter with it when she was in Lesia's room. She found it difficult to believe that the thing could so perfectly mimic someone she had grown to know so well; she had watched over what she thought was Lesia's sleeping body for hours, and not once had she suspected it was not her.

She stared at the needles that extended from the creature's claws and face, and was grateful beyond words that she had been luckier than so many others. But the Doctor seemed to be right – the creature seemed to have a limited number of targets in mind.

It stood motionless, seemingly unconcerned by their presence. Only when the human shield that protected Dmitri moved a little, allowing the creature a glimpse of him, did its claws twitch as its gaze rested on him for a moment.

But it made no attempt to attack, and so Dodo was bored. As long as she stayed in position, alongside Lesia, Nahum and Isaac, Dmitri was quite safe. He seemed not to know what was going on; he sat on the floor, facing away from the creature, whispering into his upturned palms.

Soon after the Doctor and Steven had left, the group had helped Dmitri to his feet and started to walk away from the crypt but the monster had shadowed them obediently, stopping when they stopped and keeping pace with them as they moved. They had concluded that flight was impossible, and returned to the casket to await the Doctor's return.

Dodo turned to Lesia. 'Are you all right?'

'I am cold,' her friend said with a thin smile. 'But I am glad to be alive. When I think of the others, who have died…' Dodo could see tears gathering in the corners of Lesia's eyes. 'Do you know, Elisabet used to save the finest sweetmeats for me. She was never blessed with a daughter of her own. And after my mother died…' Lesia pulled the cloak tighter around herself.

'I hope the Doctor returns soon,' said Dodo, trying to cast a more positive light on their grim situation.

'You feel more comfortable when he is with you, do you not?'

Dodo nodded. 'With him around, everything is OK. Somehow, he sorts things out.'

'And yet he has failed the people of Kiev. If what you all tell me is true, we could be the only ones alive!'

Dodo was about to reply when Isaac suddenly exclaimed 'I've got it!' They all turned to the old man, prompting the creature to stare in their direction, its claws twitching.

'Sorry?' said Dodo.

'I was mulling over what the Doctor said,' Isaac continued. 'Why does this beast not attack Dmitri when we stand in the way?'

Dodo paused, trying to remember the creature's words. 'I suppose it wants to keep us alive.'

'But what do we all have in common? Or, what do all the victims have in common?'

'The builder, various soldiers, the cook…' Nahum counted the deaths out on his fingers. 'They're all…' But his face was blank; he still did not understand.

Isaac turned to Dodo. 'It's as plain as the nose on your face!' he said, with a smile.

'They're all Russians!' exclaimed Nahum at last. 'That's why we're able to protect Dmitri, why Steven was not attacked, why –'

'Yes, yes!' exclaimed Isaac. 'It fits, does it not?'

Dodo mulled this over. 'No, hang on a minute. What about Lesia?'

'Ah,' said Isaac, gravely. 'Ah. I hadn't thought of that.'

Lesia nodded. 'My family has lived in the Russian principalities for centuries!' she said. 'We're of pure stock.'

'Let us talk of people as people, and not as cattle,' said Isaac, shaking his head. 'No, my idea is wrong. There must be something else.'

'But would it not be ironic,' said Nahum, 'if the "saviour" of the city desired to kill only its citizens!'

Dodo sighed. 'As for it being used as a weapon against the Tartars… Well, I can think of better!'

'I wonder what is going on, up there,' said Lesia, glancing towards the ceiling.

As if in answer, faint noises came from the tunnels – noises accompanied by a hint of torchlight.

'The Doctor?' she queried.

'It is too soon,' said Isaac.

'And coming from the wrong direction,' observed Nahum, pointing towards the passageways that led towards the cathedral.

The sound solidified, became more insistent – the noise of many feet, marching to a regular rhythm. The light grew brighter still.

'Mongols!' exclaimed Dodo.

# XXIII
## Bellum gerens in caelo

The Doctor's voice was grave and I struggled to hear him above the hum of the control room. Having downloaded a vast amount of information from the controlling device, and crosschecked it against whatever data the TARDIS had access to, he stood by the scanner, his head turned away from me, gripping his lapels tightly.

'Can you imagine, my boy, a war fought between people that you and I would not be able to tell apart? A war of genetic purity, based on age-old hatreds and a coexistence that shattered in an explosion of violence? A conflict where only a blood test can tell if your neighbour is friend or foe!' He shook his head slowly, as if he could scarcely countenance such atrocities. 'This creature, which has moved with stealth and guile through the hierarchy of this city, is in effect only obeying its orders. It is soldier, assassin and spy rolled into one, with limited chameleonic and psychic abilities. Launched into the heart of enemy territory, it would target one particular ethnic group. It would kill but, more importantly, it would seek out the leaders, the authority structures, and attack them with something far more subtle.'

'Madness?' I suggested.

The Doctor nodded. 'As we have seen. The most awful destruction comes from within. The battlegrounds of this alien world were littered with impregnable city-sized fortresses, or bunkers. One soldier of this type could infiltrate and destroy an entire bunker – much more efficient than sending an army, or raining down useless shells.'

'If it's as difficult as you say to tell these ethnic groups apart,'

I said, 'how did this creature do it?'

'The information is not clear, but I have an idea,' said the Doctor. 'Those spines that extend from its head and hands. Do they remind you of something?'

'I suppose… needles?' I suggested tentatively.

'Yes. Needles! Hollow tubes with which one can infect an enemy – but first they can be used to draw up a little blood from the victim. The genetic material can then be processed and checked against the expected enemy.'

'That's what happened when it attacked me,' I said. 'It obviously came to the conclusion that I was different from the Russians it had attacked. So it didn't kill me.'

'Fascinating, hmm?' said the Doctor. 'The enemy of my enemy is my friend!'

'And it's that fear of harming a potential ally that allows the others to keep Dmitri safe?'

'Exactly, my boy! Exactly.'

'But why is this…' I struggled for a name. 'Why is this bunker soldier attacking the people of Kiev? Surely it must realise they're all completely alien to it?'

'To understand that, we need to consider how it came here.'

'By accident?'

'Indeed. By accident. The bunker soldier, as you call it, has no business here. Such creatures were simply fired towards enemy positions in these special capsules. Clearly this one missed!'

'I should say so!'

'Somehow it overshot its target,' said the Doctor, whose hands were blurring over the controls. 'Indeed, it had sufficient acceleration to penetrate the atmosphere of its planet and remove itself from its gravitational pull. It must have drifted through the cosmos, possibly already damaged, for many thousands of years.'

'But eventually it was pulled towards the Earth?'

'That's right,' said the Doctor, reconnecting the controlling device. 'Completely by chance! It must have made quite an impact on the people who saw it land!'

'And they brought it to the cathedral, thinking it was some sort of religious icon.'

'Yes. A survivor of a heavenly war which, I suppose, is not too inaccurate a way of putting it. In any event, to answer your question at last, it seems likely that either the creature, or the casket that controls it, were damaged. It resorted to an earlier, and much more basic, way of establishing the ethnic nature of its enemy.'

The Doctor looked at me keenly, as if expecting me to have followed a logic. But, just for a moment, he had left me behind. 'Sorry, I don't understand.'

'Think about it. If you're shot into enemy territory, who's the first person you're likely to see?'

'An enemy?'

The Doctor nodded. 'And it seems clear that it was Yevhen and his friends who opened the casket.'

'So the creature thinks the people of Kiev are its enemies.'

'Exactly,' said the Doctor. 'I suppose Yevhen's plan was not without merit – if only he could have found a way of getting the Mongols to be the first to open the casket!'

'Now that *would* have changed history,' I said, for once catching a glimpse of the Doctor's dilemma.

'Yes, yes, my boy. Now, enough of this chitchat. I need to find some way of telling this creature…'

'Doctor…'

'Please let me finish. We must tell this creature that the "bunker" of Kiev has now been destroyed and, in essence, its mission is over.'

'Doctor!'

'What is it?' he snapped.

He turned and saw what I had been trying to draw his attention to.

Two Mongol soldiers stood in the TARDIS doorway.

# XXIV
## Auditui meo dabis gaudium et laetitiam

Dodo's face cracked into a bitter grin. The situation she found herself in was so ludicrous, so awful, it was almost funny. Almost.

With the Mongols audibly coming closer, and no sign of the Doctor's return, she and the others had agreed to retreat into the tunnels as before. Dmitri had said little on the matter: he would have followed them meekly to hell and back. But it was his life they were all trying to save, still clustered tightly around him. As they shuffled away from the creature's casket, they found themselves stumbling into each other and treading on one another's feet. It was like a three-legged race at school – with the added incentive that a monster was tracking their every movement.

Dodo risked turning her head towards the 'angel' and saw to her horror that it was again following them. Its face moved from side to side, watching them with interest. Spines appeared and disappeared on its hands with awful regularity, as if reflecting its breathing… Or its growing impatience.

'What are we going to do now?' Dodo asked, panicked.

'We do what we must to stay alive,' said Nahum vaguely. 'Only by doing so will we remain true to our humanity.'

But Dodo wasn't in the mood for philosophising. She was just about to tell Nahum this, in no uncertain terms, when the first Mongol soldiers appeared.

Given that the fear the Tartars had inspired in the people of Kiev, they weren't quite what Dodo had imagined. All were small, and lightly built. The knights of Christendom, the full-time Russian soldiers, were much more what she expected medieval warriors to be, with shining armour and elaborate helms, and shields that seemed big enough to cover a horse.

These Mongols, though, were lightly armoured, and they moved at a steady, swift trot. Most carried small bows with arrows notched in readiness. A cry went up, and the first soldiers were joined by another group with unsheathed swords that seemed to glow in the light of their torches. They appeared unperturbed by the creature, which turned towards them. They aimed most of their arrows at it, as if in recognition of its otherworldliness, but other than that gave no sign of being frightened or amazed. They had come so far, mused Dodo, crushing everything before them, that not even the monster could upset their awful self-belief.

She and the others halted in their tracks, their thoughts of escape ebbing away. The dark angel looked closely at the newcomers, then deliberately turned its back on them. It was still Dmitri that it wanted.

Dodo risked a glance sideways, and saw that Lesia was almost shaking with fear. The monster had been bad enough but, to her, each Mongol was just such a monster. She had been fed on terrible stories of Tartar atrocities for many years; to now come face to face with these 'demons' was almost too much for her to bear.

Nothing was said for many minutes, and nobody dared to move. Dodo had the impression the Mongols were sending word down the tunnels. It was as if somebody, somewhere, was trying to gather as much information as possible before putting in a personal appearance.

Eventually more reverberating footsteps and flickering torchlight heralded the arrival of another Mongol, a leader in gold-hued robes whose demeanour more than made up for his diminutive stature. He wore little armour, though his companion – who also had an aura of leadership about him

– was covered from head to toe in ornate folds of pale leather.

The man in gold stopped, flanked by the Mongol soldiers. 'Batu Khan, leader of the Mongol army on behalf of the Great Khan Ogedei, who is himself the power of God on Earth and Emperor of Mankind, has captured Kiev.'

There was a pause. Dodo wondered if he expected the news of his butchery to be greeted by a spontaneous round of applause.

'The adviser called Yevhen has been executed,' Batu continued, his voice as cold as the steel of his sword.

'No!' cried Lesia, falling to her knees. 'Father!'

Nahum stooped to comfort the young woman, whose body was racked with sobs. 'He was not a bad man!' he snapped at the Mongol leader, angry. 'He was only trying to protect his people.'

Dodo, too, tried to comfort Lesia. She noticed the creature take a few steps forward, manoeuvring itself towards Dmitri, but still it did not attack.

'The adviser was a coward,' explained the second Mongol leader. 'Others who have survived will be allowed to live.'

'Two things remain,' observed Batu, his voice cold over the sound of Lesia's inconsolable sobbing. He extended a calm finger in the direction of the skeletal creature, which had come to rest at a point equidistant between the two groups. 'Is this the great dark angel, the awesome weapon, the defender of Kiev?'

There was a pause. For a moment no one seemed to realise that a question was being asked. Then Isaac, who was towards the front of the group, spoke up. 'There are some that call it so,' he said. 'Though, as you can see, it is a sovereign creature. It does not dance to the tune of the people of Kiev.'

'To whom am I speaking?'

'My name is Isaac,' the old man replied, managing a half-bow. 'I too was an adviser to Prince Michael, and latterly to Governor Dmitri.'

Batu snorted. 'Did your cowardice make you flee down here like a rat from daylight?'

Isaac shook his head. 'We were ordered down here,' he said. 'I think Yevhen hoped we would die.'

'Then I was right to put him to the sword,' said Batu simply. His precise words sent a shiver down Dodo's spine. 'I decree that families and friends of noble adviser Isaac shall live. We are mindful of your bravery – whereas news of the cowardly flight of Prince Michael and his family has reached even our ears. How dare he leave his people behind to suffer! When we capture him, he will pay a price in keeping with his neglect of his people!'

'But my lord –'

'Silence!' snapped Batu Khan. A pause, a brief whispered conversation with the other man, and Batu continued. 'Your mention of Governor Dmitri reminds us of the second thing that needs our attention. Where is the governor? He must kneel before us.'

'He is here,' said Isaac, pointing to Dmitri, who sat on his haunches towards the rear of the group, drawing geometrical shapes in the dust on the floor. 'Though I am afraid he is quite mad,' the old man continued. 'You will get no sense out of him.'

'Stand aside, and let me see my adversary.' Batu took a few steps forward, his hand resting on his sword. 'Let me see the man who executed my trusted envoys, and then hurled the bodies over the walls!'

'He was gripped by lunacy,' repeated Isaac. 'His final orders were not those of –'

'Stand aside.'

'No!' shouted Dodo. 'He'll be killed!'

Batu turned towards Dodo, his eyes the colour of glowing ashes.

'Who are you?'

'I'm Dorothea… Dodo… Dodo Chaplet,' she stammered. She wasn't quite sure which of the two men to address.

'You have many names. Are you a woman of rank?' asked Batu.

'No, I'm nobody special. I'm just a traveller.'

'Cousin Mongke tells me he is well inclined to those who describe themselves thus.' Batu nodded towards the other man, who smiled though his eyes remained cold.

'A traveller?' asked Mongke. 'A friend of the Doctor's?'

Dodo nodded.

There was a pause, which Dodo took to mean that she should elaborate on her original interjection.

'Look, if we move away,' she said, trying hard to quell her nerves, 'this monster will attack Dmitri. The Doctor thinks it's programmed to attack just him – we've worked out that if we stand here, he's OK.' Her words came out in a rush, and she realised much of what she said would mean little to anyone living in the thirteenth century.

'Then perhaps this "angel" and I have something in common.' Batu took another step forward. 'Stand aside, by order of Batu Khan!'

The great, curved sword was unsheathed to underline the point.

Dodo and the others exchanged worried glances. It seemed they were now protecting Dmitri against the Mongols. Dodo had little doubt in her mind that the Khan would kill him, and there seemed to be nothing any of them could do to stop him.

Without warning Dmitri started to push his way towards the front of the group. Dodo placed a hand on his arm, to try to halt him, but the man looked back at her with a sad, placid smile. The insanity, for the moment at least, was gone. Now there was only grim resignation on his face, and unfathomable tiredness behind his eyes.

Dodo and the others parted for him, and he stood tall at the front of the group. 'I am Governor Dmitri of Kiev,' he said, his voice strong and unwavering. 'I hail you, Batu Khan, and your victorious army.' He bowed his head as a mark of respect.

Before Batu could respond, the beast drew itself to its full height, its mouth and claws a mess of barbs and spines. Then it flew through the air towards Dmitri.

# XXV
## Libera me de sanguinibus

I watched nervously as the Mongol soldiers stepped into the control room. If they were amazed by what they saw, they did not show it.

The Doctor turned to face them, an imperious figure. 'And what is the meaning of this intrusion?'

You can't fault him for trying.

One of the soldiers turned to him, while the other inspected the controls, the screen, the items of furniture that dotted the room. 'What is this place?' the leading Mongol asked.

The Doctor returned to the controls, pressing switches here and pulling levers there. 'I will explain everything,' he said, 'but first I must finish my work. It is vitally important!'

'No,' said the soldier. 'We must report to the Khan. He has scientists and sorcerers who may explain this. Come!'

The Doctor refused to move. 'I cannot comply, sir,' he said through gritted teeth. 'There are other matters to consider.'

'You will do as I say,' snapped the soldier.

'The creature must be destroyed!' exclaimed the Doctor, anguished.

The soldier paused, saw that the Doctor did not obey him, and nodded to the other. He strode towards me, and held my arms behind me.

I struggled, but the Mongol was surprisingly strong. In any event, he held a sword to my throat. I could feel his breath on my neck, and with every moment that passed he gripped me more closely, the cold steel pressed more tightly against my neck.

'Do as I say,' the leading Mongol ordered the Doctor, 'or your friend will die.'

# XXVI
## In extremis

*Reloading test signals…*
*Complete.*
*Reloading heuristic diagnostics…*
*Complete.*
*Loading of situational archives…*
*Skipped.*
*Loading present mission diagnostics…*
*Complete.*
*Initial summary:*
*Unassigned bunker penetrated. Provisional target GJU-435-FBK attacked and compromised.*
*Mission success index: 87.1%.*

The creature's attack on Dmitri brought an instant response from the Mongol archers. Arrows whistled through the air, raining down on its slender back. Most fell away – the skin of the creature was tougher than it appeared – but many impacted, bringing forth trickles of grey-blue blood.

None of them stopped the beast arcing through the air towards Dmitri. In the blink of an eye, it landed – its clawed feet clicking on the rough stone floor – just as a second hail of arrows fell. One arrow embedded itself in the soft tissue at the base of its skull, and the creature paused, flapping at it with its claws. Then its arms powered forwards, lifting Dmitri bodily from the ground.

A Mongol soldier ran forward, attempting to attack the beast with his sword, but the monster did not even turn to look at him. Instead its jaws and fists, now a mess of barbed spines, came down towards Dmitri's terrified, screaming face.

# XXVII
## Deus ex machina

'Very well,' announced the Doctor suddenly. 'Let us go to Batu.'

I let out a sigh of relief, and the Mongol at my back lowered his sword. He began to usher me towards the TARDIS door.

The Doctor, followed by the senior soldier, walked around the hexagonal controls to join me. 'It will be good to resume Batu's acquaintance,' he said lightly. 'I am sure he will want to see all this.' He waved a hand airily to encompass the room, then suddenly slammed it down on to the controls.

With a hum, the doors began to swing shut. Ignoring us, the soldiers ran forward, striving to pull against the interlocking white blocks. But their efforts were futile, and within moments we were all trapped in the control room.

I glanced over to see that the Doctor had used these few precious moments to resume his work at the TARDIS controls.

'Open the door!' the subordinate soldier shouted, tugging against the great white blocks with all his strength. I wondered if, for the first time, he was frightened.

'You will do as we say!' ordered the other, banging on the roundel-covered doors in frustration.

'With pleasure, my boy, with pleasure!' smiled the Doctor triumphantly. 'But I need to finish this first!'

The leader stalked towards him. 'What are you doing?' he asked in a quiet voice.

I was asking myself the same question. I looked over the Doctor's shoulders to see a small screen, seemingly connected to the alien control device, filling with random marks and symbols.

'Finishing things off,' the Doctor said, with a final stab of the controls.

The screen flashed brightly, and then became dark.

# XXVIII
# Angelus

*Reloading present mission diagnostics…*
*Complete.*
*Initial summary:*
*Unassigned bunker penetrated and compromised.*
*Provisional target GJU-435-FBK attacked and compromised.*
*Revised mission success index: 100%.*
*Verify…*
*Mission success index: 100%.*
*Mission complete.*

Without warning, the creature dropped Dmitri to the ground. Its entire body was shaking. Dodo saw its face flicker and change, melting away like a plastic doll's face consumed by fire. She caught glimpses of the governor's cook, Lesia, and many others she did not recognise – then the whole mass collapsed to the floor like an oversized puppet with its strings cut.

Dmitri rolled away, coughing. Behind him, the pool that had been the monster – a viscous mass of bone and skin and muscle – began to ebb away. Catacomb winds caught the steam that rose from the dark remains, and Dodo held her nose in disgust. It was the awful stench of a living thing being boiled into nothingness.

'What has happened?' demanded Batu. It was clear from his voice that, though he did not understand what had occurred, he was irritated it was not anything he had commanded.

'I… I do not know,' stammered Isaac.

'I bet the Doctor's behind this!' exclaimed Dodo, breathless with excitement.

'Bring the Doctor to me!' Batu growled.

Mongke nodded. 'Yes, cousin. It is time we spoke to him again.'

# XXIX
## Orbis

The tip of the soldier's sword was pressed against the Doctor's throat.

'I cannot concentrate in these circumstances, young man,' the Doctor said. 'You are trying my patience!'

The soldier said nothing, but lowered his sword a little. We all watched as the Doctor operated the controls again. With an electronic murmur, the doors opened. Beyond was the blackened shell of the governor's residence.

The Mongol soldiers exchanged whispered words, then turned back towards us. 'Come with us,' the leader ordered.

'Of course, of course,' said the Doctor, now a picture of compliance.

As we followed them from the TARDIS I turned to him. 'Is it all over?' I whispered.

'Very nearly,' said the Doctor. He paused for just a moment, examining the blackened remains of the building's once regal rooms and corridors. 'For the people of this city,' he added in a quiet voice, 'it was all over many months ago, when Prince Michael fled, and those who remained behind decided on a course of opposition. If only they had submitted to the Mongol Empire, instead of resisting it!'

'Might things have been different?' I asked.

'Perhaps, my boy. Perhaps,' he replied. 'But history, like conversation, has a habit of going round in circles.'

# XXX
# Memento Mori

'I expected more of this weapon of yours!' Batu exclaimed angrily. He prodded at the congealed remains with the tip of his sword, then turned towards Dmitri. 'Why has it died? Why was it trying to attack you?'

Dmitri, still dazed from his encounter with the monster, shook his head. 'I do not… I do not know.' He paused, then crouched on the floor, wrapping his arms around his body. Dodo thought she saw signs of the madness returning. 'I feel most unwell,' he said, and closed his eyes as if to sleep.

Isaac calmly stepped between him and the Mongol leader. 'None of us understand this creature,' he said. 'Perhaps the Doctor can explain.'

Batu nodded, and was about to turn to consult with Mongke when he noticed the flash of bright yellow on Isaac's tunic. 'The mark of the sons of Abraham,' he said with respect. 'Your faith has protected you.'

'I have little faith left, sir,' the old man said. 'Perhaps I had before your army approached, but with everything that has happened…'

'Nonsense!' beamed Batu. 'Do not your scriptures talk of ungodly nations being used to punish the people of God when they fall from faith? Perhaps, like Genghis before us, we are the instruments of the Almighty!'

'Perhaps,' said Isaac.

Lesia spoke suddenly, her voice clear despite her grief. 'I have prayed that all the people of Kiev may be saved. I do not believe that my prayers fell on deaf ears.'

'But the carnage that awaits us,' said Isaac. 'The death of your own father… What is left for us now?'

'My father once said that "No" is still an answer to prayer,' said Lesia, her face smudged by soot from the torches and by her tears. 'The Lord's ways are not our ways. For my father, this was justification for working through his own strength. That was his undoing. His faith was ill-directed, but well intentioned.'

'God smiles on you, pretty girl,' said Batu. 'There is some reason… I cannot pin it down. But there is reason in all this. Always.'

Mongke nodded. 'You are all safe now – honoured guests of the khans! Your bravery is commendable.'

'Your butchery will one day be punished!' spat Nahum suddenly, holding Lesia tight to him. 'You cannot gloss over your evil!'

Mongke shook his head. 'We merely do what has to be done.'

'Please, let's find the Doctor,' said Dodo, tiring of dances with words around the massacre of innocent people.

Batu nodded. 'We shall find him, and he shall tell us the secrets of this place… of the creature.'

He moved into the tunnels, followed by a small knot of soldiers, then Dodo and the others. A contingent of archers brought up the rear.

As the last man stepped away from the angel's crypt and into the shadows the entire labyrinth shook, gripped by a powerful explosion. Soldiers came running, through rubble and flame and falling debris, but it was too late.

The casket had exploded, scattering the walls with useless shreds of metal and quicksilver circuitry. Of the angel itself, only a dark smudge on the floor remained. In time, that too would fade.

Dodo and the others came to a halt in the main aisle of the

cathedral. It seemed barely touched by the battle, and autumnal light streamed in through the stained glass. The air was still heavy with prayer and the smell of incense; just for a moment, it was as if nothing had changed.

Batu allowed them to rest there for a moment. Dodo looked at the survivors of Kiev – Isaac, Nahum, Lesia and Dmitri. There might be others, somewhere in the city, but as far as she knew, that was it. Tens of thousands of people, whittled down perhaps to less than a handful.

She looked at Dmitri, slumped in a pew, seemingly asleep. 'Do you think he will ever recover?' she asked Isaac.

'Who can say? I shall tend him, as best I can. He shall be comfortable.'

'What will you do?' Dodo asked. 'Now it's all over, I mean.'

'We shall make a new home somewhere. And I shall continue my work, and try to bring God's words to the people.'

'After all this,' Dodo said, amazed. 'And after what you said to the Mongols… I thought that would be the last thing you'd do!'

'I have choices to make, young lady,' Isaac said solemnly. 'I have not even argued with God for many years. I either now resume my arguments, or I join the silent, awful world that is deaf to the Almighty. Does He exist? What form does He take?' He glanced at a crucifix attached to a nearby wall. 'Did He do something as undignified as *that*? These are weighty questions. I have been asking them all my life.' He sighed. 'Perhaps little has changed.'

'And we need to find if mother has survived,' said Nahum, his voice breaking a little.

'Yes,' said Isaac. 'So much death,' he added quietly. 'So much death.' Then he closed his eyes tightly against the tears, and said nothing more.

Dodo touched Lesia's arm lightly. 'I'm sorry,' she said, the words tumbling over themselves. 'I'm sorry… Your father. What happened to him was terrible.'

Lesia gripped Nahum's hand tightly. 'I have lost a father,' she said, 'but I have gained a husband, and a father.'

Dodo beamed brightly. 'You mean… '

'There is no one for us to hide from now,' Lesia replied.

Dodo was about to say something else, but she left her words unspoken in the scented air. It felt as though she was saying goodbye, and that was how she wanted to remember her friend: strong-hearted, even while staring into the gaping maw of death.

Escorted by soldiers, Dodo walked from the cathedral, and did not look back.


The Mongol attack had destroyed those parts of the governor's residence that had survived the fire. Only a single tower remained, and Dodo found the Doctor and Steven at its top, looking down on the ruined buildings of Kiev in awe-struck silence.

They embraced in silence, and stared at the city where thousands of innocent people had died. The walls had been breached in many places, falling on to the hovels that clustered for protection at their base. Residential areas had been razed to the ground, and every state building over a storey tall was little more than a pile of rubble. Of the Church of the Virgin, little remained. The collapse of its roof had done more damage than any Mongol siege engine or gunpowder shell.

Only the Cathedral of St Sophia was untouched, its towers seeming close enough to touch. And, underneath them, the catacombs that had for so long concealed an alien secret.

The air over Kiev was thick with the stench of death and

infection. Crows wheeled overhead, the only beneficiaries of the battle.

The Doctor turned as Batu and Mongke appeared behind them. The wind tugged at the Mongols' beards and hair and, perhaps, irritated their eyes. Only that could explain their tearful gaze as they, too, looked over the city.

'You must let anyone who has survived live,' said the Doctor. 'A dead city is of little use to your empire.'

'Of course,' said Batu, without looking at him.

Mongke turned to the Doctor. 'The weapon under the cathedral, the "angel". What was it?'

'A poor trapped beast, far from home,' said the Doctor. 'Still trying to fight its own war, and make sense of a puzzling world.'

'As do we all,' said Mongke.

'You too have behaved with honour,' said Batu, addressing the Doctor. 'You shall live to travel to other lands, other cities.'

'Thank you,' said the Doctor.

'We have heard that your blue box contains rooms,' said Mongke. 'How is this possible?'

'A mere trick with mirrors,' the Doctor said. 'You have listened to my many tales of strange beasts and stranger lands with great interest. It is time, at last, to see my magic at work. As a mark of thanks, for sparing our lives, I will show you the greatest trick you shall ever see.' He turned to Steven and Dodo, managing a half-smile. 'I will make my blue box disappear before your very eyes.'